COLD GRACE

Author's note

This is a story about colonialism, about the lengths to which white communities will go in protecting the idea of their purity. The book contains scenes of sexual and other physical violence, as well as violence against disabled people. In editing, we've worked to avoid the kinds of dehumanising language which were used at the time in which the story is set. Nevertheless, some characters express beliefs and ideas which are violent and distressing. Please look after yourself while reading.

COLD GRACE

Meredith Miller

Thanks so much
for coming, lovely
friend.
Meredith

HONNO MODERN FICTION

First published in Great Britain in 2025 by Honno Press
D41, Hugh Owen Building, Aberystwyth University, Ceredigion, SY23 3DY

1 2 3 4 5 6 7 8 9 10

A catalogue record for this book is available from the British Library.

Published with the financial support of the Books Council of Wales.

978-1-916821-06-4
978-1-916821-07-1 ebook

Cover design by Ifan Bates
Typeset by Elaine Sharples
Printed by 4edge Ltd

nhad

Or is it that it shadows forth the heartless immensities of the universe, and thus stabs us from behind with the thought of annihilation ... is it for these reasons that there is such a dumb blankness, full of meaning, in a wide landscape of snows...

Herman Melville, 'The Whiteness of the Whale'

A Way Back

For a long time she whimpers in the dark, trying to find something to lean up against. It feels slick and smells rancid. Wet ash. The way you smell after a bonfire gets doused by sudden rain, the smell that won't come out of your clothes and makes you feel like a hobo begging in the dooryard.

Her legs hurt, and the blood is pounding between them. And it's dirty right up inside her, too. Her body is full of ash.

She'll maybe have to beg like a hobo in front of her own house now, if she can face it. Standing outside with the chickens, asking for grace. Them inside will cross themselves and shut the door, leave her looking up, holding her mouth open to the rain until she drowns.

Later, she thinks she must have fallen. She opens her eyes and it's just as black as with them closed. The taste of ash has made it into her nose and throat, and this is all there is ever going to be. There will never be light or sight again. This is hell, maybe. Not fiery, but the cold aftermath of fire.

Then, somewhere in the hours, streaks of light appear, coming through the edges of whatever it is they've stuffed in the smoke hole. They stab down at her like the light that comes through the clouds in pictures of God, then they go again. Maybe that will be how time passes now, a slow tolling bell made of sunlight, separating the pieces of darkness.

She isn't dead, then. There is something outside of where she is, space and sunlight and time. But of course, there will be something else. If they weren't coming back she would be dead now, or bleeding along the side of the road somewhere.

She chokes, her throat closing in. She coughs until bile comes up and then she is cold.

The sound of metal ringing wakes her up. Someone is making something, doing or undoing something with tools. Something made of metal, done in the cold dark. God knows what it is, what's next. There is a thump and then a long stillness.

The smokehouse door swings open. It is night but the moon makes it seem as bright as day. A horse nickers somewhere. The little brother, Eddie Allen, stands in the doorway with a finger to his lips. There is a bigger boy with him, one of the boat people from the lake. Eddie is so scared he's shaking, and for a minute that makes her feel older. Steadier. She stumbles as he pulls her toward the paddock fence, and the world crashes down onto her.

'I can't go home,' she says, and doubles over with the weight of it.

Little Eddie goes blank and stiff, looking at her like she's ruined everything. She can see he hasn't thought himself past that smokehouse door, and she can see what that cost him, too. She looks at the other one, T-Roy.

'Where can I go?'

Why is she asking them? They're both younger than her. Eddie ten, and T-Roy maybe fourteen. She almost feels she shouldn't leave little the little brother there, in that house full of blood and cold eyes. He's only a child. Then, so is she, according to her dad and her brothers.

She turns toward Eddie, reaching down to hold both sides of his face so he'll have to look into her eyes, and mouths a silent thank you. T-Roy gives him a shove and he turns back towards the house. Then T-Roy one puts his wool shirt around her and rolls himself over the fence, holding out a hand to her. Swinging her leg over the lower rail, she tears herself open again. Blood falls on the wood, black and thick in the moonlight.

The cuffs of his shirt don't even reach her wrists, but it's warm and dry and scratchy. It smells like earth and things rotting in the water, instead of like ash.

Under the trees the ground slopes down. After half a minute, the Allen place disappears into the dark behind them. He has hold of her hand, pulling her through the fallen leaves, but the weight of the dark is stronger than him. It isn't long before she falls.

She curls around herself and crumples the wool shirt in her fists, pressing it into her belly. Sick tremors come through her body, like it's trying to shake the flesh right off the bone. She could vomit herself up until she's inside out, a pile of meat lying in the leaves, waiting for scavengers.

He keeps right on pulling at her, saying nothing. In the end, she has to gather the body back around herself and stand up. When the grey light turns into pink and gold, she can see the soot and blood on her skin. Looking like this puts a girl outside of everything good. There is no way back from here. Her mind circles around, trying to picture herself anywhere warm, indoors. But there is no warm indoors, no family anymore. The saving you get from young boys in the night is only ever temporary.

The crows are talking over their heads, telling each other about where they are. When she turns towards the place where she thinks the road will be, they are higher up and not at all as far from the Allens' as she thought. There is Jerusha Prichard's spring house. She could clean up in there, but the sight of the lock on the spring house door makes her stomach clench. She leans her hand against a tree, bleeding again.

'Well, you two're up early.'

Jerusha is standing at the side of her cabin in the pink light of the new day. This morning that is the sharp edge of some new life. Her grey hair is braided down her back and she's wearing a nightdress and work boots. Jerusha looks down at the blood and holds out a hand.

She lets the boy's soft, slick hand go and looks at Jerusha's calloused one. The hours pass in her mind's eye, the black smokehouse, the stabbing light, the whites of Eddie Allen's eyes. She feels like a doe being coaxed out of cover. Like there is probably a bullet waiting to cross the space between herself and Jerusha's comfort.

3

Jeanne

Of course, I remember.

Listen, sit yourself down and leave your recording machine alone. I'll make coffee. Well, yes, I can see you're from the city. Nobody local woulda worn those shoes up here. You're new, but government people come along every once in a while. They go again.

You'll have to take my country coffee as you find it, government man. I said, sit down. The chair's clean.

Yes, I've seen a recording machine. Whatever it is you think you're collecting, you can save your questions. They won't do you any good in my house. You want me to talk, you'll have to just take what I give you and be satisfied. I'll tell you the things I'd as soon give away anyhow. Certain things still come back to me every day, even though they're small inside the whole size of it.

Maybe you have a time in your life that carries on through everything that comes after? Things move forward, but it's like you haven't. You're always inside that time, underneath it all. Well, I'll tell you mine. It was the end of the year I turned from fifteen to sixteen. The end of wandering through the woods and chasing things, or hiding behind things and waiting. You could think of it maybe as the year I became visible, stopped hiding inside my mother's name. That fall, I finally arrived. Ripped a hole in the side of the world and walked right in.

Cream? You don't get it like this where you're from, city boy.

Them days, people used to shake their heads and roll their eyes when they said my name. They'd look at me and huff a big breath out and say, 'Jeanne Delaney'. It was a name with a meaning all its own, at least while I carried it.

My mother laid the name on my head before anybody could stop her, with its too many letters and all. Still covered in blood, the both of us, that's the way Jerusha told it later. Both names my mother's and nothing in the middle. 'Jeanne Delaney,' she said, and then died.

Guess there could only be one with that name breathing at a time. If that's the case, I suppose I appreciate her passing it on. But what if she was only saying her own name? Expiring it on her way out, like? In that case, I never even had a name, did I? Well, everyone calls me Jeanne anyway. How they say it depends on who they are. The people from the Children's Aid always made it rhyme with bean.

'Twasn't until I was nearly grown Grampy and T-Roy told me Delaney used to be deLaneuville. I said, 'Why disguise one kind of Catholic under another?' Grampy just said, 'My father lived through the Aroostook war, girl. Don't even ask what happened to us after. Just take the Delaney and be grateful.' Don't look at me; I don't know what he was talking about. It was better not to be French if you could help it; I did know that. They called us vagrants, and pirates because we lived on a boat. They were wrong, and then right in a way, too.

Well, all right then, I'm grateful for the name she gave me and the life too. All of it. Look around you, city boy. See how much I have to be thankful for?

The fall I turned sixteen was 1913, I guess. That was the year we all went together into winter, me and Eddie and Jerusha and Eddie's big brothers. All of us together into the whiteness and the cold, and also into the can't-see-your-own-hand-in-front-of-your-face, can't-even-find-your-own-soul darkness.

The first of it was the day I met Eddie in the woods. Well, see, I'd known Eddie Allen all my life, but when we ran into each other that day it was a shock, like tripping and falling into a cold lake. It woke me up and changed me without any warning or sense.

Summer was ending but our boat was still docked at the bottom end of the lake. We were still living our warm weather life, swimming and ferning and soaking willows. Haying was past; we'd made some money helping Bud Crook with his.

It was the end of a lot of things besides summer too, the day I chased after that car and then cut up into the woods towards the beginning of the next thing. 'Course I didn't know any of that at the time, me all tripping over my feet and not looking down at what was in front of me.

I'd gone out that morning to get some blackberries for my Grampy. Already, Grampy couldn't get around much.

T-Roy, that's my big brother, had made a little gangway we could throw out to the dock for him, instead of just a plank, but mostly Grampy stayed on the boat. By the end of that winter, he wasn't moving from in front of the stove except once a day for the necessary. So I wanted to make him some blackberry jelly because he said it reminded him of his own *me'mère*. See, I was a good girl. Believe me or don't, I don't care.

There weren't any women living on the boat but me. T-Roy had always wanted Etta Grace, but she'd been ruined and gone since before the time I'm talking about. He didn't get another woman until later, and that wasn't exactly by choice. For almost all the time I was growing, summers on our boat was just me and T-Roy and Grampy.

In the winters, once we dry-docked the boat and the water froze, the men headed up to the north end of the lake and I went to Jerusha. From her house I went to school as much as I had to, to keep the Children's Aid away. Jerusha taught me quilting and canning and things. She braided my hair and washed the blood out of my clothes without saying anything. Like I said, I pushed my own mother out on my way into the world. She took up the slack, I guess. After Jerusha lost Etta Grace she was all alone in the cabin, unless it was me there. So I spent the winters with her even after I was old enough for work.

I went to school on and off until I was nearly fifteen. If you stayed still too long and didn't get yourself to a school, the people from the County or the State started eyeing you up, wanting to 'help' you. You didn't want to give them any excuses. The most important thing, according to T-Roy and Grampy, was that you never asked for money. I never have, still, and that's kept my name mostly out of their filing cabinets all my life. Mostly.

Up at the north end of the lake there was a one room schoolhouse with a potbelly stove, the kind of thing they put in aspic and show to the tourists from Boston these days. The teacher there was Miss McLaughlin. I remember I thought it was funny calling her Miss, because she was older than Grampy. She gave me a book about Joan of Arc, written by Mark Twain, and some other ones where the people they called Iroquois were all bloodthirsty or else very noble and entirely without feeling of any kind. All the white women were terribly virtuous and fell down praying all the time when they should have been wetting themselves with terror on account of the bloodthirsty ones. *Leatherstocking Tales*, that was called.

Down in the town there was a bigger school with five classes. I went there some, too. I liked Miss McLaughlin, though. It was her who inaugurated the tradition of huffing my name out while shaking her head. As in, 'Jeanne Delaney,' huff, 'you're bright as a button, but you're hanging by a thread,' sigh and shake of the head. She rapped knuckles with that ruler, but we didn't mind. It felt kind of loving. Sometimes, there'd be a kid who wasn't so well taken care of. She'd send us all outside to play and make them take a bath in a tin tub by the stove. They'd come out all pink with miraculous fresh clothes on, looking like new-born eight-year-olds.

Anyway, it was from Miss McLaughlin's books that I learned about courage and swashbuckling sort of stuff. Blame them, if you like. Once when I cut myself with the gutting knife, T-Roy said that's what school did to you, made you practically cut your fingers off 'cause you were dreaming about knights in armour while you were supposed to be paying attention to gutting the fish. Grampy said school could save you and that's what the country was here for, and we should take advantage of it. Old people always said that. They didn't have the Children's Aid when they were young to disabuse them of that particular kind of starry-eyed notion. Me, I wanted the shining armour, not the scholarship to Bryn Mawr. I'm still glad about the books, though.

So I went to school some and never asked for handouts. You say the government is paying you and a bunch of others just to gather up our voices? Well, they wouldn't pay a mother and baby not to starve. Not without making files on them, maybe tearing them apart and locking them up somewhere. Maybe worse.

Delinquent, degenerate and dependent: they could only ever pin two out of three of those on me, and those were the two that depended on which way you looked at it. I ducked them and dodged them like I was the Pathfinder and we moved ourselves up and down the lake, back and forth across the borders, county, state and nation. The last of my going to school was about a year before that day I saw Eddie Allen sleeping in the woods. That fall I'm telling you about I was done with classrooms, but not with Joan of Arc.

That particular morning when I saw the car, I don't think I even noticed the fall coming, let alone the rest of it. I paid my own kind of attention to things, on my own time.

I couldn't help running after a car, could I? A passing car was an event, them days. I saw it coming up the valley, with the sound that was like purring from far away and like you couldn't hear yourself think when it was up close. It was painted the colour of dried blood, a kind of red brown, and the sound of it echoed off the sides of the valley, changing pitch as it came. The roof was made of canvas and the man driving actually had on a cap. The lady in the back seat was reading, like she couldn't even feel the wind from the open windows, like she wasn't excited by any of it a'tall. One of those charity ladies from the hospital, I guess, used to riding around in automobiles.

I knew I'd never catch the car. I chased after it just to make a breeze of my own, get in the road for a minute and feel the power of my own legs. Call it vanity if you like. I don't care what you call things, I'm just telling them to you. I gave chase.

We both slowed down going up the hill past Jerusha's cabin, the car and me. Then the car dipped and disappeared and by the time I crested the hill it was twice as far away and that was when I saw two crows (joy) swooping into the trees above the creek. I had to follow them into the woods, because you do, don't you? The lady in the car kept going down the hospital road and I cut through into the trees behind Jerusha's place, all hollow and echoing the absence of Etta Grace. But I didn't stop to feel that either. I was keeping an eye on those crows. I just knew, that time, they were flying towards joy.

And they were. Joy among a lot of other things, as it turned out.

So, I followed those two birds up into the woods, then later forgot all about it; only just thought of them, now I'm telling you. When you get older, memories put themselves back together. You had that yet, government man? Might not happen for you if you keep carrying around that recording machine, using that for a memory instead of your own head.

I knew where the best blackberries were and it wasn't even a mile, but I was taking a long way around on account of the birds. I went into the yellow birches and stood still for so long I saw a quail with her nearly grown children still tagging behind her, and later a fisher cat, travelling on some kind of fisher cat mission.

You see? I could be still and notice things when I wanted to. It was a game I liked to play, practising stillness, seeing what would come out if I was quiet enough. That practice made a difference later. If I wasn't so good at quiet, they might have seen me there, watching while they did what they did to Eddie. Or worse, Eddie might have known I was watching. But I'm getting ahead again. Like I said, it runs through everything.

After the crows and the quail and the fisher cat, I came out under the pines and Eddie Allen was sleeping there in the woods like it was his own house. Even though I knew Eddie from when we were children, somehow I'd never seen anything like him before that day. He had on a plaid wool shirt like a logger would wear, working in January with the steam coming from his mouth. I pictured him like that, swinging a hatchet and sweating. I just stood there in between the patches of sun, picturing him in every season. Swimming in the red pool in the summer, too. I guess I was staring, but he looked like a song or a prayer to me. He just struck me different all at once. I don't know. Anyway, I wished he'd just keep on sleeping.

Now there's two pictures lying over each other in my mind. It's only now I can see that the shape of him was the same at the beginning and the end, sitting with his legs stretched out, leaned up against something. Except that first day his hands were free and in front of him.

Later, Eddie told me he came out that morning because he smelled it, the good rot in the woods that means summer is over. He said he could smell me coming too, before he even opened his eyes. You felt like an animal around him, like something hunted, but it wasn't a bad thing. It was like he could reach into the silence around you, feel what you were about to do without you having to say anything. He thought of everyone like they were an animal he was tracking, but you need to understand that was a kind of love. He loved the deer, even while he skinned them.

When he did open his eyes, I stepped aside and looked down. I think that was the first time in my life I thought about what I was doing with my arms and legs. Jerusha would have been happy; she was always telling me to watch my limbs and quit knocking into things. Right then, though, they seemed too many, in the way.

Eddie just looked me up and down, stopping at my boots.

'Ain't you got a button hook, girl?' he said.

A Carpet of Needles

The autumn of 1913 is warm, dry and long. It makes Eddie feel sleepy and light, like his lungs can't get enough of the cooling air. He can't keep from drowsing under the trees.

Coming in from milking in the blue dawn, he catches the taste in his breath. He cocks his head and takes a deeper breath. The dog looks up and whines.

'You smell that too, Don?' Eddie says. 'Gimme a minute, then.'

He gets a canteen and a hard apple from the kitchen and lets Don out the gate. The dog runs down the road toward Jerusha's, looking back once to check he's right, then disappears around a bend.

In the woods, mulch is making itself under Eddie's feet, and the shelf fungus is brighter even than the leaves will be in a few weeks' time. Don runs before him up the slope behind Jerusha's cabin and off onto the deer path.

Hoof beats pound from the edge of his hearing to the centre and Eddie Allen's heart speeds up to match them. The doe flies out of the scrub not five feet in front of his face. Her belly slides past at eye level, then she drops and pounds away again on the other side of the road. There is something about the way a doe is made that always startles Eddie. He might have taken her skin off and separated all her parts dozens of times, but she still seems longer and rangier, more sinewy, than the picture in his head.

Anyway, she's got nothing to fear from him. Don yaps and chases her a little way. He knows they're not hunting. Not legal for another few weeks, but that's not what stops Eddie. Hunting just isn't why he's here. He's come for that smell of disappearing leaves that blew past the kitchen door this morning.

The woods up here have all been cleared once, likely in his grandfather's time. Since then, the pines have had sixty seasons or more to make a carpet of old needles springier than his Sears mattress that's been in the house since who knows when. He's not so simple he'd sleep out here at night without a reason, but you can't help yourself resting on that ground on a fall afternoon if the sun's out. Eddie can't, anyway.

Maybe he's just as alone in the woods or the house, now they're all gone away, but the house stifles. It's full of scratchy whispers and things half made in the shadows. Memories, you could say, but that word isn't really enough for it.

Even though there are four different beds, he still sleeps in the same little room off the downstairs parlour he's been in from a boy. He hardly goes upstairs at all. The thought of sleeping up there unsettles him if he's honest. It's like if he closes his eyes and lets go, the rest of them who used to live up there might slide into his dreams and take over. His own bed is haunted too, of course. Sometimes he thinks he's woken up and can't see or move, his mouth full of ash, or a knife sliding into him, or his brother Hank pushing a pillow onto his face while Micky holds his legs down. Then he'll wake all the way up and there will be just the dark window and the lumps in the bed.

He'll get up and go outside then, tie his boots on the back porch and walk through the yard. He's knocked all the latches off the outbuildings, but nights like that he checks them all anyway, looking for what was trapped there years ago. Once he's opened every door and shut it again, he heads out the gate. Sometimes, he crosses the road and walks through the near field up into the woods, where he can stop and breathe his silver breath into the trees, listen for the night animals slipping by. After a while, his thoughts slow down to match the air around him. It's better than a drink or a smoke to calm you, breathing in and out with the whole breathing forest.

At the farm, inside the fences, the things that have been done can still be felt. The yard and the near fields have been cleared maybe two hundred years, and full of Allens for at least half that. They say the first settlers ploughed right in between the stumps of the old trees they felled.

But Eddie stays for the forest, not the farm. The house makes a stopping place in between walks, a place to store things up and clean his gun and make biscuits. Anyway, someone has to do the work, with Micky not able and Ma taken him to live in town. And, too, it doesn't matter where Eddie goes. The ghosts are inside him, making themselves at home in his head. Moving away wouldn't change that. In the daytime under the trees, his dreams are different, though still not what you'd call restful.

He eats his apple with his back against a pine. Don takes off, but he won't go far. He'll circle around, checking for threats or excitement, then come on back. It isn't cold yet, the rotting smell is just a foreshadowing, a telegraph of the coming change. Eddie slides down into the patchy sun and shuts his eyes. He startles and then settles again when the dreams fall down between the trees.

He can feel Grampy Pliny's bowie knife in his hand, but how he got it from Hank he doesn't know. There is a wet peeling rip as he separates skin from muscle, slipping the bowie knife along in between. It's a satisfying sound and it excites him in his dream.

He's taking the doe apart, but she's still moving, flying past him while her skin falls away under his knife. He is like a god, or some kind of hero, making and unmaking things. The deer goes past again, and her skin is whole. She flies in front of the sun, interrupting his tall, godly shadow. It goes all the way dark then, night pricked with stars. She is a constellation. He throws his knife at her, but it falls short of the sky, misses its mark. Then his brothers are behind him, snickering.

Don barks once, somewhere nearby. Eddie panics and shrinks, then feels his shirt scratching him. There is someone right there between himself and the light, a dark outline close enough to touch if he stretched a leg out. He keeps his eyes half closed, trying to hang on to the dream. He can feel Don, moving the air in front of his face with his wagging tail.

13

Eddie knows the shadow belongs to Jeanne Delaney, even without all the way opening his eyes. Who else will it be, wandering around behind Jerusha's cabin, now that Etta Grace is gone? It's somebody Don knows, and nobody else would stand staring at a sleeping person like that.

When he does open his eyes she steps sideways, smiling and letting the light through. Well, it is her, but then it isn't either. She's grown tits and a light fur on her legs that shows in the slanting light, and then there's a smell coming off her like the woods. How long has it been since he's seen her? Long enough for spring to turn to summer in her body while summer moved across the rest of the world. Jeanne Delaney seems to have turned into a woman, and for a minute he wonders if he's still in his dream, where things are changing into each other.

She used to be part of a mismatched pair with Jerusha's Etta Grace, the two of them running around in the woods behind the old logging camp where Jerusha lives, their bird voices startling the deer away and stirring up dust between the pines. He came on them once, splashing in the oxbow with their shifts pulled up and their stick legs all red from the cold water, the light stabbing up from the creek in all directions, blurring them and making coloured spots in Eddie's vision so they seemed like angels.

It was Etta Grace's body Eddie saw that day, with the sun coming through, making that thin cotton into a halo around the shadow of her. The shape of her was singing into his eyes. When he saw it he felt sick, like he wanted to throw a cover over her and then run. He wanted to find a secret place and hide her under the leaves where his brothers couldn't find her. That day, he shook the feeling off without even asking himself what it was.

Jeanne is standing there now, wearing her new body and waiting for him to say something. He's caught up, though, trying to remember when he last saw her, when she changed.

She must have been one of that whole gaggle of kids, standing around the day they took Etta Grace away to the hospital, Crooks

14

and Delaneys and stray kids come down the lake with their families to plant potatoes. Surely Jeanne was a child then? How long ago was that? Two years, maybe three? He can almost see Jeanne there, staring down at her feet while the doctor helped Etta Grace into the back seat of his automobile and Jerusha screamed the only scream of her life.

Everything that Moves under the Trees

A flash of white in the trees brings Jerusha to the back door. Everyone is traipsing through her yard this morning. First Eddie with the dog, now Jeanne.

The girl looks like a ghost, wearing nothing but a white thing that's more of a shift than a dress, her boots all undone except for the top button. She's chasing something that flies, running with her face thrown up to the trees. You'd think she might suddenly lift up too, and take off like a water bird, rising. But no, not her. Flighty isn't exactly the way you'd describe that girl.

Maybe it's the feeling of fall coming that makes Jerusha think time is working its way around in a circle. It isn't that Jerusha mistook Jeanne for the ghost of Etta Grace, not that at all. You wouldn't, not even with the way she runs with her head thrown back. But the minute she sees Jeanne flapping through the trees she knows things are coming back on themselves. Somehow, she just understands right away that Jeanne will run into Eddie Allen back there. She feels like she's watching a story being told the second time. Not even the names are different.

Eddie went up a couple hours ago. He didn't stop to talk, but that's nothing. He's the type that talks to trees more than people. He'll stop when he likes, and he'll be glad when she comes into his yard, too. In his flat kind of way he will, anyhow. He needs the company, whether he admits it or not.

He shouldn't be alone up at that farm. It isn't natural, and that family of his won't help. Got something broken in the blood, that bunch. Turned in on themselves. Well, it happens up here. The grandparents are supposed to guard against it, make plans and see the marriages aren't too close. Raise the children up right. That wasn't going to happen for Eddie and his brothers though, was it?

Grandfather poison, too. Jerusha has always known exactly who and what they were, since the night she brought Eddie out of his mother.

It was this time of year when Eddie was born, must be a birthday around now. Twenty-two?

The night his mother gave birth to him, the summer heat had just started dropping off quicker after dark. Back then, Jerusha lived up in the *garçonière* behind Seb Crook's house, doing for old Seb where she could keep an eye on Etta Grace at the same time. She couldn't let Etta Grace go to the school. They'd have taken her away. Taken her sooner, that is. So she kept quiet back there on Crook's farm and never took the child into town. Old Seb was sweet to Etta Grace, showed her how to peel an apple in one long piece and sprout beans in the windowsill. Made her laugh at the stupidity of chickens.

By then, people around the valley knew Jerusha as the one to call when their babies came. The trick to midwifing is to make folks feel like you're there to make calm out of chaos, like they can finally let go of themselves, now you've come.

Hank Allen, the big brother, came to get her in the pony cart the night Eddie was born. She went out the door to feel the air and then went back to wrap a second blanket around Etta Grace before she laid her in the back of the cart and got in on the seat beside Hank. It was dusk but you could still feel the heat of the sun coming up off the road. A porcupine snuffled in the grass along the edge, and she had a sudden urge to shout and scare it away from that boy and his cart. Right then she didn't know why, but she knew later.

She'd been expecting them to come for months, ever since Mrs Allen started showing. That woman didn't bring out many live babies. There were big spaces of time between the Allen boys and in the intervals Julia Allen's body coughed up half-formed, bloody things. Time Eddie come, she was more than forty. You'd have thought Eddie would be the broken one, the way change-of-life babies sometimes are. The way Etta Grace was, perfect to look at, but what people call not all there. In the end, though, Eddie seems

17

like the only one whole. In and out of the world all backwards and twisted, those Allens. It's easy to think of Eddie as a kind of saviour, a sort of redeeming angel, the way that family throws him into relief. You have to guard against that kind of thinking, though. You don't want to put a halo around anyone, in case the light blinds you.

Well, if Eddie is a saviour, she was there for the miracle of his birth. Which was an ordinary thing in itself, considering.

It was nearly full dark by the time Hank got her over to the farm, sky the colour of the Virgin's veil. She climbed down out of the cart and had to remind Hank that it was polite to lift Etta Grace down and put her in her mother's arms, not make a woman who's come to help your ma lift all the weight herself. No doubt it was the first time Hank Allen touched the girl, and it was Jerusha who suggested it. Most of the sins we commit happen all unknowing.

Things were going slow with Mrs Allen. There'd been no need to rush. She was silent about it, just went stiff with every pain and lay against the headboard like a statue until it passed. Not a good way to be at all, better she should be screaming than that, but you can't soften a woman's soul all at once at the same time her body is doing them kind of things to her. It either happens or it doesn't, and usually not till the baby is out. Anyway, there was plenty of time to lay Etta Grace on the couch, get a pot of water on the woodstove and change the bedding under Julia. She'd piled up all the old quilts and they smelled clean. Bit proud, in fact, Julia Allen.

A couple hours after dark, once the room was in order and Mrs Allen as calm as a stiffened-up woman was ever going to be, Jerusha tucked the blanket in around Etta Grace and stepped out into the yard. She made a circle around by the barn, just to stretch her legs. A fox screamed somewhere so far away in the woods you could barely hear it. She could hear the creek, though, playing over the rocks at the bottom of the hill. It was that kind of night, with heavy, open air that carries sound in ways you don't expect. There was a light in the dairy barn and the door was slid open. She looked in, thinking to say something comforting to whoever was in there.

It was Hank, sitting on the floor in the aisle. He had something in an old chicken carrier, curled in the corner as far away from him as it could get. The creature was doing its best to be smaller than it was, and she couldn't make it out at first. After a minute she realised it was a fisher cat.

It took time for her brain to put together what her eyes were telling it. It didn't make any kind of sense. What she was seeing frightened her before she all the way understood it, but she didn't stop looking.

Hank Allen had strapped a hunting knife to the stock of a hoe or some such, lashed the blade to it, so it was a knife with a handle three feet long. He had this long knife stuck through the side of the cage and he was poking holes in that fisher cat while he looked right into its eyes.

Jerusha felt like she was seeing something enormous in the landscape, an ocean or a ten-year storm or one of the giant falls in the Seaway, something so big it would crush you or wash you away before you'd hope to comprehend it.

Had to have been a while he'd been going at that fisher cat, because the thing wasn't spitting or snapping or trying to look fierce. The situation was past any of that. Hank Allen was master already. The creature didn't look away from him, didn't seem to know how. It was already as far away as it could get and all it could do was curl around itself and keep its eyes on the danger.

Hank's arm jerked forward again and Jerusha gasped. Surely, she made a sound he could hear out of the dark, even if he couldn't see her? She took a step back and cast her eyes around, looking for the best way out. That was when she saw the other boy, on the edge of the lamplight. Micky Allen was sitting up on the door of a stall, holding a post to steady himself. His eyes were shining and he was breathing through his open mouth. He was so intent on what his big brother was doing, he never looked her way, even when her feet scuffed against the dirt in the yard. That night, Micky Allen was maybe eight years old.

19

Jerusha never made a move to help the creature. When she pictured herself stepping into that circle of light to get between them, she could feel the knife going into her own thigh, then her belly, just as though it was actually happening.

Those boys were somewhere west of reason, as her William used to say. People like that make no sense; the next thing they do could be anything. It never occurred to her that what she'd seen was something small, done by boys who will grow out of such things. That scene didn't strike her like one thing by itself. It gave her a feeling like thunder building up in July. In the thrust of Hank Allen's knife hand, she could see a future stretching out over the valley like war and famine and burning rain. She backed away and stood shaking by the kitchen door for a minute before she went inside again.

What if she had stepped in and scolded them instead? Would everything have come out the same anyway, or could she have bent them in another direction?

When she went back into the house, the Allens' sitting room seemed like another world. In the firelight it looked like something in a magazine picture by N. C. Wyeth. The heat from the stove was extra and unnecessary and it made Jerusha feel sick. Mrs Allen was sweating silently and Etta Grace was breathing into her hand, covering her own mouth, the way she always did when she slept. The water on the stove hadn't even boiled. Jerusha'd been gone maybe five minutes, if that. Looking back now, though, she can see that those few minutes held their whole future.

In the end the baby came without much fuss. It took Mrs Allen a while to harden up inside after, but that was to be expected at her age and there wasn't too much blood. Wiping the thick whiteness off the baby who was about to be Eddie Allen, Jerusha had a sudden urge to hold him to her chest and run. She even spent a crazy minute trying to figure out how she could wake up Etta Grace and get them both away before Julia could call her men to chase them.

But then she shook herself and laid the boy down next to his mother. Julia Allen looked at him for a long minute with no expression at all, and then got him into the crook of her arm and closed her eyes. Jerusha cleaned her up as best she could and then woke Etta Grace, so they could walk the dark road home. *Mère de Dieu*, she was never getting in that pony cart again.

It's not like she usually wanted to steal other people's babies. It was just an impulse, an instinct like the one that made that caged animal get as small as it could and stare its pain right in the eyes. In the face of something like that, most creatures run or fight if they can and cower if they can't. And the mothers want to protect the young.

How could you leave a newborn baby in a place like that?

Twenty-some years later, Eddie is still there in that same house. The rest of them have gone, either to hell or to town. He's there by himself on the farm, and Jerusha living in the old logging camp, right at the edge of Allen land. Who'd have imagined all that, twenty years ago? Jerusha and Eddie Allen, both clung to the same woods, and him with so much love for everything that moved under the trees, it seemed again like redemption.

Eddie ought to have a woman there, or some farmhands if a woman's too many for him. He has one of those souls that belongs to the woods, and that isn't always a good thing. Sometimes men like that lose sight of everything. The sharpness goes out of their eyes and they forget how to talk to people, forget about people altogether.

And there the two of them come now, out of the trees together just like she knew they would. Jeanne Delaney the younger, daughter of her friend, stomping her feet like a bear walking upright while her hands flap around like two upset birds. She's chattering non-stop, the way she does. Eddie looks in front, instead of at her, but Jerusha can see he's listening with his whole self like Jeanne is something he's tracking.

21

The girl is tightrope walking on time right now, still running around in the woods playing pretend, but with a woman's body on her. Jerusha can see that body, ringing out there between the two of them and, too, she can see that only one of them notices it. She'll have to talk to the girl. Even though Jerusha is the worst possible choice, considering history. There isn't anyone else and she owes it to the memory of the first Jeanne, who breathed her last breath into Jerusha's ear the night little Jeanne breathed her squalling first.

Seems like Jerusha's lived long enough to see everything come back full circle. Here she is, older than she ever thought she'd get to be, and maybe this is why? Counting everything up together, Jerusha isn't sure her body has a right to rest. Not yet, anyway. Since the night Eddie Allen was born, she's been failing to do things, leaving things out. Those mistakes started small, in a way, but they've been moving forward and growing. There'll be no fixing things. Broke stays broke, she knows that. But she knows that she's part of it, too.

Seeing little Jeanne all the way grown is maybe the last thing she has to do. Once the girl is as safe as anyone can be, the memory of her mother might rest. Maybe Jerusha can die quiet, too.

If it's winter when Jerusha finally goes, who'll be there to find her? Jeanne will have gone off into her woman's life. It'll be a good, long time before anybody else notices, even Eddie. Like with old Campbell, the foxes and the wolverines could be through the windows and gnawing on her frozen limbs before they come to haul her out in the spring. Well, fine. Might as well be food for innocent creatures and go the long way back, into the good dirt under the beech trees.

She can lie there with maybe some owls and a jack rabbit to keep her body company. The moon arcing over the cabin and the slope down to the bend in the road. Crows and coyotes to break her up and take her away.

Jeanne

Eddie Allen didn't laugh. He smiled at me sometimes, when I was jabbering on about things I imagined. Guess you think I'm still doing that now, eh? Well, I haven't talked this much in years, certainly not about them days. Only doing it now because you're a stranger. You'll see.

Later, when Eddie touched me, he never smiled. Sometimes he did after, just one slow, sad one, without teeth. I never seen him just let go and laugh though, big belly laugh because you just can't help it, the way people do when they drink or otherwise let loose because they can't hold onto their feelings anymore. That is why the world invented stupid jokes, if you ask me. Okay, so you didn't. But you said you want my story.

People are vultures, city boy. All they want to know about is other people's ugliness. Well okay, I am telling you, if you're listening. Eddie Allen just didn't know how to laugh. Boy and man, I never seen him do it. Think on that for a minute.

Get it?

Anyway, what I want to tell you is about the fair in Harmony. It was maybe a couple weeks after that day I found Eddie sleeping in the woods. I need to tell you the whole day of the fair. It's one of the sharp-edged pieces of the thing, one of the parts that cuts when I think about it now.

It was still warm, but the light was turning and the trees were, too. He was waiting beside the path when I came up from the water, standing in front of the half-turned leaves. Both the Allens' horses, the fine one and Betty, were snuffling the mulch behind Eddie. When he saw me he didn't move his head. He just looked into the middle distance like maybe it was a raccoon or a bobcat he was waiting for. He was listening with his whole body. Then his eyes brought me into focus and his gaze closed in. I lost my footing under the weight of that stare.

'Come with me,' was all he said. It wasn't a question. I don't know why it didn't worry me. I never suspected him of anything mean; it just wasn't possible. You'll hear people say a lot of things about Eddie Allen. Those things go with his last name, but not his first.

So anyway, I went giddy instead of feeling everything that was lying there waiting for me in the air. That's the way you do when you're that age, isn't it? I looked Betty up and down, pretending I was only then seeing her for the first time. Betty was slow. She was meant for pulling, not riding twenty miles with a saddle.

'This supposed to be my *beau cheval blanc*?' He just looked at me. I guess he knew I meant to joke, but like I say, Eddie Allen didn't laugh. 'Never mind,' I said. 'Where we going, Eddie?'

'Not telling. Get up.' He locked his fingers and stooped beside Betty.

I pushed his hands away and swung up. Once I was in the saddle, I realised that was the first time I'd touched him. Not the first time, you know. I mean, the first time since we saw each other in the woods. I kept feeling it, long after it was done and we were riding. First time that happens to you, that sting on your skin, it knocks the sense right out of you. You forget what you're about. You must recall that yourself, city boy. Try to keep that in mind while I tell you the rest. I'll be needing a lot of leeway if you're gonna keep companionable, sitting in my chair till the end of the story.

Betty kept wanting to scratch her sides on the trees. I had to push off all the time to keep her from crushing my legs. She was trying me out, just like people do. They learn, and so did she. By the time we got to the road, she was doing her best.

After a while, I realised we were headed for the fairground outside Harmony. You need to understand, there wasn't a lot to do in those days. There was the woods and the water. They could keep you busy for months on end, but that was every day. In the way of events involving people and novelty, there wasn't much. I was nearly

24

sixteen and I'd never seen a moving picture. Don't laugh, it was like that. The fair was the most exciting thing that happened all year, in that kind of way. I'd only been once before in my whole life.

Sit still while I tell you about the first time I went to the fair. T-Roy and Grampy took me when I was nine. Everything seemed enormous then. I held T-Roy's hand and looked at the hocks of the horses and the dynamos grinding underneath the rides. That was my eye level.

On the fairway there were hawkers and carnival people yelling about everything you could have and see, people who weren't made right and animal foetuses with two heads and ladies from far away, dancing. I remember I needed to pee so bad I just kept tugging on T-Roy. He was rushing me along the fairway, wouldn't let me look at anything. We got to the end behind the exhibition house, and he said he'd stand right there and wait for me outside the ladies' restroom.

Grampy was off somewhere. Thinking back, I guess he was playing dice behind the barns, but I didn't know that at the time. I just knew T-Roy was mad and in a hurry. So I was rushing when I went in the bathroom and threw open the door to one of the stalls without looking first or thinking.

Now listen, people talk about Catholic girls like they know nothing and they'll do anything. First off, I knew all about monthlies and where babies came from. Christ, I spent half my childhood with Jerusha Prichard. Even Etta Grace had her monthlies. You don't need a sound mind for that.

Second, sure I'd do anything. If I wanted to, I would. If you wouldn't you're stupid. Life moves past faster than a motor car. If you don't jump in and take a ride, you missed most of it. It's that kind of plain thinking the ladies at the Children's Aid called 'degenerate', or maybe it was 'delinquent'. I can't remember which was what.

So anyway, I flung open the door. At first, I couldn't make sense out of what I was seeing. There was more blood in that toilet stall than there should have been. Least it looked like it to me. The toilet water was full of that bright red Jerusha always said wasn't healthy. 'Too thin, bad colour,' she'd say, when a woman shed blood like that. Jerusha would make those women drink molasses tea. Blood was all over the seat too, and some on the floor. The little bit of air in there smelled like rust and mushrooms.

So I come skipping through the door and that whole sight hit me like a hard slap. Things have a way of jumping from around the corners of life and flinging themselves at you. I don't even know why I'm telling you, it just stayed with me and fell together in my mind with things that came after. I can't figure whether I've exaggerated it inside myself over the years, remembering with little girl's eyes. All that blood was saying something, but without the woman who made it I couldn't tell what. Had some poor girl let a baby go in the toilets at the county fair by accident? Poked herself with something on purpose? Or did she just get caught out in a pretty new rayon dress and have to sit bleeding too much in the public restrooms while her boyfriend waited with the bearded lady? I can't be sure now, but at the time it looked more like a murder than a natural bodily function to me. It scared me. Like I say, that's not because I was a Catholic girl who didn't know what was what. You'll see about that as I go along.

Later, Etta Grace made blood like that. If I couldn't make sense out of it, how was she going to?

I guess I'm saying, the bloody bodies of women are what tie this whole thing together, even though they weren't the worst of it. I saw plenty of sights like that later, things that make you realise that the difference between nature and violence is just a story we tell ourselves.

I stared for a bit, then remembered how bad I had to pee and turned away. I took that sight with me, though, and I still have it. Little pieces, little broken pieces we carry around with us until we die. They don't necessarily hang together or make sense, and I won't apologise to you for that. The life behind you is just a bunch of moments that are heavy enough or sudden enough to sink in.

Sure, I didn't consider anything like that ever happening to me. At nine, I thought I'd grow up to be Joan of Arc. Spirit shining right out of my body and nothing like blood to hold me down. When the night came and T-Roy said don't wander off into it, I looked up at the lights on the Ferris wheel and thought somehow my life would be full of that kind of shining movement. Without the motor and the grease and the people who spit from the top just because they think it's funny, of course. All I could see was those lights and the sky behind them, and me brandishing a shining sword.

I would have been good at that kind of thing. Don't laugh.

At fifteen, walking through with Eddie, the fair seemed smaller and dirtier than it had then, but I still thought I was a hero. The lights at the fair reminded me of that earlier feeling, and even the smells seemed like they came from the place of heroes, deep fat and burned sugar. Those carnival people had no borders at all. Some of them had probably been to California, but they didn't even stay there neither. They just kept on the move and did as they liked. In those days, the hoboes were already everywhere, collecting the dust that rose up on the roads and getting their dinner at people's kitchen doors. The carnival was moving too, but above everything instead of underneath. From where I stood, it seemed like they lived in a perpetual shower of nickels and dimes, all raining down and flashing under strings of coloured lights.

Me and Eddie got fry bread and cotton candy and then Eddie wanted to see the pulling. He was concentrating and I got bored. Eddie had a way of shutting people out. He was one of those men who could be all alone in a crowd, just watching the cows and the horses. The noise and the shoving didn't seem to touch him. Turned out later, Eddie could shut us all out. He had a shell like a scarab, or maybe a turtle. He could pull his head in and pretend to be a rock, let people kick him around or just walk by. I know he had a kind of

27

strength, because I felt it that very day, and after. But it usually wasn't the showy kind. You'll see.

Later, Eddie paid for us to have our picture taken. The photographer had a pony caravan with his name painted on the back door. On the ground by the wagon he'd pitched the tent where the pictures got took. There were three different painted canvases and a stand where he lit the flash powder. He ducked under a black cloth, just like you see now in the movies. Eddie let me pick and I chose the backdrop with a moon and clouds. The moon was silver and blue, but you wouldn't know it in the photograph.

The photographer gave Eddie a fine jacket, and got me to turn a bit to the side and look up at his face. Eddie didn't smile, of course, but I did. I couldn't help it. When people didn't want me to, I always got giggly. Miss McLaughlin said it was a devil in me, but she didn't make having a devil in you sound like a bad thing. She always liked me, I could tell.

In my mind's eye, me and Eddie look like vaudeville stars in that picture. Both of us heroes in a frozen moment that could never be touched by what came after. I still have it with me, just as if it got printed and put in a frame. In fact, though, we didn't ever get to see that picture. It got ruined before it got made.

I said I'd wait for the photograph while Eddie went to see the last round of the pulling. I asked the photographer a lot of questions about where he'd been and how it was out west, but all he wanted to talk about was what he called 'the science of the photograph'.

'This right here is silver,' he said. 'I paint silver on the paper.' He tipped a big jar full of clear liquid back and forth a little.

'It looks like water,' I said, 'not silver.'

He laughed and explained the whole thing to me, about how photographs worked. He said his daddy had made that caravan and all its machines. I'll tell you what struck me. That man just trusted me to understand what he was saying, didn't talk down to me at all. He said how the light burned the picture onto the glass, and then you reversed it and burned the paper with light again. He lit a red lantern and told me I could come in if I shut the door. He put the latch on and explained that the white light of the sun would ruin everything, you couldn't risk anyone opening the door while the pictures 'developed'. The chemicals didn't respond to what he called the red end of the spectrum. Well, then he had to explain about that. I'd never seen anyone so happy with his own work. Grampy and T-Roy had a kind of still satisfaction about the things they did, but the photographer was like a kid at Christmas. He had a coat like a mad scientist from a magazine picture that he put over his clothes before he poured out the chemicals. Inside the caravan it smelled like vinegar, and something else that clung inside your nose.

The only reason we see anything at all, he said, is because our eyes are made to capture light. When we look out over the hills and valleys from a distance, it's just patches of light and shadow, which is just less light. That's the only way we can tell the shape of the land, or even the people we love right up close. Light falls into the eyes of the blind same as it does into ours, it just doesn't register. Something in them doesn't respond. He used a lot of words for that, but I don't remember them now.

Well, he had a machine with a lantern inside. He pegged the paper up to the wall and put his glass plate into a frame between the lens and the light. He lifted a little hatch and the beam of light travelled over his different trays of liquid to hit the paper on the opposite wall. There we were, our image travelling in that beam, but ghostly and backwards. Our shadows were shining and our shining places were black. Eddie's eyes looked like empty white sockets.

I don't know, maybe I'm just remembering it like that now, considering everything. That picture of me and Eddie made out of light is like the blood in the toilets from the time before that. It's etched into me just the way it is. Right or not, I can't shift it.

The photographer took the paper carefully off the wall and put it in one of his trays of liquid, tipping the tray back and forth to make a little ebb tide. While he was doing that, Eddie knocked and tried the door. When he felt the closed latch, he let out a bellow like a mother bear. I'm saying it was that terrifying, and either you've been in front of a moaning bear, or in between someone like Eddie and the thing they wanted, or you haven't. In the latter case, just forget it. It's not a sound a person can describe. Maybe you heard it in a nightmare, but I bet that's the closest you've got.

I was up on the one seat in that little caravan room, a high stool I suppose the photographer normally sat on when he worked at his counter. Eddie bellowed my name and it sent me back into the corner of the wall with my heart pounding. It felt like maybe a cow had kicked at me and just barely missed.

One time, I got caught in the river in the spring. It was stronger than I expected, and I'd forgot just exactly about the cold. Up here, see, the water is freezing coming down from the hills; you get dizzy just from putting your feet in it. The river was high and fast and the cold knocked all the breath out of me and stopped my limbs. Whatever I tried, I just kept going under into the ripping cold. Well, crouched there on that stool in the red light, I felt just like that, like I'd jumped into something without looking and now I couldn't even struggle for the surface.

You can probably guess the next thing Eddie did.

After he broke the photographer's door, we left quick. The photographer, who was about as threatening as Miss McLaughlin, didn't even look outraged. He just blinked at Eddie and looked at the door, hanging askew. Then he looked over at me and held out his hand to help me down off the stool.

'Your picture's ruined, Miss Delaney,' the photographer said. 'I'm sorry about that.'

I pushed past Eddie and walked down the fairway as fast as I could. I wasn't mad or scared anymore. I just knew I didn't want to be the person at the other end of that sound that had come out of him. Like the sting on your skin when you first touch somebody, it sends you sideways the first time you realise you can cause that kind of reaction in a person. I was no way prepared for that. I wanted the dark to come, the lights to come on, the hawkers to keep shouting and chanting. I wanted all that to never stop and leave me alone with Eddie Allen. Why didn't I run away then? I could have left town with the fair, surely? Imagine if I'd turned in another direction that day. I'd be in a whole different life. Likely, I wouldn't be sitting here telling you about it, neither.

After that day my eyes were never the same. Sometimes I look out over the lake, or the snow on the fields, and I think, it's just light. Everything your eyes have ever shown you is just the world throwing light back at you. Just patterns and pieces of brightness and shadow. The whole world might as well be just a flat piece of special paper. The effect is the same.

'Course I calmed down after a bit. I didn't run away because I didn't want to, is the truth of it. It was scary, but it was hypnotising, like the time after that when me and Eddie saw a mountain lion through the trees. Something was drawing me in and making me want to run at the same time. I don't scare easy. I stayed.

We took the horses home down the middle of the road; you could in them days. Like I said, almost no one had a car, and anyway you could hear one coming for miles. With the dark it turned chilly. Eddie reined up and clucked at Betty to stop so he could reach over and put his wool shirt on me. You could lean those horses right into each other. They were family. The moon came up late and huge over the mountains east of us. White, though, still a summer moon. It was so bright the trees threw blue shadows onto the road. We heard the owls, and when we got closer to the lake, loons. All night long they cackled like the folks in the colony for the feeble-minded behind the hospital.

Every once in a while, Eddie'd bump that quarter horse up against Betty and give me a little shove. Just letting me know he was there.

I said, 'You gonna tell me why you scared that poor old picture man half to death, or what?'

'Jeanne,' he made it sound like a boy's name in English. That was him making an effort to say it right. 'Jeanne, how old are you?'

'Sixteen in two weeks. Old enough for you to answer me straight.'

'Jeanne, you're both too young and too old for that man to have you behind a locked door.'

'You don't need to keep repeating my name like that. Look around, Eddie Allen. No one else here. I know who you're talking to.'

I was mean to him like that. I couldn't help it. That was the contradiction in him. He had a kind of power, but, too, he had that in him that just made the other person take the high ground. Well, yes, I saw why later. He'd been bred to it in that family. You smelled it on him without even realising.

It was only a human thing, though. The animals in the woods never tried to bully Eddie. He was one of them. He followed their rules of calm and violence, killing and giving way.

'He did wrong, Jeanne.'

'There you go again. You sound like a charity lady. He wasn't trying to do anything. He was showing how you make a photograph. They're made of silver, Eddie. Did you know that? Silver that burns.'

'Ay-uh, you said that three times already. You shake around a jar of silver and bring a girl child into your red light; only one reason a grown man does that.'

Innocence was not a thing Eddie Allen understood a'tall.

'He wasn't even thinking about anything but his science stories, Eddie. I'm telling you. He reminded me of Grampy. He was that kind of man. Anyway, what about you? I'm fifteen, since you asked. How old are you?'

'Turned twenty-two and you know it. When you were born and your mama died, I was six. I remember it because of how Jerusha told it to my mother.'

'So, what are you doing with me? We're on a dark road between Harmony and just about nowhere; you went crazy and broke my photograph and now the silver is smeared all over the sky. Why are we under all that in the dark, Eddie Allen?'

32

'You shouldn't talk like that to people, Jeanne. You sound like a poem in a book. People might think you're soft in the head.'

'Stop telling me what to do and answer! It's close enough to midnight. I'm fifteen, just like I was a few hours ago. Aren't you wrong, Eddie? What're your reasons?'

He looked like I'd kicked him in the gut. That was because what I said was half true and we both knew it. It was the ugly half, though. And anyway, it was too soon to say it out loud. I could've broke the whole thing right there. Eddie dug his knees into the horse and took off. He didn't leave exactly, but he stayed a quarter mile ahead and never said a word to me the rest of the way home.

I rode on and watched him from down the road. Which is why I saw it when the stillness took him over. I swear he just soaked it into himself from the air underneath the trees. That was Eddie Allen's special power. No matter what had happened to him five minutes before, he could turn himself into a creature from the woods and shine out calm like a lamp shines out light. It wasn't something everybody could respect, or even see, but it was a particular ability he had.

We didn't get back to the boat till near midnight. I caught up to Eddie waiting there at the top of the bank above our dock and jumped off Betty. When I landed, I reached my hand over and steadied myself on Eddie's leg. I didn't need to, but I was afraid to walk away without closing the space between us first. I just wanted to touch him one time. I said thank you, but he didn't answer. We looked at each other for a minute. His eyes were set back in two shadowy pits, just the opposite of that picture shining on the old man's wall. He wasn't gonna say anything and I didn't know how to, so after a minute I just went.

That bank was so steep the only way down it was to run and let your feet catch you and slow you down every step or so. The only way if you were fifteen, anyway. So, I came stumbling out of the trees onto the *batteur* with my boots in my hand and found T-Roy sitting smoking on the dock. I said something stupid about the Ferris wheel and the two-headed pig foetus and ran up, thinking to steal a drag of his pipe and sit on his shoulder. He grabbed me so hard by the arm, I nearly pissed myself right then and there.

You need to understand, T-Roy had never once even looked at me cross-eyed since the day I was born. The worst he ever did was roll his eyes at me when I did something stupid. When he grabbed me like that, it was probably the worst shock I'd had in life so far, including what happened with Eddie and the photograph man. My stomach turned to water all in an instant.

When he raised his other hand, I jumped off the dock. My body just grabbed me and took me away into the water. I didn't have time to think or make decisions before I was swimming out into the dark. I'd had to twist out of his grip as I jumped. The next day there was a rake mark of long bruises around my arm.

'That boy ain't strong enough to protect you from what's around him, Jeanne,' he shouted after me. 'That's a fact.'

I didn't answer. The moon was well over the trees by then, throwing a path across the water. I stayed out of the light and swam right out. The water was warmer than the air and I turned over onto my back to look up at the moon and stars. The loons were cackling and they made me think of Etta Grace and of what Eddie said about the way I talk. I could still feel T-Roy's fingers on my arm and in my mind's eye I could see Etta Grace, swaying under the trees. All of that was jumbled up in my head and my heart was pounding. Maybe words would stop meaning things and everything would just come apart into craziness. It was like anything could happen after T-Roy raised a hand to me. He was still shouting from the dock, saying, what was wrong with me and didn't I know I'd scared him and Grampy half to death.

Lying on top of the lake, I started to cry a new kind of tears that'd never come out of me before. They didn't heave up from down in my chest the way they do in kids. I didn't have to use my whole self to make them. They just rose up into my eyes and slid down my face into the lake, warm and black, burned silver.

34

After a while T-Roy got scared and called me back. I waited till his voice calmed down and he started to begging.

That highway of moonlight cut the lake in half and ended in the overhanging trees near the floating dock. I rolled over and pushed into it, so T-Roy could see me, then I swam down the light home.

We went inside to where Grampy had a candle lit under his Saint Barbara on the little shelf behind the stove. There was no other light in the cabin, except the glow from his pipe. I sat with a quilt over me and looked at the flames around Saint Barbara, moving in the candlelight like real flames, like it was all one fire. I always liked her. She looked as if no one had ever managed to come anywhere near touching her. No doubt she'd set plenty of men bellowing the way Eddie did that day, but it didn't trouble her. She was all calm in the quiet place inside that roar of fire.

'Jeanne Delaney,' T-Roy started in.

'I know. I scared you. I'm sorry. Sorry, Grampy. Really.'

'It was in here you know, Jeanne. *Maman* died in here.'

'Okay, you don't need to try to make me feel worse, T-Roy. I said sorry.'

Grampy kept quiet, leaning over to throw some driftwood in the stove. I wished T-Roy wouldn't bring all that up around him. I felt bad enough for being the reason his little girl was dead without going over it with him.

'I was nearly ten,' T-Roy said. 'I missed her.'

Not one for overstating the case, T-Roy. What he meant was that he was broken forever from losing his mother right when he needed her so bad. Did he think that hadn't already occurred to me? My poor brother always seemed to be losing his women. *Maman*, Etta Grace. Me.

'Could you yell at me in the morning, T-Roy? Grampy's probably tired and I've made him enough trouble for right now.'

But he wasn't stopping. He brought it all out, how I got born and what happened to Etta Grace. T-Roy told it like it was something I wouldn't already know. Like girls were some kind of delicate things

35

that might shrivel up if you exposed them to the light, but he had to tell me for my own good. Poor T-Roy, he didn't even see how ridiculous that was. It was my mother and Etta Grace who did those things, and Jerusha who had to live in the shadow of them. I've been a girl all my life, having to piss in toilet stalls full of gore. Maybe I didn't know the details, but it's not like I couldn't see it all coming from the minute I opened my blood-covered eyes.

He meant well, and I won't say T-Roy was stupid. Just simple, and mostly good.

We all three sat there in Grampy's cabin, me drying off and Grampy smoking. The smell of his pipe usually made me sleepy, but that night was different. I didn't want the story, but I couldn't shut it out and go to sleep either.

Grampy stared into the candle flame with miles and miles of distance in his eyes. Never said a word. Maybe he wasn't listening. Saint Barbara stood in her flames and gazed right over our heads. It occurred to me, Grampy spent most of his life sitting under that stare, in the room where his daughter died. All of a sudden I could see how that must have been from his position. Why'd he stay there like that?

We sat until the lake turned pink with the morning and the candle sputtered, until the flames were just orange ink on paper and Grampy was asleep in his chair.

I wished then that I could go back into the lake and live there. I could become some kind of fairy creature that breathed the rusty water and swam through the star grass. I wanted to live in some element besides air, where no one could follow me without drowning, in a land where everything wasn't made out of blood.

In the Small Hours

T-Roy is on the deck before dawn, the only one still awake. Even Jeanne finally wore herself out. Their *pe'père* sleeps as much as waking now anyhow, sliding back and forth between the two at all hours. The problem seems to be left for T-Roy to think on. Again.

There's a strong wind blowing down the lake and the boat rocks them like they're all in a cradle together. Eddie Allen will be at home now, waking up on that farm full of restless ghosts. There's no point talking to him. Not that he won't listen, just that it won't be him that moves whatever will move between them two. It'll be Jeanne. She always has had more than enough force, and no idea at all.

Eddie Allen only ever took charge of one thing in his life, and that was just long enough to throw it off on T-Roy. He might be kinder than his brothers in one way, but it's just that where they have acid for blood, he has water. Boy's weak, is what. T-Roy's known since they were both kids.

T-Roy was fourteen the day Eddie Allen showed himself down on the lake. He came out on the dock and sat for nearly an hour saying nothing while T-Roy cleaned an eel and three trout. He looked at the eel, wide-eyed, but not at T-Roy. He looked at his feet, and over at the far shore, then twisted himself to look up at Mary's Peak behind him. It was obvious he had something to say by the way he tried so hard to pretend he didn't.

Yep, he showed himself that day, more ways than one.

'You ever break the law, T-Roy?' He'd waited a good long time to come up with that opening.

'Well, would I tell you if I had?'

'You ever been in a fight?'

'Kind of hard to avoid when your mother's dead and you live on a boat.'

Eddie made him feel older somehow. Responsible, which was what he was trying for. He was troubled and terrified and needing someone to do what he wanted done. There was no one on that farm who defined responsibility in any way that was normal.

He must have been nine or ten that day, but already there was something showing in him that put him apart from that bunch. Or maybe they'd put him apart, treating him like a runt since he could crawl.

'Did you like it?'

'Like what?'

'Fighting.'

'I like the quiet. I don't have many thoughts, but I like to be able to think 'em. Up close, fighting's noisy and confusing.'

'I like the woods. You like the woods, T-Roy?'

'Yep. You gonna stop asking me questions and help?' T-Roy held out the bucket of offal. 'Bring all this in to my *pe'père*. He's in the galley with the baby.' The baby was little Jeanne, of course.

After he done that, Eddie came back around the stern and startled T-Roy. Even then, the boy was soft in the world. Good at coming up on you quiet.

'They've got a girl.' Eddie talked at his back and T-Roy didn't turn around. He knew it must be bad because he didn't want to look T-Roy in the eye while he told it. Thinking on it now, he had to suppose that was a sign of character, him knowing enough to be ashamed. Where he'd learned about shame in that house is anyone's guess.

'A girl?' T-Roy said as innocent as he could, trying not to startle the kid and make him run away.

'She's in the smokehouse, T-Roy. I need help.'

'What kind of help?'

'We need to let her out. She's crying. My ma won't talk about it.'

'We?' T-Roy turned around then, because he had to and if the kid ran maybe it'd be just as well. 'You have any idea what you're asking me?'

Well, of course he didn't. He probably didn't all the way understand what they were doing to the girl, even.

In magazine stories the heroes sail boats through storms and survive in jungles where they have to eat their dead companions. They scale the tops of giant waterfalls and fight lawless warlords in the mountains of Afghanistan and Colorado. When danger presents itself they square up and step in. That night was T-Roy's only taste of that kind of thing. Afterwards, he thought he'd prefer to be one of those thinking heroes that walks through wilderness alone, dealing with mountain lions instead of men.

He gave Eddie the hourglass from his bunk, told him after everyone was asleep he should turn it and let it run through twice and only come get him after that. He got that from a magazine and all. After little Jeanne and his *pe'père* went to sleep, T-Roy rolled into a blanket on deck. Rain was sprinkling down on the lake from between the stars when he heard Eddie scrambling over onto the *batteur*.

Up at the Allens' farm it was dry, nothing in the air to stop the sound from carrying clear. But there was no sound. No one crying in the smokehouse, not even the animals shuffling in the barn.

'Where's the dog, Eddie?' He whispered it even though they were in the trees at the far end of the paddock.

'Spark's dead. Coyote. Crook's bringing a new pup tomorrow.'

Maybe Eddie had imagined the girl. He was maybe upset about the dog, seeing it after the fight with the coyote. That could be ugly, and he was only little. Probably gave him nightmares, not to mention living with those brothers he had. Or maybe T-Roy just didn't want to believe it. People just up the road from him who could do something like that and then sleep on it, all through a night of clear air.

Eddie led him up to the back wall of the smokehouse and gave three little knocks. After a minute the knocks came back from the bottom of the wall.

She was in there. It took them an hour to get the lock off because they needed to be quiet. T-Roy lit a match and studied a bit, then decided the best thing was to dig it right out of the wood. Every so often he had Eddie hold up a match again. They burned the wood some too, to soften it.

He lay down the lock gently on the ground, took a breath and swung the door. Then they all three stood looking at each other for a full minute, in three different kinds of shock. The girl was covered in soot and as soon as she met his eyes she started to cough. They should have brought water. By the time they got her back across the paddock she was trembling like a telegraph wire. You could feel it spitting through her, the nervous electricity that's left in the wake of being terrified.

Once they were over the fence, T-Roy sent Eddie back to the pump for water. He came back with a milk pail from the cow barn. The girl drank some, coughed and puked a little, then started shaking harder. Finally, there was a sound from the yard, a horse nickering.

'We should go,' Eddie said. 'They wake up all kinds of times. They listen.'

What in the world was T-Roy thinking? People didn't get in the way of Allens. If you did, they came into your dreams and circled like crows until you felt the shadows of them passing even in the daytime. Then one day, once you were all unnerved, they'd swoop. T-Roy may have been only fourteen, but he knew that just like anyone in the valley did.

Somehow that didn't stop him. 'If you'll trust me,' he told the girl, 'I'll take you somewhere safe.'

He can hear those words of his now, bouncing off the trees and travelling straight up into the dark. Looking back, he can see it was one of those moments when the world was witness, but you don't know it yourself till later. The words bounced back into T-Roy and stuck like pieces of glass, waiting inside him to do their cutting work. He never should have brought that girl anywhere near Jerusha and Etta Grace.

T-Roy felt his way down hill, trusting her to follow him. It took over an hour to get to the dip in the road where they could cross. He looked through the trees when the sun sent its feelers up over the lake, and she looked too.

'Well, you two're up early.' Jerusha didn't sound surprised to see them. She was used to bleeding women appearing at her door. She knew how to make calm from a tortured body, that was her work. That was why T-Roy took the girl to her.

'She's been at the Allens,' he said. 'Maybe no one should see her.'

Jerusha snapped at him then. 'You're not old enough to be out here at this hour. Go home.' She meant he wasn't old enough to see what'd been done, but the girl couldn't have been much older than him.

T-Roy could hear Etta Grace singing inside the house. He wondered if she would come to the door, if she'd laugh at him or maybe sit on the porch with a needle and thread, listening to him tell a story about the lake or the other side of the border or the eel he'd caught yesterday. Yesterday, when he'd been on the dock with the fishing knife thinking only about skin and guts so small they'd fit in your hand. Thinking only about the jobs to be done and about Etta Grace.

Soon as Jerusha took the other girl into the house, he stopped worrying. That's how it is when you're that age. You pass your troubles onto someone else and forget them, so maybe it isn't fair him blaming Eddie for doing the same thing. He dropped all his other thoughts and stood there hoping Etta Grace would come to the window and he'd be able to see her throat with the song ringing in it.

He honestly wasn't afraid right then. He knew Eddie wouldn't tell on him. The boy would suffer in silence and never do anything to free himself. That was Eddie Allen, even then.

And that was T-Roy, too. He didn't think for a minute about what kind of trouble he'd brought to Jerusha's house, though it couldn't have been more obvious.

41

He knows now that the girl wound up in the colony for feeble-minded women behind the hospital. He's seen her there, circling around the lawn and pulling at her hair, winding her way between the other mumbling, shuffling women. Jerusha told him later that she had a lace-curtain Irish family that wouldn't even look at her when she tried to go home.

He never knew her name.

Now Eddie is messing about with Jeanne. Really it was the sight of his own sins coming back that had called up the fury in T-Roy the night before. He heard Jeanne saying goodbye to Eddie up on the road, then saw her running down the bank looking just the age of that other girl. Hadn't they all paid enough not to have their women tangled up with Allens again? He'd been rough with Jeanne, telling himself it was for her own good.

Really it was just fear, swelling into anger. Just the malice and dread that passes from one to the other around the place, like electricity or disease.

Jeanne

We're all animals. Even you, city boy. We all have fears and other nameless things driving us, right underneath what we can notice or control. Just like a rabbit or a vulture, a person in a certain situation will do a certain thing, every time. Good and evil are only ideas we lay on top of that. The preachers say we can choose, and we can. We should, too. Right up until we can't.

Not long before I finished at the school in Harmony, a teacher there told us about evolution. She said two things made people different than all the other animals. Thumbs and brains. Those made us what she called successful. By successful she meant the clear-cutting and the paper mill.

Where am I going with all that? Well, like I said Eddie made me feel like an animal. Hunted. Tracked. He was learning my habits. So, I put my human brain to it and set out to do the unpredictable. Turns out I had a pattern, once I stopped to notice it. You won't know this, government man, but a deer never goes more than a mile or two its whole life. They just travel their little patch of woods in circles, with no idea how easy they are to figure if you have a brain, and a thumb to cock triggers with.

A fox too, will circle back to its own den eventually. So did I, back then. Every day, up the bank to the hospital road, round to Jerusha's cabin, up the creek to the pools between the falls, round and back down to the ledge over the lake. One direction or another, I made that circle most days. Once I noticed Eddie watching me, I changed it. Took it in a different order every day. Sometimes, I sat in one of the pines halfway up Mary's Peak and watched Eddie and Don drive the sheep or disappear up into the larches with the .22. I pretended I was the hunter then.

I carried on telling stories to myself and spying on things, all unaware what it was making me skittish in the first place, what exactly I was trying to outsmart. I thought I'd done it, though. I was proud of myself. That was me back then. No idea about the good or the bad that was waiting. None at all.

Then one lunchtime Eddie come round a bend in the road right at me, carrying short rails for his fence in the pony cart. It was so all of a sudden, Betty shied up and shook her head to get me out of her blind spot. I stepped to the side and said hello to Betty, then ran around to jump up on the back of the cart. The rails were laid longways in there, and I put my arms out to the sides to run up them like a girl on high wire. Then I threw my leg over to climb into the seat next to Eddie.

'Where you been all morning?' he said.

'What do you mean, where? Where *you* been?'

'Don't you never go the same way twice?'

Ha! I'd got him. See?

The whole of his thigh was stretched along only an inch from mine, but it wasn't touching anywhere. There was a shivering in that inch of air like right after you strike a bell. Even I noticed it, idiot as I was then. I did what I always do when I get flustered, kept talking.

'I go every which way, Eddie. You know that. Have I told you about the Pathfinder?'

'Some. Cold's coming, Jeanne. Where are you all gonna go?'

'I don't know. T-Roy wants to go over the border after they dry dock, but I'll be with Jerusha anyway. One time, he was with his Mohican friends and they were being chased by the bad ones. Down on the Hudson this was, right? And the Mohicans knew this place where you could go behind a waterfall that was like a curtain.'

'Who? T-Roy?'

'The Pathfinder! Pay attention, Eddie. It was an island, like, right in the middle of the river and no way to swim to it or bring horses. You could hole up there for months if you had the stores. Wouldn't you like that?'

'Not this time of year, you couldn't,' Eddie said.

44

'That head of yours is never gonna get into the clouds, that's for sure.'

'It may do. Getting so I can't keep it stuck to anything lately. The change of the year, must be. I'm saying, when it's cold you want a fire and a few of Jerusha's quilts. You want windows and doors.'

I laughed at him. He looked at the road and then up at the pines, a little flush climbing up his face. A shiver went through him and he reached for his jacket. That made him seem what people call human, by which they mean a little helpless, exposed. Up till then, I hadn't thought Eddie ever felt the cold.

We come out of the trees up to the fallow field that backed onto the pines. The sun was burning a good smell off the long grass. The chicory flowers and the white campion still shone in it like daytime stars. Eddie jumped off the cart and waded in. A redwing blackbird stopped singing and shied away from the far fence.

'Whyn't you have a wife, Eddie Allen?'

I guess it was that ringing space between us that had me thinking of it. I wasn't conscious that was why, though. Animals, like I said. I was like Betty, shaking my head at a blind spot.

'Jeez, girl, I'm only twenty-two.'

'Who mends your shirts, though? Who does the bread?'

'Jerusha mends my shirts, you know that. I eat biscuits and I like being on my own. I like the quiet.'

'You think I talk too much.'

'Well, yes, but I just imagine you're a bird chattering. It doesn't signify.'

'That you trying to charm me?'

I'd followed him over to the fence up between the woods and the field, wondering if he could feel the space between us, too. Like he was the moon of me, always at some exact distance I couldn't figure out how to widen or close, something invisible pulling on whatever in me wasn't anchored.

I was asking for it, but I didn't know what *it* was. I think Eddie couldn't work out how to feel about it. Did he think I was a creature from the woods or a girl from around the way? It seemed like half and both and it made each of us a little sick, a little scared, I think.

I was stuck in that distance, anyway, weaving some pieces of tall grass while he fitted rails. The grass had been yellow a while then, and getting brittle.

'So, why don't you marry somebody, put her in that kitchen and make her have a few babies. Pretty babies. Don't you get an ugly or a stupid girl, Eddie Allen. I won't forgive you if you give your features to a bunch of half-witted, homely things.'

You maybe think it's queer, me dreaming of Eddie marrying some other woman. Thing is, the women in my family don't marry people. I may have been fixed around the whirlpool of Eddie Allen, but I had no idea of attaching myself to him in that kind of way, the way you do inside buildings or laws.

'I don't like slow girls,' Eddie said.

'What about Etta Grace? You seemed to like her enough. All the men did, even though she could barely count to ten.'

Eddie looked at me, then over his shoulder at the cart, like there was something he needed but he couldn't remember what it was. Something worked in his throat, and for a minute I thought whatever it was would strangle its way up and out of his mouth. Then he turned to walk across the field, and stopped on the crest of the hill looking down at the river and the hospital grounds. He stood staring for a while.

'I didn't want to marry Etta Grace, or do anything else to her neither.' He said it with his back to me, talking into the space above the valley.

'You mad at me, Eddie?' I walked up and put my hand on him. He startled like it burned.

'No. I can't get mad at you. You don't stay still long enough.'

'That doesn't make any sense.'

'Not to you. You don't make the same sense as other people, Jeanne Delaney. I guess you noticed that before now. Make yourself useful and carry a rail. I gotta get this done and go.'

He didn't really have to go; he was just saying that. After we finished, we left Betty in the field and walked into the pines. Eddie'd gone somewhere inside himself and still hadn't come back. I guess I'd changed places with him and become the hunter after all, because it was me that had to sit still and braid my breaths into the breezes, waiting for him to trust me again so he'd come out and show himself.

Finally he said, 'If we were to stay until dark we'd hear a horned owl up there in the larches, maybe see them wolverines that've been down around the side.'

I could picture it, too. My stillness had paid off. Me and Eddie were in the same place again, looking together at something that wasn't there yet. I could picture everything moving in the quiet, all the creatures with their souls open in the night air.

Nothing in the woods hides itself really, that's just something people think.

'Every creature in here is honest,' Eddie said like he was answering my thoughts. 'They'll all kill each other, if they have to and they can manage it. And they all know it.'

'Maybe that's the difference between animals and us,' I said. 'People have the killing all mixed up and they aren't as ready to do it.'

'Well, there's two kinds of creatures, too. There's the gentle ones.'

'The ones that get eaten, you mean.'

'And creatures like Betty. Only way she'd hurt something is by accident.'

'Don't be silly, Eddie. She'd kick you square in the chest and kill you if she liked.'

'She wouldn't. Not me.'

'People, though. Carefully not killing each other seems to me the main thing people spend their time on. The thing that makes us human is not letting our natures out.'

I guess I said that then because I had yet to see Eddie's brothers up close. If you asked me now, I'd say it's the lack of reason. If Betty kicked you or a mountain lion tore you open, they'd have a reason.

47

'Crook would like to expand up here and clear all this,' Eddie said.

'I thought this was Allen land?'

'I guess.'

'What do you mean, you guess? Is it, or isn't it?'

'Allen land. I don't even know what that means.'

'It means you're the one that's allowed to shoot everything in here and cut the trees down, that's what it means.'

'You're forgetting the rest of 'em.'

'They're not here, Eddie. It's just you.'

The strangled thing came out of his throat then. 'They're always here,' he said.

And then we saw her. A mountain lion was padding across the next ridge. It was like we'd called her up out of the things we were wondering. She wasn't in a hurry or stalking anything, just come out on the rocks up there to put her feet on the heat from the sun. Even from a quarter mile away, I could see the shape of her shoulder and the way her skin rippled over bone and muscle like wind on water.

'The other difference between us and them,' Eddie said, 'people sometimes kill themselves.'

Many Returns

The maple leaves have turned the colour of blood, splashed all down the hill to the creek. Jerusha sits on the little back porch Eddie built her, mending a quilt she pulled down from the rafters.

Looking out from the porch, she can almost see all the girls that have run through these woods over the years. They've left impressions; sometimes it's like they might all be there at once, ghostly shadows in white shifts slipping through time. Etta Grace, who will always be there, swaying back and forth under the leaves. The girl T-Roy broke out of the Allens' smokehouse and brought here bleeding, one morning years ago. Little Jeanne Delaney, not so little these days, who lately found Eddie Allen in among the pines.

They're all there inside Jerusha, all the lives they've lived together and all the children they've made. Her and Roy deLaneuville, Jeanne's *pe'père*, are the only ones left who remember. Everything's returning to her in the pieces she's stitching, her Will's old trousers and Jeanne's mother's dancing dress.

This is the first quilt she made with the girls, when she looked after them both together. Jeanne was somewhere around seven years old then. She mostly ran around the quilting frame in circles, picking up the needle every once in a while, bumping into the pan handles on the stove and not even noticing, while even Etta Grace was concentrating on the work. Able to keep her mind on one thing for hours on end, Etta Grace. All the while they worked, Jeanne was firing a string of questions that cut right through things like the cold outside.

'Why do ya live *here*, Jerusha?'

'Why not?'

'Well, you could have a real house.'

'What's so pretend about this one? You live on a boat, child.'

'Yep, but it has rooms, and Grampy and T-Roy.'

'I have Etta Grace. She's prettier than your Grampy.'

Etta Grace laughed then, with her hand under the frame, pushing the needle up. She was maybe fourteen.

'Etta Grace, wouldn't you like an upstairs on top of here?'

'How would I get to it? There's no staircase.' Maybe Etta Grace was joking when she said those things, maybe she wasn't. Or half and both all the time.

'Jerusha, if Etta Grace went to school would she know more?'

'Etta Grace isn't going anywhere. I'll thank you not to ask again.'

Little as she was, Jeanne could see she'd said something wrong. Rebuke never made a dent in that girl, though.

'I know a lot.' Jeanne puffed herself up tall and stuck out her chest.

'Yep, and you don't know a lot, too. Cut me another thread.'

Those flinty eyes didn't suit her mother, but they suited little Jeanne from the start. Sharp as tacks, that girl.

Looking at Jeanne the other day, chattering down the path to the road beside Eddie, you'd never know she came into the world on a wave of blood that looked like something out of Revelations.

Jerusha closes her eyes on the trees and the stream coming down along the back yard, feeling the little scrap of velvet in her hands. She can smell the sun heating up the mulch under the maples. She can hear the water on the rocks, singing down to the road. In the dark behind her eyes, though, she can see the first Jeanne Delaney, swinging her little shoes in one hand, twisting her waist around while she stands on the dock in the dress that Edge-Crockett man sent her.

T-Roy's father, Ted Prichard, didn't stay long. It was Jeanne herself who pushed him off. Ted would've married her and put her in a house, but the life Ted Prichard was offering was too ordinary for her. She had an idea she was special. Got it from a magazine, probably, the way her daughter does from adventure stories. Or maybe it's just in them through the blood. Just the Delaney girls. Their men are steady enough.

Ted Prichard went off west with a long face and enough logging money to buy a farm in Ohio or somewhere, leaving T-Roy with his *maman*. Ted was cousin to her Will, Etta Grace's father, both of them Prichards. That's one reason Jerusha looks out for Jeanne's children. Calculated scientifically, little Jeanne Delaney has got no blood of her blood, but somehow Jerusha feels the tie, same as she does with T-Roy.

That first Jeanne now, the mother, she had an idea she was something men wanted. Her nose was too sharp and her eyes were flinty, but she didn't need to be pretty to be a magnet for a little time, like all girls just turning into women are. Like bitches in heat, to tell it plainly. Difference was, Jeanne's mother got fooled and thought that was her permanent state. She breathed out pretty like it belonged to her. Do that and men'll pretend to believe you, but not for long.

Even after T-Roy was born, she didn't come down to earth. She seemed to throw motherhood off and turn back into a virgin thing, twisting her neck around and smoothing out the front of her dress, which incidentally she kept cleaner than anything that ever came near it. She kept that up after she was old enough to know better. By the time that Edge-Crockett man came up from the city, T-Roy must have been nearly ten years old. That would make his mother nearly thirty. She looked better than she had when she first stepped out with T-Roy's father, though. It was all artful, all contrived with powders and girdles. That's what she spent her money on, but she was a good woman underneath all that. It was just there was nothing for her to do with all her dreaming except save up and buy beauty creams from the backs of magazines.

Nobody knew how they first ran into each other, the first Jeanne Delaney and Edge-Crocket. It would likely have been Jeanne who contrived it, though. Edge-Crocket was in one of the hunting camps up the lake, him and a lot of other people with expensive shoes that wouldn't have lasted the winter if they'd stayed. The sort of people who come in the fall with their guns and their nets and their broad hats. They stood on the porch and got their picture taken, the women too, with a couple guides posed like bronze statues either side of them. They'd clomp through the woods, and the guides, both Nadeau boys, would somehow manage to get something killed with the gun in the hands of one of those city men.

In the evenings it was all single malt and cigars and self-satisfaction on the porch. Sometimes a dress-up to-do at one of the camps, like a little play about civilisation acted out under the moon. They'd pay pennies for beadwork and take the girls that made it into the bargain for free.

It was when Edge-Crockett sent Jeanne a dress and an invitation that Jerusha first heard of him by name. Tell the truth, the dress was too big for Jeanne, and not warm enough for the season, but she had a way of looking like she felt, and none of that showed. It was made of silk velvet and had marcasite buckles at the front of the shoulders.

Jerusha tried to talk sense to her, but there was no room for sense in her head.

'Oh, Jerusha, take T-Roy back to your house? Please?'

'How are you gonna get home later, Jeanne?' That wasn't really the question Jerusha was asking.

'I don't know, but men like that don't leave you to walk. Send a dress like this and then make me walk home?' She laughed and swung her little shoes some more.

It was very evidently someone else's dress, but Jerusha couldn't bring herself to say that.

Instead, she said, 'I read a book once where a man did that, made the woman walk home after taking her to a party. The girl died in the snow because her father wouldn't let her back inside the house. All the villagers carried her away and buried her.' In fact, that wasn't how the story ended, but Jerusha needed it to end like that, in the current emergency.

'I just want to feel good one time. I want to dance in the house with those people and drink champagne. Anybody ever ask *you* to do that?'

Well, that was mean.

'You know they haven't, but they do leave me to get the babies out after.'

There.

There was no moon that night, and the lake was flat as a shingle. The dark was sliding down like slate from the hillside, but Jeanne had it painted in her mind like something by Maxfield Parish. Jerusha was sure there was a moon and stars and a glowing blue sky behind that girl in her own imagination. Stars on the buckles of her dress and her shoes, everything spangly and a down quilt laying on a bed somewhere, waiting.

He came with one of the Nadeau boys driving the cart and hollered up on the road, leaving her to scramble up the bank toward the carriage lamp. Later, he had her up against the side of the house.

Edge-Crockett's friends weren't even as shocked as he wanted them to be when he brought Jeanne Delaney through the front door and gave her some frilly pieces of food and a glass. No doubt it became a joke they told behind their hands while they sat in theatre boxes in Boston waiting for plays to start.

Of course, Henry Nadeau told the whole story up and down the lake.

Jeanne showed sooner than she had with T-Roy. She never thought Edge-Crockett would come back to marry her. She wasn't that stupid. In fact, she was so afraid of him coming back, it got morbid. By the time her belly slowed her down she'd eaten away her fingernails and her hair looked limp. She kept saying he'd come for the baby, she needed to leave the baby with her *père*, would the baby be a girl? Edge-Crocket wouldn't want a girl. If it was a son, he'd take it away. Couldn't Jerusha tell what it was gonna be?

Right at the end she got so she didn't make much sense at all. Her blood got thin with all the dreams drained out of it. She couldn't see a future anymore, and that told her there wasn't one. When the labour started, she came to stand at Jerusha's door, not saying a word. The salt water had already come out of her and was all over her under things. Right from the start, there was more blood than there should have been.

And it was bright as maple leaves turning, which is what reminds Jerusha now. The colour of the maples moving like weak blood in the sun.

That night, Jerusha gathered up some clean cloths and motherwort and they went back to the boat. On the way they stopped three times so Jeanne could crouch down moaning and bleeding on the grass at the side of the road. Jerusha chased T-Roy and his *pe'père* out of the room. The two of them spent the night wrapped in blankets on the deck.

The sweat stood out on Jeanne Delaney in the lamplight till she looked like she was made of polished wood. She kept saying, 'Please Jerusha, keep the baby up here. Don't let anybody take it off the lake,' and things like that. She'd made a deal with death before the thing started.

When Jeanne spoke while Jerusha was cleaning off the baby, it nearly made her jump out of her skin. Surely there couldn't be enough breath left in her to make words with? But Jeanne laid her hand on the child and said, 'A girl. Thank God.' Then she put her lips against the top of that bloody head and said her own name, marking that baby, willing her to keep her mother inside herself. She died then.

Sometimes they do.

What it feels like to be a person who can sing on softly and keep rinsing cloths while your best friend dies in front of you Jerusha has never told anyone yet. Memories of blood and water and souls breathing out sit heavy inside you. A family pays the midwife to take those things back out of the house with her.

Sometimes they call nurses angels, and that, really, is what they mean. They mean women who can set themselves right outside of caring so they can take care. They mean the being that drops down into their houses and takes all the responsibility for life and death. The one who can just about manage not to be crushed by that. Angels are heartless, inhuman beings from the fiery sky.

Well, the men were still out of the room when Jeanne breathed her last breath, and they only seem to have one woman at a time on that boat, so Jerusha was the only one present. It was up to her, and she chose to take Jeanne's words as an act of naming. It wasn't right, shouldn't have been part of what she did. It was for Jerusha to pull nameless things squalling out of the dark, and for the mothers to make them into people with names and dreams and things hid under the surface of themselves. The thing wasn't Jerusha's to decide, but she burdened the girl with her own mother's name, telling the father and the brother before she could stop herself. Maybe she was just trying to keep the sound of her friend in the world.

Really, Jerusha thinks now, Jeanne Delaney was just saying her own name. Whispering it into the soft spot on the top of her daughter's head, getting it in there before the bone closed over, before she died. She was missing someone she was never going to meet, trying to anchor that about-to-be-orphan child with its mother's name.

It wasn't until the other day, seeing the girl tripping through the trees behind Eddie Allen, that Jerusha realised it might be a curse she'd laid on that child.

Well, done is done, and in some ways the name fits. To look at, Jeanne Delaney could be the ghost of her mother, but when she's moving you'd never mistake them. Her mother made every movement like she was aware of the eyes on her. Little Jeanne Delaney moves like she doesn't even know she has a body at all. She's forever flailing around and knocking things over.

That first Jeanne Delaney spent her last few years thinking there was going to be someone on a white horse to come brandishing a sword and lift her off the water into the sky. Once she understood that wasn't going to happen, it killed her.

Little Jeanne? She thinks she's the one on the horse.

Anyway, the name fits now. Little Jeanne made it a hero's name. If only they'd been alive at the same time, she might have galloped in and done her mother's rescuing. Children do that, take a name and make their own. It works even if you remember the first bearer. Those other ones stay in the name somehow though, returning sometimes like ghosts in a house, halfway displaced by the new owner.

All this thinking has made Jerusha's stitches crooked. All those girls parading through her head and chattering at each other. She must have stirred up their dust when she pulled the quilt down after all these years. Or maybe it was Jeanne, pulling Eddie out of the woods and through the back yard like that, starting the whole dance all over again. It's spooked her if she's honest, the way it looked like a circle coming around again and closing. Like it's one year turning over and over again, with all its seasons made of violence.

Tearing out her work to do over, Jerusha realises her fingers are stiff. The shade is getting brittle and the wind is filling the yard with leaves. A shiver runs through her nerves like a ripple moving on the lake.

Something's coming with the cold. Go ahead and call her superstitious. That's what old women are supposed to be, isn't it? There's something out there in the time in front of them, waiting for the snow to fall, waiting to come out of the silence and the whiteness.

Back Along

T-Roy walks the pony all the way back along the road from Harmony, the wind off the lake whispering a lie about summer over the last bit of road. He's got a full sack laying across the withers: fishing line, lineament, molasses and a book for Jeanne's birthday. She'll be sixteen tomorrow.

'Get the biggest book you can find,' Grampy told him. 'Bring back as many words as possible. Keep that girl occupied.'

Words won't do that. Not anymore, but how can he say that to the old man. Jerusha knows.

T-Roy can remember the work it took to distract himself from his wants at that age. Then again, when Etta Grace started growing, he held himself back off her like she might sting or burn him.

The day before Etta Grace turned sixteen herself, T-Roy came back from Harmony with a brass bell. It wasn't something she'd asked for, only a fancy he'd had. She understood, though. Etta Grace always understood what mattered. He stayed up all night making a knot to hang the bell from, so pretty and complicated she'd never be able to undo it. He brought the bell and an extra piece of rope for Etta Grace to practise knots on. He was teaching her to make a bowline.

And he retaught her practically every other day all that year, because things took a while to stick with her. In the end they made a game and a story out of it.

Loop it over, so it makes a snake. Once the two of them had seen a milk snake out on a rock on the side of Mary's Peak, lying in the daytime sun. That was back when they wandered together like any two kids in summer.

Pull the rope around and through, like two arms dancing and fiddles playing. There used to be a fiddler that came with the pickers to Crook's place every fall. At least once during their stay, they'd make a big fire and he'd play so they could all dance. You couldn't keep Etta Grace away from any kind of firelight. When the dancers lifted their arms and turned them around each other, her joy would shine right out of her skin.

Pull the rope through, like Jerusha threading a needle. 'That's easy,' Etta Grace would say. 'I can thread a needle. Let me.'

After that she said the knot looked like a butterfly, which T-Roy couldn't see. She called it that, anyway. The butterfly.

When she was just toddling and T-Roy was already picking Crook's beans, Etta Grace used to try to grab for the yellow swallowtails on the butterfly bush. Laughing and laughing.

'Those colours on their wings are only powder,' Jerusha said to her. 'If you touch it and it rubs off, they'll die.'

She spent a long time thinking about that. Later, in that final year, she said to T-Roy. 'The only beautiful thing that you can touch is water. Water just moves itself around you and lifts you up.'

'Not in the winter, it doesn't,' he said.

'In the winter, the water is sleeping. Under the ice.'

You would have thought Etta Grace was nothing but simple, until she said things like that. She often made him wonder how saints and poets were made.

On her sixteenth birthday, Etta Grace had a box of animal crackers and they lit every lamp and candle in Jerusha's house. He gave her the bell and she rang it while they sang. They were at the old camp by then, of course.

All that year, he helped her practise the bowline until one day she could do it without him. He stood behind her shoulder and watched, hands itching in his back pockets, saying nothing at all.

Good God.

Jeanne

I guess in the city you have your children's birthdays with cakes and music and politely sitting on sofas. I read how when your daughters turn sixteen, you announce them up for auction in the newspapers like yearling quarter horses. Well, my birthdays were never quite celebrations, though they did try. My mother died the day I was born, remember?

When I turned sixteen, they got me an old volume of *Harper's* for a present. I spent most of the morning with that book up on the bank above the *batteur*. It was chilly out of the sun by then and I brought a blanket. The air bit into my lungs. It smelled like leaves turning back into dirt. I could smell the water below me too, slowly giving up its heat.

Jerusha come down in the afternoon, hauling a crate full of canning. There were three jars of wild strawberry jam, some relish made of squash and two jars of pickled beets. Whole days in the woods it takes to get enough wild strawberries for the jam. Jerusha always set aside some for my birthday.

She stopped at the top of the bank to give me my good wishes, to shake her head and say, 'Sixteen!', the way grown-ups do. I held all her canning jars up into the sunlight to look at the colours inside them. T-Roy come up and took the box, tutting at Jerusha, saying whyn't she leave it for him to go get?

She smiled at him like he was her own boy. She'd been doing that ever since Etta Grace went.

Oh and I forgot, there was a hobo cake in the box, too. That was for me. You ever have a hobo cake, government man?

Jerusha sat and slid right down the bank on her bottom. She didn't mind her dignity when there was somewhere to get to. I followed her in, which is why I heard her mumbling at Grampy, 'Roy, we need to talk about Jeanne.'

Grampy sat in his chair by the cold stove, presiding. 'Jeanne, how about you take the pony back up the lake to the Nadeaus?'

'I don't have to, Grampy. It's my birthday and I want to read to you all.'

'You're too smart by a mile, that's your problem,' Grampy said. He said that all the time.

'Oh, come on!' I was sort of whining. 'Just lemme read you this one thing.' I'd been all wrapped up in 'Some Talks of an Astronomer', where the man told why an eclipse happens and how they can tell which planets are nearest.

'Take that poor pony home and get her comfortable,' Jerusha said. 'She needs brushing.'

'Why can't one of the boys come get her?'

'What am I to do?' Grampy tried looking helpless, which was getting easier for him by that point. 'Should I telegraph and let them know T-Roy's back from town? Just go on. You know *maman* Nadeau'll give you some molasses cookies, seeing what day it is.'

He couldn't ever really get hold of my age, Grampy. Right up to the end, he still thought sometimes he could buy me off with sweets.

I realised if I said yes, I had a better chance of hearing what they had to say about me. I had to stomp all the way off the gangway and scramble up the bank, then take my boots off and come back around from up the lake, all quiet. Otherwise, they'd know I hadn't left. Don't forget, those were the three people who'd known me the whole of my life.

You going to judge me for eavesdropping? You might want to store up your disapproval for the rest of what's coming.

I had to climb back up without tossing the boat, and that's not easy. It took ages, so I missed a good bit of what they were saying. Luckily it was mostly in English, only slipping out once in a while when one of them got really agitated. I didn't know much of the other, since English is all they ever talked to me.

'I seen those two come out the woods and my stomach dropped right out of me.' That was Jerusha. 'I'm telling you boys, it's like the turn of the year, all come round and happening over again.'

'Yeah, but how do you stop something like that, Jerusha?' T-Roy said. 'We can't lock her up.'

'Listen to me, both of you.' Grampy had a certain quiet, rocky kind of voice he used to get your attention without shouting. 'I learned about those people the year I took T-Roy's and little Jeanne's *grand mère* to live with me.'

'I know you did, Roy. I'm sorry to bring it up.'

'Well, T-Roy don't know and I'm telling him now. Everett Allen had Agnes up in the logging camp and the cold was coming. She was freezing up there without enough wood for the stove. He didn't bring coal, though he hung half a deer and two turkeys in the shed.'

I was leaning on the outside wall of Grampy's cabin, under the flue, trying to figure out where he was going with all of it. I could just about hear T-Roy asking, 'Which one is Everett?'

'That was Eddie's Pa, the one who died just before little Jeanne come. But this was long before he married Julia and had those three boys. Everett was only just about a man, time I'm talking about. His father Pliny was still alive. The mother, Eddie's grandmother, had gone with diphtheria the year before.'

I pressed my ear against the outside wall so hard it got sore.

'That was a sharp winter, but it come late, I remember that. That year, them from over the border didn't go back up till the start of October, because the warm weather lingered and there was still fruit and beans. When the rest of them went back up, Agnes stayed. I think Everett Allen went up to the camp most nights, but he never put a child in her somehow.'

There was a long stillness then, so I almost thought that was the end of the story. Then Grampy coughed and started again.

'So, Everett had your *grand mère*, Agnes, up at the logging camp. To look at, she could have passed for Allen kin, but she didn't speak any English at all. Far as Pliny Allen and them was concerned, she was the other kind of people. Our kind.'

The sun had dropped behind some cloud cover, making a gold lining in the sky and a cold breeze on the lake. If I was going to ride to the Nadeaus' and then walk back down before they got worried, I shoulda been hurrying. I was shivering in the shadow of the cabin wall, but I didn't care. I was in a trance there, listening to the most words in a row I ever heard my Grampy say in my whole life.

'Everett Allen loved her,' Grampy said then, 'no point in denying it. But that won't help you to understand what I'm telling you. I was there working in the near field with the rest of them the day he told Pliny he was going to marry Agnes. You could hear the yelling right down the valley. I thought that was the end of it, until Everett asked me to bring her things up to the camp after everyone else was gone for the day.'

'He was hiding her?'

'No, honey,' Jerusha said. 'I think he thought they could wear Pliny down. Don't you, Roy? I remember your Agnes well enough. She had a kind of sweetness neither of the Jeannes got from her, if you don't mind my saying. She looked like a girl who'd never even seen her own dinner butchered. I think she'd seen all kinds of things, in truth. It was just they washed over her and made her all the more clear. Sorta like Etta Grace, but she wasn't simple.'

Grampy got worked up then, and said something I couldn't understand.

'Well, yes,' Jerusha said. 'That, too.'

'Well,' Grampy said, 'they was paying me day wages then, the Crooks and the Allens, different times. I did all kind of work around both places. Now listen to me, T-Roy. There was an evening I was out late after a missing heifer that'd got through the fence and across the creek. I took Mitch with me, one of the Allen dogs. The heifer wasn't hard to find; she'd headed straight for the sweet grass in the nearest bottom. It took two hours, though, by the time me and Mitch got her up the road and past Crook's turn-off. It was in the trees right there I saw them, Pliny Allen and Omar Sloat. That's Harold Sloat's dad. See what I'm telling you, T-Roy, back then people enforced their own rules. If you stepped outta line, there was men who'd whip you back in, even if they were your own family.

They had that boy hanging by his wrists from an elm. Wasn't even far enough off the road to hide what they were doing. Anybody could have seen. They wanted everyone in the valley to see what would fly and what wouldn't.'

'See what, though?' I wished T-Roy would stop interrupting. I had cramp in my calves and had to stretch my legs out real slow, one at a time, trying not to gasp while I did it. It was getting late.

'I'm telling you what, boy. That man had his own child strung up and was lashing the bottoms of his feet with a bundle of raspberry canes. I could see the bloody cuts from where I was standing. The heifer had stopped too, and I didn't want to make a noise slapping her. I just kept hoping Mitch wouldn't bark or run over there. He knew better, though. He went right into the drainage ditch other side of the road and slunk down, hiding.

'Everett Allen had on nothing but blue jeans and there wasn't a mark on him, excepting the bottoms of his feet. He was so young, he had no more hair on his chest than me or you.

'"Go on it, say it!" Pliny was shouting at him.

'I thought Everett's arms were going to pop with the weight of hanging. Maybe they did. I know he didn't come out of the house for two weeks after. I expect he couldn't walk for most of that time.'

Until that day – my birthday, remember – I had no idea Grampy could tell a story like that. I didn't even care if I got caught. I wanted the end of it. Needed the end, maybe. I was the one they should have been telling, anyway.

'I was stuck fast right there,' Grampy said, 'and Pliny was still yelling so loud he didn't notice me. There was a moon coming up behind me and I suppose I was only a shadow in the road, but Omar saw me eventually. He said, "Move the hell on, boy." Everett mumbled something. Pliny hit him with the cane again and said, "What was that?"

'He was just saying, "Okay, okay, okay." I don't think he knew what he was agreeing to or who was there watching him. I don't know when the message sunk in or how they broke him. I didn't wait for Omar to tell me twice. I put that heifer in the barn and went on back to the lake. I expect they left Everett to crawl home to the farm.

'Next day, I took some beans and a blanket up to Agnes at the camp. I found her bleeding there. I guess they'd been to her after they were finished on Everett. They'd made their point. I took Agnes up the lake with me that winter, and we got the boat in the spring. She was broken so, we lived like brother and sister for a year, at first. Sorry, T-Roy. Everett worked the summers and drank away the winters for three years, then he married Julia Allen and had those boys.'

'It's living in them,' Jerusha said. 'All of it. That's what I'm trying to tell you two. We have to keep Jeanne away from there. How many times does one thing have to keep happening?'

'I don't think Eddie's like it,' T-Roy said. 'Eddie's got a sympathy to him.'

'Well, I feel that, too, honey. But I ain't willing to trust it. We're not gonna know what that quiet inside Eddie Allen really is till it comes out and shows itself.'

Well, they could have asked me, couldn't they? I was the one looking at Eddie right up close.

'The thing is, he ain't strong,' T-Roy said. 'That family'll just run him whichever direction they want. I still don't see we can do anything about it.'

Of course, T-Roy didn't see. You'll find, government man, that in the country the women are the ones that organise that kind of thing. It's called meddling and gossiping but we'd all be animals without it. The men do the brute work and aren't supposed to think so much. I suppose that was one thing wrong with Eddie Allen.

'Get that down, son, will you?' Grampy said.

From the sound of T-Roy moving to the shelf over the stove and the noise of the lid coming off the cracker tin I knew what it was.

'Your *maman* said give it to the baby when it was old enough.'

I nearly laughed and gave myself away then. What did them three think, I never looked in that tin before? I knew all what was in it; I just hadn't known it was meant for me.

'That belonged your *grand mère*,' Grampy said then. He must've been showing T-Roy the pillbox with the enamel shepherdess on it. Inside, it was gold. They finally gave it to me when Grampy died. I sold it years ago now, way up in the Maritimes. Needed the money to get back here.

I could finally stretch my neck and turn my face to the sky then. I didn't need to listen; I could see the other things from the tin just by closing my eyes. Only two things in there besides the pillbox, a two-dollar bill and a calling card. The card was dirty, with raised black letters. It said, 'Arthur Quentin Donald Edge-Crockett, Boston, Attorney at Law'. It was only that day that I realised it must be the name of my father on that card. Two middle and two last names, my dad had, government man. And all the way from Boston, too.

Well, I climbed up the bank and put my boots back on, then took the dirt road around the lake, riding the Nadeaus' pony bareback. She didn't need a hackamore, even. Me and that pony had known each other since we were both babies, and anyway she was lazy. She wanted her bed but she wasn't in a hurry. Neither was I.

I lay forward on the pony's back and had a good think. She was warm and a little scratchy. Jerusha was right, she needed brushing.

Was I thinking about the strength of Eddie Allen? The pain his family passed down among them like it was their fortune? No, I wasn't. Listen to the story I'm telling you, city boy. It's about how I spent a whole year walking through the world with a hammer-blow hanging over me and never stopped to notice it.

I was thinking about Agnes, the grandmother I never got to know. And I was thinking, like I always did in the woods, about my mother. The three of us – me, my mother and my grandmother – had spent our lives circling this same lake road, one at a time. Each one had sent the other out of the light. It made me think of the eclipse in my book.

And, give me some credit, I was thinking about my Grampy's sadness, which never really come home to me before that day.

I remember it was one of those evenings when the moon comes up huge and yellow in the east just when the sun is going down. I was in under the birches and the hemlocks, but those two balls of light were shining on either side of me through the turning leaves.

The Nadeaus house was full of people, like always. They were one of those big noisy bunches that make you feel like you can't count them even when they're all there at the table.

'I brought the pony back!' I shouted from the porch. 'It's my birthday.'

She did give me some of her cookies, but she did that every time I came. She kept them in a tin in the pantry. More like little cakes they were, the colour of T-Roy's eyes and smelling like molasses. She dusted them with light brown sugar that felt like sweet sand on your tongue.

The Nadeaus' kitchen was warm and full of light and their table stretched from one end of it to the other. I sat down with my cookies and milk and asked Mrs Nadeau if she knew my *grand mère*.

'Agnes? Of course. She got to be friends with my *maman*. Well, sort of.'

'Didn't they like each other?'

'Oh, yes. Everyone liked Agnes. She was quiet, though, kept herself on the inside. Not like you!' She laughed then and ruffled my head like I was turning six instead of sixteen.

I didn't ask her about my mother.

Sitting at that table gave me the feeling it was impossible to be lonely. Folks seemed to stay in that house until it was the proper time to go. There was no one missing from them.

I said goodbye and ran back along the edge of the lake. The moon was all the way up then, and spilled its trail over the water. There was so much light I could cut through the trees across a loop in the road. The creek came through there, but it was nearly dry that time of year. I thought I'd splash through it and home, but when I came out of the trees there was a moose standing right there in the creek bed.

She was twice as tall as me. Ugly, gangly things they are, despite what Eddie Allen might've said. Certain times of year, a moose gets nasty. I wasn't gonna get in her way, but I didn't want anybody to shoot her either. I got myself next to a tree and looked her in the eyes. 'I won't tell,' I said. She turned her head away from me and tossed it at the moon.

I never did tell anyone I'd seen her, not even Eddie. Never told anyone until you, right now. Funny how things come back, isn't it?

When I got back to the boat, T-Roy had made watery hot chocolate on the stove. They pushed the hobo cake out of its coffee tin and sliced it. Nobody sang; we never did any of that. There was the lantern, shining next to Grampy's Saint Barbara, and the boat rocking, and Jerusha told a story about the people from way up north.

So, I guess you can see, my birthday wasn't all candles and singing and everybody glad I was born. It was like every year, my celebration that was really a remembrance, for the other Jeanne Delaney. When I was littler, I used to think maybe if I died, she could come back.

'You go on up and stay with Jerusha, Jeanne,' Grampy said, sometime after the moon was down. I felt like they were passing me around. The second-place prize, the sorry comfort for the thing they'd all lost. Well, I was turned sixteen. Everybody's stupid and cross at that age, aren't they? Or maybe it's just the women.

'Jerusha can't walk alone in this dark,' T-Roy said.

I kept waiting for them to give me those things from the cracker tin. They didn't, and of course I couldn't ask.

It was the next day T-Roy went off and disappeared. I didn't put the two things together at the time.

A Short Stretch of Grace

Eddie feels tired already. He puts Betty in the traces and thinks about the drive to town. The thought of the houses along Main Street presses on his lungs, the smell from Sloat's yard and all that coal smoke coming from the chimneys. Already he's breathing hard and shallow. It has to be done though, and he'll do it. Regular, too, else Ma and Micky will miss him and send somebody out this way. They'll want their provisions and whatever cash he's got from the dairy and the apples and the weekend hunters.

The valley is still dark below him; even up in the dooryard it's barely light yet. He'll hit the valley bottom before the sun, but he could drive it in the pitch dark if need be. It's the outdoors but it's inside him, too. Every tree stump has some kind of memory attached.

There's been a little rain. The dirt in the dooryard is soft and sticks to his boots while he loads the cart. The apples in the crates are too green to smell much, and the rest is just a coonskin for Micky and the milk, packed between the crates of apples with a tarp over it all. Just as he's ready to go the little Nadeau girl, Alma, comes with her nickel in a pail. He stops to go back into the dairy barn and fill it with milk.

He opens the gate and looks out at the waiting road. The earliest thing he remembers, maybe, happened right here at the gate. His brothers called him to come see a load of carnival folk go by in a painted cart. He could hear the noise and see the man on the seat driving, but he couldn't see anything else through all those legs. When he tried to push through, Micky scraped his boot down Eddie's leg and stomped his toes on purpose. Eddie fell back into the yard bawling, so Ma picked him up and took him back into the shadows in the house. She smiled at Micky though, in a way that said they both knew something Eddie didn't.

When Eddie was that small, it was like each limb of Micky's had a life of its own. Every separate piece of him was mean. If he'd had words that day, Eddie would have cursed the foot his brother used on him. That's maybe why he remembers it, now that very foot is gone.

It's like that right down through the valley. A memory at every turn in the road. He's been putting off the journey all week, not wanting to live in those memories anymore.

What is it that's changed in him now? What's making him shy away? Is it iron or water inside him, or blood on his hands? When Ma and Micky smell it, will they back off or come in for the kill? He can just picture Micky sniffing at him like a hunting dog, then throwing his head back and singing out.

He's hoping the milk and the money will keep them away. There will be a next batch of city men up from Boston soon, too. At least that'll be him busy and blameless for a few days, earning. Micky and Ma won't bother him then. Them city men'll put up at Harold Sloat's inn and Eddie will collect them in the mornings. He'll take them into the woods and they'll make a lot of noise and fire at everything without ever seeing a thing. They'll love every minute, then drop some money and take the train back south, hungover and stowing mangled raccoons in the baggage car. Back to the banks and the law offices and the state legislatures, so they can make some more regulations to stop people like Eddie from fishing and trapping fur.

The pony cart is down in the bottom before Eddie realises, rolling between the fields and through an arch of trees. He and Betty startle the rabbits away from the edge of the river with their clattering on the road. Not that the woods are silent, or peaceful either. Those are things only people who don't live in the trees call them. The air is full of crackling and whistling and rustling. All kinds of little killings, happening or waiting to happen.

There are pockets of fog in the hollows and the first maple leaves are coming down. The air has a bite that'll disappear in the warmth of the sun later. Right now, Eddie's exhalations make him feel like a ghost, like his soul is coming right out of his mouth to join those pockets of mist.

At first, the long shadow by the river looks like just another memory. Eddie wonders what it is that's come to haunt him now. Then the shape resolves itself into someone breathing and familiar. T-Roy Prichard, Eddie can tell by the hat.

'Ho, Betty! Morning, T-Roy. Climb up.'

T-Roy looks at him without answering. He nods though, and hauls himself up the wheel to the seat. For a minute there, Eddie thought he was going to go round and sit with the apples, just to make his point about his little sister.

Eddie moves Betty along again, while everything the two of them aren't saying rattles around between them on the seat.

'When I was little, Hank and Micky told me those wisps of wet air in the woods were the souls of burned witches, waiting to swallow up cowardly boys.' Eddie says it just to fill the air between them, then realises he's called up another memory he doesn't want.

T-Roy makes a sound that might be an answer. That isn't unusual, though. No one's ever called the man garrulous.

'They said you never saw them at bright midday because the witches shied at the light. If your nerve broke at dawn or twilight, though, they'd be right there to get you.'

Still no response. Well, all right.

There's no kind of silence that scares Eddie these days, not outdoors anyway. At the bend in the river, T-Roy lays a hand on his arm.

'I'll get down now, and thank you.'

'Where you going? I'll take you.'

'Pull up, Eddie.'

'I mean right, T-Roy. You know that, don't you?'

'You've always meant right, Eddie Allen. That's not the question. I'd appreciate if you didn't say you seen me.'

'Does your Grampy know where you're going?'

'I meant to my sister. I won't be back for a while. She'll work on everybody, and if she gets a hint she's as likely to follow me as do any other thing.'

'So, you're not telling me, either?'

T-Roy just nods and throws his leg through Crook's fence. He might be cutting across to town or he might not. That's just the way of him. Eddie watches while he climbs the field and disappears over the rise.

The sun is all the way up now. It burns into Eddie's shoulder and the side of his face. He takes off his wool shirt and drives in his white undershirt, looking down at the blonde hairs on his two good arms. That again makes him think of Micky, waiting for him there in Ma's parlour.

Hank and Micky were always like magnets, carrying some invisible force. Their bodies are only the half of the power they have. The most scared of Micky Eddie ever felt was the day Micky should have been helpless, the day he lay tangled up in the wheel of Crook's hay wagon, right here at the bottom of Widow Road, with a vital piece of himself hanging off.

It was a day sort of like this one, only hot when you were right in the sun. The hay cart was high and full and they were riding on top with Alice Crook. Bud was driving. They'd climbed on up by the high field, from where they could see the whole world dipping down to the river. There was nothing in the sky but two red-shouldered hawks, gliding against a holy kind of blue. Eddie put himself on the other side of Alice, feeling too good to be next to Micky. He was eighteen so Micky must have been twenty-six. Him and Hank were still working the farm then. Well, the three of them, sort of.

The cart sped up heading towards the bridge, overloaded and getting faster than the horse. It twisted and went up-end and there wasn't any time for them to grab for the rails or each other. It always seemed to Eddie like time wrinkled and skipped that day. First, he was on top of the hay wagon, then he was in the grass by the river with a rock digging into his back and Micky was screaming and cursing. Try as he might, he can never create any memory of flying through the air or falling like he must have done. The hay was everywhere around him and one of the wheels was rolling away while Micky kept cursing and groaning. Once his brain started up again Eddie's first real thought was, *even in front of Alice he talks like that*. Then he looked.

There wasn't much blood but he could see a jagged something, sharp and white at the end of Micky's leg. After a minute he understood what his eyes were showing him and saw Micky's foot laying along the axel in the wrong direction. There's a kind of sick excitement you feel when the inside and outside of creatures trade places. When he saw Micky's foot like that, the first wave that hit him was the same kind of feeling he always feels when he skins something. Like the world had opened up to him and the truth was suddenly plain. He rose up out of himself then, and his own insides fell away.

A chain inside him had been cut; he was like a hunting bird suddenly let out of the hood and up into the brightness. All bets were off, he thought. He'd never have to avoid sitting next to Micky again.

The next thing he thought was about that girl in the smokehouse. You can't do that anymore, he thought. You won't be able to run after anything. He sat staring while Alice and Bud did the panicking. No one noticed him for a long few minutes while Bud checked the horse's legs and Alice made a fuss over Micky, bringing him water and putting her sweater under him. Then Bud ran up through the fallow towards the house, startling a nesting bobolink up out of the grass.

Eddie just sat there, tethered to his flying soul and wondering.

After a while he looked away from the sky and into Micky's face, and came crashing down. Micky's look wasn't scared or anguished, it was burning. The string of filthy words coming out of him was his own native language, found at last.

It was then Eddie started to shake, all over in little coughing fits like a motor trying to start up. Bud caught Alice's eye and nodded in Eddie's direction. She came over, but he waved her off and stood up, sputtering and bending over to hold his stomach. Even now, thinking about that moment makes Eddie curl into himself. It wasn't his brother's bone, come out of its proper darkness into the sun. Nor the horse that had to be shot later. What comes when he passes the spot now is the feeling of crashing down, of that thirty seconds of false freedom and the way it ended in the expression on Micky's face. That pain had come into Micky's life like the friend he'd been waiting on all along. He didn't get helpless. He got meaner. Even lamed, Micky Allen can knock the wind out of a man just by looking at him.

Up Widow Road now, today, there is a vulture circling the side of Mary's Peak. A kingfisher is gliding over the river. As far as the eye can see there isn't a creature besides himself that can make language. There should be a roadside shrine here in the blessed quiet, he thinks. A historic marker. It's what, four years later? Ma and Micky have taken their meanness into town, more than two years ago now. Hank works the quarries and doesn't come home much at all. That day was kind of a linchpin in time. In a way, Eddie's first feeling was right. They did all start to change places that day. Allens started drifting out of the valley until now Eddie is the only one left. All in all, things've worked out better than he ever thought they would that night he and T-Roy pried open the smokehouse door.

Eddie keeps telling himself that, the rest of the way into town.

'You ain't made cider?' is the first thing Micky says.

'It's only just September, Micky.' Eddie pulls Betty into the drive at the side of the house and tries not to meet Micky's eyes. Betty has a nibble at the pyracantha under the window, then gives up.

In the living room, the smell of fermentation is the most noticeable thing. It's before noon, but they're both burning alcohol of some kind or other, either from this morning or from last night.

Coming from Eddie's mother it smells obscene, somehow. On Micky it clashes with the washed and pressed rest of him. Ma tries her best to make Micky fit right in with all the other ornaments in her front room. Maybe she dusts him every day.

'My two boys.' She's looking back and forth between the two of them and smiling an empty smile like there's someone else there she needs to impress. A preacher maybe, or an alderman.

'At least one of us is a man, Ma. Maybe both, even.' Micky puts one hand on the armchair and slides his crutch out while he hoists himself down into it.

'Eddie, I'm making fish chowder. Will you like that?'

'What the hell you doin' up there, kid?' Micky says, ignoring his mother. 'I don't like what I'm hearing.'

'It's September, Micky. I'm sure you can picture what I'm up to. First apples, last fences in the sheep fields, haying done, potatoes still coming, cabbages.' He doesn't mean about the haying on purpose.

'Ay-uh, that's what the Allens are known for. Last idiots in the county with sheep. What a distinction. You know what I mean. I heard you got a whore right in the house. That true, or what?'

'Micky, speak civil in my living room, please. Have you got a girl, Eddie?' Her smile gets wider and shallower.

'It's not *a girl*. What I hear, it's some kind of teenage delinquent from one of them pirate families on the lake.'

'Eddie?'

'I forgot to get my boots off, Ma. Be right back.'

In the mud room it's cool and musty. There are some fishing rods in the corner and a blackberry brown betty on the shelf with a kitchen towel over it. He puts one hand on the work bench and uses the other to untie his boots. The clapboards let in streaks of light and Eddie can see the cobwebs behind the canning jars.

Micky lumbers into the open doorway, blocking the way out.

'You fucking that little piece in my mother's bed, Eddie?' His breath is like the exhaust from an automobile or a train. Chemical and flammable. Hypnotising.

74

'No, Micky. I'm not.' It comes out too high in spite of him.

She looks good, he wants to say. *Not like people would notice, but she does. She makes me want to laugh, but my insides are too tied up. You might be able to crush her, but you can't get hold of her. Not really.* Instead of saying any of that, Eddie keeps his eyes down and leans his boots on the rail under the work bench.

'You keep the little bitch in an outbuilding where she belongs. Hear me?'

He turns to reach for some slippers down on the shelf among the spiders. Bent over, he takes a slow breath. Those were the words you either do something about or not. Not is forever. But when he stands up and turns around again, Micky is already heading back to his chair. Eddie'd been too slow, and his brother hadn't even considered he might fight back.

He wonders if things could've been different if he'd hit back. People are like animals, there is a language past words you can use with them. A set of signals that makes a man back down, same as a bull or a wolverine. But the rules with people are different and it seems like Eddie never will learn them.

He steps out into the yard and leans his face against Betty's wither. She pushes into him. He lets her take his weight and hold him up, breathes some more before he lifts down the milk can and rolls it into the mud room.

'Brought you a coon skin, Mick.' Eddie holds it up in the doorway to the front room.

'Kill that yourself, did ya? Big man.'

'Shot him in the birches up the side of the hill over the hospital road. Big bull, have a look.'

'When you gonna bring us down half a deer?'

'Sit down, Eddie,' his mother says. 'Let me make some coffee. I done some ginger snaps.' Julia Allen wanders off into the kitchen, leaving them both looking out of place on her chairs.

'She wants me to talk to ya. I ain't doing it.'

'You notice she seems different these days?' Eddie says.

'No. You just hardly stop to see her.'

'She seems like a girl to me. More gentle, like. Talks more than she did at the farm.'

'You're just remembering wrong, Eddie. She wasn't any different then than she is now.'

That sinks like a stone and leaves a silence behind it too big to break for a little while.

'What you want to talk to me about?'

'Me? Nothing a'tall. Nothing to do with me.'

Julia comes back with a plate of cookies in one hand and a tray table in the other. She makes two more trips for coffee and cups and a pitcher of milk from the can Eddie brought.

'Micky tell you we got a mortgage on this house, Eddie? We're in a bit of a worry.'

'Why? You don't need anything. I'm banking the money for you same as always.'

'Well, 'twasn't enough this year. Hank and Micky needed some things, you know. Anyway, there's nothing to worry about. We just have to do some figuring about the farm.'

'What things, Micky?'

'Things, Eddie. I can't work, case you haven't noticed.'

'I thought you said this had nothing to do with you?'

'Isn't me wants this house. I don't need a *parlour* and a bed of dahlias in front. If Sloat'd let me, I'd live over the office at the slaughterhouse.'

'Hank send you any money, or is he just taking it the other way?'

'A family has to decide things together, Eddie. We don't all get to please ourselves. Your brothers always did understand more than you. Micky, explain it to him.'

'If we sell off the pines, Bud Crook'll buy that for a field, turn it back into pasture. The three of us are ready to sign. Just waiting on you.'

Eddie looks at the unlit stove. He looks at the colour print on the wall, showing a storm over some trees and a road winding into the distance. He looks back through the kitchen, thinking about going over to the inn to see about the city men coming. His mind does these things for him while he sits in the quiet, waiting for it to pass. Julia stands up and goes to the dining room door.

'You say what you need to, Micky. We all know it has to be done.'

'See, she hasn't changed. She just thinks living in the town means a woman's supposed to pitch her voice a little higher. She's still the same woman that made us.'

'I won't do it, Micky. Just so you know. I won't do it ever. We sold off enough already and I'm not selling more. I work what's left and I take them weekenders hunting in our woods. Where's the game gonna go without the trees? We'll lose more in the long run. I'm doing my bit and more.'

'The long run, is it? Wiser than your years, eh? You think you're gonna live up there with that dirty teenaged trollop *in the long run*, you're dead wrong, Eddie Allen.'

'I ain't living with anyone, Micky. I suppose Bud Crook's been gossiping.'

'Well, right here's a good time to explain yourself. What kind of grandchildren you planning on giving ma.'

Eddie opens his mouth, closes it, shakes his head, then opens it again.

'I need to go over to the inn. I'll be back to eat.'

By the time Eddie is on the road home, the sun has gone behind Mary's Peak and even his wool shirt can't keep him warm. Comes of sitting still all day, you get cold. You get heavy. Micky's getting a beer belly on him, even. A whole good fall day indoors, breathing in second-hand booze and the smell from the slaughterhouse.

Just out of town, a fox watches him from off the road in Sloat's near field. And then there is no one and nothing for a long time. Bud Crook's cows are away at the top of the hill, crowded by the gate and moaning their heaviness. The swampers have been and gone home from the valley, leaving the log piles waiting to be chained. The mists are gathering again on the water. He pulls Betty in by Crook's gate and gets down to climb the hill. He just wants to pump his muscles and get his lungs to burn, scorch all the poison out of himself. But he's come the wrong direction for that.

He's walked right into the spot, there by the pond, where he killed his first thing that wasn't a fish. Why is it fish don't seem to count? He's been killing fish so long, he can't remember the first one. Yes, you can see a kind of something expire. It's there and then it leaves, but it isn't like it is when you kill a thing with feathers or legs.

That first thing was a rabbit, the spring he was maybe ten years old. One night a few hours before dawn they took a covered lantern and went lamping. Eddie was just sprouting up then, and Ma had started calling him bean pole when she was happy with him. Hank and Micky had been teaching him the .22 all week. Been measuring him every so often the whole year, to see when he was tall enough and had enough reach. They wouldn't let him fire the shotgun yet.

In the first few hours, Micky and Hank startled some squirrels and a raccoon and shot them. An hour before the light, they stopped right here by the pond and waited. The yellow birch was a man-length smaller then. They all stood in the willows behind it, breathing slow and shallow. Hank handed Eddie the gun in the dark, feeling for him and putting it in his hands the way it should be. He said nothing at all. Quiet is the first thing you get taught, in the woods.

The moon had set and they'd found their way over to the edge of the pool half by feel, half by memory, travelling below the breeze. You get a careful memory too, in the trees, else they all look the same when you're agitated. Else you stumble when it's dark.

After a long while, things started to resolve out of the night. There was a crowd there by the pool, including a doe with a belly on her. A deer only startles for a second. You have to be quick, and to be quick you have to be ruthless. That's what they were teaching him, really. That's what they were always teaching him.

Whatever people call human feeling just gets in the way of hunting. One thing those city weekenders have going for them is the total lack of that. Problem with them is different. It's being convinced they're the centre of the action, that the woods revolve around them, just like the rest of the world does. In the woods, you have to know your own smallness and be cold-hearted at the same time.

That dawn when he was ten, the doe made herself out of the darkness and Eddie raised the gun and held it like they'd taught him to. When he sighted though, the doe turned her gaze on him. He wasn't ready for that. He must have spent five whole seconds looking in her eyes, but Micky and Hank didn't poke him or say anything at all. Hank just stayed stock still behind him, waiting to finish it with the big rifle if need be. You don't talk or move at a time like that, not for anything. First rule.

There is a short stretch of grace, between the raising and the firing of a gun. As long as he was convincing, they wouldn't speak or move. The size of that moment was bigger than the space it took up. It was the first time Eddie was master of them and he knew he'd be able to make it happen again and again. Just hold the gun, put something helpless at the end of the barrel and his brothers couldn't touch him. It would only be a string of instants, but that was the beginning of something Eddie could live with. It was a small, good feeling, like warmth or water.

Meanwhile, Eddie was seeing the doe, getting to know her while they looked at each other. That's part of it, too. The trick is to be able to feel that closeness and then kill the thing anyway. Knowing them like that, you'll always be able to find them and know what they're going to do next. And because you can really see them, look at them, they don't see the bullet coming. It's a kind of trust you make, and then you break it.

Well, Eddie was only ten that day, and those things don't take all at once. He came back to himself and panicked, realised there was no way he could shoot her after they'd looked at each other like that.

There were three rabbits by the edge of the pool. Eddie moved the barrel and fired without steadying himself or thinking much. They were so close it would have been a miracle if he didn't hit one.

The spell of the raised gun was broken. The doe startled away and Micky poked him, hard. Hank just laughed out loud.

'Go get the rabbit, then. She's yours, Eddie, you little milksop shit,' he said. Or something like that.

The rabbit was breathing in that panicked way they do. Eddie couldn't see any blood on her anywhere. She was looking at him, too. He was still in the middle of everything. Everybody waiting for him, and him standing there stupid and staring with the doe still in his eyes.

His feelings took over then, and he gave up being one of them, being big, being allowed to hold the gun. He just knew they would always be stronger and that was how it should be and why should he be in charge anyway? He took in a breath and let go of all that, thinking he didn't care anymore. He only needed somebody to tell him what to do next.

'She's still alive, Hank. Am I supposed to brain her now?' He wouldn't do it. No way.

'Get on, kid. What you talking for? You know what to do. Hurry up and do it. I want to go ahead and kill something before it gets all the way light.'

The rabbit had those eyes the gentle things in the woods have, black and bright and full of some dark language. In the wild, ruthless things have yellow eyes; that's pretty much a rule. Eddie noticed it early on.

He didn't want to take whatever those two would give him if he didn't do it. That's the truth. Eddie never had the courage for that but once, later that same year, and it turned out to be temporary. Thinking back now, he guesses it was right he saved his only bit of backbone for the girl in the smokehouse.

Right then, by the pond, that small heart and those little lungs pumped on the ground by his feet. He threw his head from side to side, looking for the nearest, biggest rock. He hit her twice, because it wasn't hard enough the first time. Hank laughed at him and that made him hit her harder. Her little skull cracked and flattened out. He'd made a mess. If nothing else, he's carefuller now.

Once he turned the rabbit over, he could see where the bullet had gone into her. The pelt wouldn't be much good, but Ma could use it for some slippers. Micky told him to tie her legs and wash his hands. You don't walk around the woods smelling like blood.

It was only after she was in the sack that Eddie missed her. All of a sudden he realised she wasn't there anymore. Something was absent, gone. He'd put something out of the world, and he could feel it. It was different than anything he'd ever felt before. It changed him, no doubt about that.

It's true, fish don't count somehow.

Down to the Minute

Years ago, T-Roy thought he'd walk everywhere. He wanted to walk into Mexico and disappear like Ambrose Bierce, then keep walking, invisible, outside of what everyone who'd ever known him could imagine. Into the jungles and up the green mountains where people had made cities like mazes thousands of years ago and stuffed them full of gold. He didn't want to fill his pockets or come back home, just to keep walking so far the land turned white again, the ice made itself on his eyebrows and someone helped him to sheepskin boots so he could keep on going.

And here he is now, grown, not walking but on a train clicking away the minutes of the night, the windows so black he could be anywhere and never know it. It's a sort of mail train, timed to arrive in the city first thing in the morning, bringing everything the city people will want all day. There's a cold car, full of lobsters from up the line, milk and butter and cream. In the seats, there are mostly men just like T-Roy, nodding in their best shirt collars and wondering what Boston will be like.

Turns out, Boston is windy. He steps out of North Union Station and turns around to look back up at it. He bought a hat just for this, but it won't stay on, so he holds it. Arthur Quentin Donald Edge-Crockett has an office on Tremont Street. Either the paper boy outside the station gave T-Roy the wrong directions or Boston goes around in circles. He finds it in the end, in some place he could swear he's already looked.

Number 420 has a gold-braided doorman and paintings of the battle of Bennington along the walls. Well, he didn't know it was that until he asked. There are Burgoyne's men, looking exhausted with their clothes in tatters, and some Mohawk men and Yankees looking too full of strength and goodness to speak, even.

Edge-Crockett is on the fourth floor and there's another gold-braided man working the elevator. The hallways are made of green sprinkled marble, with long windows at the end. T-Roy steps out into the corridor and all he can see is a long, tall rectangle of light. It blinds him at first. The walls are lined with glass cases sitting in the gloom, full of things with labels beside them. Up close, T-Roy can see there are arrowheads and insects and a tall case with glass shelves full of Abenaki beadwork and Haudenosaunee wampum. At the far end under the window is a case full of bones. T-Roy recognises the snakes and lizards and the bones of hawks, but there are other things, something like dogs or coyotes but not exactly either of those. The names underneath are written in Latin and don't help him.

A clerk comes out of a side room full of piles of paper and looks askance at T-Roy.

'I need to see Mr Edge-Crockett, please,' T-Roy says, hoping that's the way he's supposed to say it.

'What is your business, sir?' The clerk smiles a canine kind of smile. T-Roy recognises that animal thing in his expression. He stops caring about whether he gives the proper impression.

'It's personal.'

The smile goes. 'Do you have an appointment?'

'He'll want to hear me.'

Edge-Crockett can already hear him. He sits behind his desk at the other end of a long room with the main door open. Still, it seems like they're going to go through the whole play. On the door is a metal plate with Arthur Quentin Donald Edge-Crockett's full name engraved on it. 'Prosecutor,' it says in larger letters below.

'Let him in, Norman,' Edge-Crockett says. In spite of the distance, he doesn't have to shout. His voice is made to travel across marble rooms. 'It's all right.'

The clerk steps aside, looking down pointedly at T-Roy's country shoes. It takes a full minute for him to cross the room, making his way between a leather Chesterfield and a row of wooden filing cabinets. When he gets to the desk, Edge-Crockett still seems far away. T-Roy hides his hat behind his back and says his name.

'Sit down, Mr Prichard,' Edge-Crockett makes a gesture at a chair and then returns his long fingers to their steeple shape, the ends resting on grey lips. 'I'm sorry about Norman. He views himself in the character of a watch dog.'

T-Roy says thank you and sits.

'Now. What is it you assume I'll want to hear?'

'I'm sorry, sir, but it's about your daughter.'

Edge-Crockett lifts himself half up out of his seat and says, 'Margaret? What could you possibly have to say to me about her?' For a moment, he is both angry and frightened. Both things pass visibly across him and then go again, like spring clouds. He settles back down and opens his cigar box.

'No, sir. Sorry, I wasn't plain. You have a daughter up north out of state, near Harmony. Did you know that, sir? It's her I've come to talk about. She's my sister.'

'Are you claiming to be my son, boy?'

'No, sir. My father was Ted Prichard. Jeanne is my sister, and you are her father. We had the same mother.'

Edge-Crockett relaxes and cuts the end off his cigar. 'How on earth do you construe that?' he says. 'Have you come here with some kind of proof of paternity?' Knowing T-Roy hasn't, can't possibly have.

'No, sir. I don't think you've understood me.'

'Does she look like you then?' Edge-Crockett moves his eyes to T-Roy's hands, resting one on each knee. T-Roy follows his gaze and lets out a long breath.

'Like I said, we had the same mother. My father was Ted Prichard. Jeanne's father was you.'

'I haven't been up north into the woods for twenty years. Used to go hunting and collecting up there. Did you see my collections when you came through? You seem like an intelligent young man. Have you been to school?'

84

'Not much.'

'Last time I was up there was for a probate. That was years ago.'

'Just about seventeen, sir.'

'What?'

'You were up there nearly seventeen years ago, for Everett Allen's funeral and again the summer after.'

'And you're in a position to prove that conclusively, are you?' Edge-Crockett laughs and the light in the window behind him gets suddenly brighter, so that T-Roy can't make out the details of his expression. He is a silhouette with both arms stretched forward now, white cuffs shining in the light and all ten long fingers spread out on the top of the desk. An eleventh one standing up straight with smoke coming off it.

'I'm guessing you think I've come to fleece you,' T-Roy says. 'I haven't. Jeanne, she's about to get herself in trouble. We, her family, we want to do something before that happens. She's a good, strong girl, quick and clever, but she's mixed up with the wrong people. She's always done the right thing, looks after the old ones and works hard. I thought you might be able to help us get her away, a school maybe, or a job if not. After all, she's here because of you.'

T-Roy hasn't said any of it right, and he knows it.

Edge-Crockett stands up slowly. He's so thin, even his hand-tailored suit hangs off him, but he's tall. He seems to keep rising for a long time. T-Roy has to strain his neck to look up into his face.

'I think you've mistaken me, boy. The law is my business. I have no intention of owning to any child who wasn't borne by my wife. If I were to help you, that would arguably be an admission of paternity and I will not compromise myself in that way. I can see that the child is no better than her mother, and will soon go the same way. I'm sure it's very sad and I'm sorry that your women seem to run that way. I donate to the Children's Aid here in Massachusetts and I'm sure there are good people in your area who do the same. Clearly it's too late for your sister, if the situation is so dire you've come to me. There must have been more likely options closer to home.'

'She died!' T-Roy stands up and drops his hat on the floor without realising. He's still a head shorter than Edge-Crockett, but he's madder, too. 'My mother died having Jeanne. You might just as well have shot her! What kind of a man denies his own child?'

'Your kind, if the annual reports are anything to go by. Myself, I can't deny a thing I never owned.'

'She isn't a thing. She's a girl. Her body's grown all past herself and she'll likely die too, if you don't help her.' T-Roy shouldn't have said any of that, but he's lost himself now.

It seems like the smoke from Edge-Crockett's cigar has filled the whole room. T-Roy can smell the leather and the dust and the piles and piles of paper stacked all around him. He can smell ink. He realises he's still yelling when someone touches the back of his arm. It isn't the clerk; it's a policeman.

'Thank you, Norman,' Edge-Crockett says to the doorway behind T-Roy.

Then he looks past T-Roy's shoulder and says, 'I believe you heard the boy threatening me. Occupational hazard, you know.'

'Have you got a name for the man, Mr Edge-Crockett?'

'He claims it's Roy Prichard, but hasn't any papers that I've seen.'

'We can check our records, sir. Do you want to make a formal charge?'

'I don't think that will be necessary, as this is his first visit. We do get the odd vagrant with a general sense that "the law" is the cause of all their troubles. Drink, I don't doubt. Perhaps a few days' quiet contemplation will assist his recovery. If he were to return, we'd have today's record to corroborate further charges.' He looks T-Roy in the eye, just to bring that home.

A few days turns out to be three. Three days and four nights. The jail is full of hungry, cold men and silverfish. There are small windows high up, but still there isn't much difference between night and day. Sleep happens whenever there's a lull, because they bring men in and pull them out all around the clock. There's oatmeal and johnny cake and water twice a day and an old man who tells good, long stories into the dark. There is no heat.

He comes out on the fourth morning into another windy day, painfully bright. There seems to be too much light in Boston.

Back in North Union Station T-Roy asks and finds that the night train back up leaves at eighteen minutes past ten. He stands in the wind that whips up the platforms and looks through the window at a mother rocking her baby in the ladies waiting room. When she sees him there, she looks scared. He realises he's all unshaven and staring like a criminal. He is a criminal now, he supposes. He's been to jail and they've made a file that says 'Roy Prichard' with marks around it to show they don't think of it as a real, believable name. 'Vagrancy', it says.

Who decides to make a train leave at eighteen minutes past the hour? What is the purpose of a little, sliced up number like that? The angry wave comes up in him again, and he throws back his head to scowl at the ceiling that sits between himself and God. Then he smiles and nods at the young mother to show he means no harm and turns away towards the doors.

Leaves have blown in onto the marble floor. When he pulls at the door, it gives so fast with the wind behind it, he nearly falls back. Outside, he looks around at the steaming coffee wagons, the newspaper stands piled up with words and the huddle of cab drivers spitting and smoking at the curb while their horses snort into the cold. Cities make no sense. He turns his back and heads north into the wind, walking towards home, doing just the opposite of all his childhood imagining.

Jeanne

It was a couple weeks after my birthday I went up in the night and hid in Eddie's smokehouse. I guess where you're from, government man, the girls sit nice with their hands in their laps waiting for things. I'll tell you again, since you seem a little behindhand getting it, if we did that up here those city ladies of yours'd never get their cream or their fox collars. Anyway, I'd rather be called delinquent than sit indoors waiting for somebody to come along and tell me where my life was going to happen. Women like Julia Allen twist themselves in circles trying to do both, trying to make their own lives out of the meanness around them. I'm not one of those.

You had to get up so early to be before Eddie Allen, you might just as well not sleep a'tall. Not only he was a farmer, he was up sometimes just to wander out under the trees before even the songbirds started. That was just the soul of him, sort of dark and watchful. Why was I up in the small hours watching Eddie? Like I said, I wanted to be the one doing the hunting. The one in charge. Maybe that was the trouble with me. So everyone told me, anyway. There was a thing happening and I couldn't figure it, so I wanted to get the jump on it.

I waited till Grampy was asleep then went up and slipped into the Allens' dooryard in the dark. First, I had to throw Don some fish guts and gentle him from under the fence. Once he knew it was me, he didn't make a fuss.

In that smokehouse it was darker than the dark outside. It smelled like metal and carbolic soap. I guess maybe I dozed off waiting, because my head started to fill up with sounds and pictures of things that couldn't possibly be there. There was laughter and whimpering and the smell you get when you open a pig. Blood and the rotting world. I woke myself up and paced for a while, and then leaned against the doorframe and dozed again. When I'd decided to hide and stalk Eddie, I thought I was having fun. I hadn't considered the presence of whatever was seeping into me in that smokehouse, making me feel like there was engine fuel in my veins instead of blood.

I'd always thought Eddie was alone up there, but that night I found out he wasn't. No, I'm not asking you to believe in ghosts. It wasn't like that. It was just, time worked different up there. Things overlapped around that valley. When everything else was quiet, you could hear the crying and the laughter seeping through the gaps between tomorrow and yesterday. I don't care if you believe me, but if you don't at least let yourself picture it, you won't understand all what comes next. It was a place where things came back around and echoed themselves. Things up there didn't happen just the once.

When the light came on in the kitchen I was tempted to run in there and push myself up under Eddie's chin so I could smell him. I'd never been inside the Allens' house before, though I'd been working their fields and wandering through their outbuildings all my life. I wasn't quite ready.

I stayed behind the smokehouse door while Eddie carried a lantern through and did the milking. I watched through a knothole in the side wall while he mucked out. Yes, I watched him wash all that off at the pump. I can see you're thinking it. He left his boots and his coveralls right on the porch, and then came back out wearing jeans and two shirts.

He took Don and the rifle and a couple traps in a sack, and went on foot down into the bottom of the valley. He was on the road, so I had to stay well behind him.

There was only a toenail moon and not even a wash of light to the side of Mary's Peak. I knew right where the dawn would happen in a little while, but a stranger wouldn't have guessed. The sparrows and the cardinals had started in, though, and I realised the tanagers were already gone away south. Eddie Allen didn't talk to himself, though he said a word or two to Don now and then. I went just close enough to make out the shadow of him, and tried to decide whether I'd recognise the shape if I didn't already know who it was. I liked seeing him as just another shade of darkness, me and him the only human shadows out on the road. I wondered what it would take for that man to frighten me. If he was just an unknown shape without those two names and all my memories, would I still feel that quiet coming off him? Would I still want to climb right inside his clothes as soon as I smelled him coming, or would I feel my heart in my mouth and try to hide?

I knew Eddie was after beaver or muskrat 'cause he went in along the river. No way I could hide from him down there, so I went over the other side of the road and got up into the old oak at the corner of Crook's pasture. He emptied three traps and laid two more, then he leaned his back up on a willow and took the bolt out of the rifle. There was a bag full of dead things on the ground beside Eddie, but Don didn't even nose it. He went down into the water, then around up into the field before he settled down.

From up in that oak, I could see the pattern of what they were doing in a way that made a whole different kind of sense than it did from the ground. The world was so changed up there, it startled me. Lift yourself fifteen feet off the road and you're in a whole new layer of life, everything at a different angle, wider and further. Things change in their importance. While Eddie rested, I got sort of caught up being in that gliding, sliding world. I thought how it would be to swoop down out of that tree and startle something like a field mouse or a garter snake, rise back up with a racing heart squirming in my claws.

After a while I saw Bud Crook come over the crest of the high field. Eddie and Don couldn't have seen him, but Don must've heard him shouting at his cows. He raised his head, yapped once and tore away up the hill.

What was I watching for? I don't know. Listen to what I'm trying to tell you. This boy, or man, I'd been seeing all my life had just acquired some kind of quality I could feel but I couldn't see. I thought it was him had changed. Don't laugh. How was I supposed to know it was me changing? My *maman* was dead and my brother was like to get violent if I even mentioned it.

Anyway, my brother had all of a sudden disappeared and nobody would say where he'd gone. I couldn't seem to get anyone to act worried about it. If you asked Jerusha anything, you got a long story about something that seemed suspiciously like what was happening to you but took place somewhere far away where everyone's name was different. I thought I'd scream if she started in with that again.

So I was on my own. If I observed Eddie closely, maybe I could figure out what had shifted in the air around him. He'd slid down with his back against the tree and laid the rifle across his knees. Once he closed his eyes I dropped down into the ferns and sprinted across the road, circled up behind him and came down behind a poplar tree.

I hid there, taking deep breaths and trying to follow him into his quiet. Don came back and looked at me like I was ridiculous, but he didn't bark. Far as he was concerned, I'd been there all morning; there was no need to greet me. I tried to breathe the same breaths as Eddie Allen. If I could get comfortable, maybe we could slide on into the same dream and he wouldn't notice me till we got there.

'Whyn't you come on out, Jeanne?' He didn't even open his eyes when he said it.

'Oh, come on, Eddie. How'd you know I was here?' I spoke from behind my tree.

'Don told me.'

'No, he didn't!'

'Me and Don got a secret code. Come on out. I'm done here anyway.'

It wasn't Don. I think Eddie just felt me with his extra senses, the ones only Eddie Allen had and nobody else even had names for.

I had to step on the willow roots and hold on to the branches to get around to where he was sitting without getting wet. I told Don he was a traitor and jumped up onto the dry ground. As soon as my foot landed everything changed, quick as lightning. Eddie opened his eyes and then shot right up and started cursing. Don caught the feeling from him and growled down in his throat like I was a bobcat or a coyote. The two of them were acting like I was something that might pounce and tear their guts out. One minute we were one way, joking with each other from behind the trees, and then we were another, facing each other and Eddie bristling like a wolf.

There was water in Eddie's eyes; I could see it from where I was standing. If you took that away though, you'd have thought he was about to kill me, for sure. He actually picked up the rifle and dropped the bolt in. Then he threw his head around, like he was checking where he was, like he might suddenly be somewhere else without having noticed. Next, he looked all around my face, making sure every detail was where it was supposed to be.

'It's me, Eddie. What the hell is the matter with you?'

'How'd you get like that?'

'Well, I believe the county say it was my mother, committing what they call offences against chastity.'

'I'm not joking, girl! What happened to you?' I'd never heard Eddie Allen shout before. I hadn't thought shouting was in his nature a'tall. He took that rifle in both hands and used it to push me back up against a tree. Then he brought his eyes right up to mine. His voice went all the way down low. 'You need to tell me how you got like that, right now.' I thought he might be able to draw the insides right out of me, using just the vibrations in that voice.

'Got like what, Eddie? I don't have a single idea what the hell you're talking about.'

That year, the gentle boys around me had all gone violent. T-Roy grabbing my arm, Eddie pushing his rifle up against me and both of them shouting. Something invisible was welling up all around me, running like electricity into the men.

Other girls would maybe cry right about then, but I got mad. I was pretty sure he was about to hurt me, but that just made me want to fly right back at him. Remember that as we go along, government man. In the face of danger, I rise up like that. Always have and never could help it. Every so often, Jerusha would call it stupid and dangerous, but she knew there was no point trying to change the way I was made.

I followed Eddie's eyes down the front of me and saw my dress was covered in soot and my shins were scraped. They were always scraped. Eddie's nose was flared open and he was breathing in the charcoal and blood smell of me.

'Sorry I don't look proper enough for you, Mr Allen.' When I heard myself, I was shouting too. 'I spent half the night in your smokehouse.'

'Jesus fuck!' Eddie never talked like that.

He spun away from me, took the bolt out of the gun and put it down real careful. After that he picked up his insulated bottle and hurled it at the trees. It hit the poplar where I'd just been hiding and I heard the glass inside tinkling apart. Eddie walked away up the hill without looking at me again.

Me? I sat right there in a still, empty space, not knowing what to feel.

He was gone a long time. I got bored after a while and opened the bag of bloody muskrats. Then I put one eye against the stock end of the rifle barrel, trying to see what Eddie saw in that long, hollow darkness. I skipped a few stones and then shouted for Don.

He come back along of Eddie, and they both looked tired. Eddie didn't look scared or mad anymore, though. Maybe a little sheepish, in fact. He wasn't gonna say sorry, though, and I wouldn't have wanted him to. I'd wandered over to the Allens' in the dark to find out about things, and I did. Never mind it was written in some other language I didn't understand; I knew more about Eddie Allen than I had the night before, no arguing with that.

He didn't want to look at me, just messed around with his sacks and picked up the rifle. I saw him drop the bolt in, load and sight up in the trees. I realised he was aiming at a crow. When he took a long breath in, I jumped over to him and knocked into his arm.

The rifle went off and the crow squawked away, thinking we must be pathetic. Don whined and looked at us like what should he do.

'What'd you do that for, Jeanne Delaney?' Eddie said it quiet and offhand, like we were at the kitchen table and I'd laid down three cards that didn't match or something. Most days, he was particular about me being careful of the gun. Normally that would have got a sharp word at least, me touching him while he was about to fire the rifle. But he'd washed himself out and wasn't gonna get mad again that day, I guess. Wherever he'd gone off up the hill to, he'd stayed until he'd got almost too much hold of himself.

'You only wanted just to hear a bullet, to feel that little kick on you. You didn't want to kill anything, Eddie.'

He thought on that for a minute.

'No. I guess not. I'm going back. You're planning to follow, at least be honest about it.'

'Eddie, anybody tell you anything about T-Roy?' I took the sack with the sprung traps off him and went to pick up the useless insulated bottle from under the poplar.

'No. Why would they? T-Roy in trouble?'

'T-Roy ain't nothing. He's not even here. Day after my birthday, he worked all day, then disappeared.'

'Don't they go north around now, up the lake?'

'He didn't go with Grampy, Eddie! I'm trying to tell you my brother just disappeared. Jerusha and Grampy keep acting like it doesn't even matter. They're not even worried. He might be in trouble. He might've got tired of us and run off. He might be dead and they think I can't take it. I don't know.'

We were quiet for a long time, then, climbing the hill.

Finally, Eddie said, 'T-Roy isn't dead, Jeanne. You got no reason to think that.'

'Really? In case you haven't noticed, everybody's dead around here. It's like a stinking boneyard up in this valley.'

'T-Roy's a grown man, and he's a careful one. He wouldn't leave the three of you alone, but a man's got to go off sometimes. He'll be back.'

'You're not supposed to sound like them two, Eddie. I'm following along of you because you're not them. You're my thing. You're supposed to see what I mean, not tell me I don't mean it.'

'I ain't nobody's thing, girl.' He was funning then. Whatever happened down along the river was sinking behind us as we climbed up and out past the Allens' fields. I was so glad of that, I forgot about T-Roy for a while.

Back at the Allens' I still didn't want to go in through that kitchen door. I wanted to think a bit before I stepped over Eddie Allen's doorstep for the first time. I said I was going to visit with the horses and ducked under the fence into the paddock. They come snuffling up, sticking their noses into the collar of my dress and pushing each other sideways. I went in where Eddie kept the apples and brought some back into the paddock.

When I couldn't think of anything else to do, I turned towards the kitchen steps and called all the boldness up into myself. Like I been telling you, there was plenty. Way I figured it back then, that was what made me a good candidate for the reincarnation of Joan of Arc.

Okay, go ahead and laugh. I have to, and all. What did I know?

Eddie had dumped those muskrats right out on the kitchen table and brought out the knives. The very first time I came through the Allens' kitchen door, what I saw was Eddie with his hands full of blood. He looked a little happier about it than most people would, tell the truth. He was in his element, holding the short, sharp knife he used to separate the muscle from the skin.

'Sorry, I poked something and made a mess,' he said. 'Wasn't paying attention.'

'I never seen so much blood come out of a muskrat before.'

'Funny how creatures come apart so much easier than you'd think,' he said.

'What you gonna do with all that?' I was pointing at the mess of innards and bone sitting at one end of the Allens' table.

'I'll keep the legs; I want to bait for bobcat. Throw the rest in the road, it'll be gone in an hour,' he said. Then I listened and heard the crows and the vultures already circling up over the house. They must've known Eddie better than I did.

Thinking back now, I'm not sure what I saw in Eddie Allen's eyes right then, but at the time I thought it was a kind of challenge. People all around knew the Allens as a ruthless bunch. There were plenty stories. Some ridiculous girl part of me wanted to prove I was equal to whatever lived in that house.

Of course I'd seen it all before, but skinning and butchering anything other than a fish or a chicken was T-Roy's job. Or otherwise, we took an animal up to the Nadeaus' and the men divided it, some for everyone.

I made a fire and put a big pot of water to boil on the stove, so we could wash the table after. When I was done with that, I got another empty pot and piled all that mess into it, then carried it out through the dooryard. From the Allens' gate, a person could see down along the whole valley. If the birds were far enough away, you were sometimes as high as they were. It was a sweeping kind of view, and I could see how it bred a sense of power into those people over the generations.

I tossed that jumbled-up pile of recently being out into the middle of the road and stayed about ten steps from it. Tell the truth, I wanted to be up close to those vultures while they gulped down guts. All this killing and things swallowing each other seemed to be part of the secret of whatever lived up there. I wanted to know about it. The crows were swooping and screaming at me and the vultures were circling up above them, but I stood my ground. I could still smell the gore from where I was. The crows gave in first and came down. Then there was one vulture couldn't take it and dove in with his wings open wide. He grabbed hold of as much muscle and guts as he could and then flapped away. If I'd blinked, I'd have missed it, but I wasn't blinking. That was my point, such as it was.

You think I proved anything that day? Well, I don't know. You disgusted with me yet, government man?

In the Dooryard

The men'll have to come out and fill these ruts. Jerusha has to walk right along the raised middle of the road up to the Allens, even at this time of year. It'd be slow going even for somebody young, which Jerusha certainly isn't.

There's a second shawl in her basket, and a good pair of garden gloves she made last year. The hens are all around the gate in the Allens' dooryard and she has to clap and shout at them before she can open it. She goes to the kitchen door and yells in, but Eddie's splashing in the tub.

'Just me, son.'

'Ay-uh.'

'Been seeing you and little Jeanne traipsing around together lately. What are you two getting up to?'

He says something in between splashing, but she can't hear what it is. He's left her a pile of mulch for the asparagus like she asked him to. She puts the gloves on more for warmth than anything. Her fingers stiffen up easy these days.

Here she is, tending vegetables in the Allens' yard. While ago, all she wanted was to come up here and burn down the barns. Who'd have thought? Well, things rearrange themselves, and you can sometimes wait a whole lifetime for revenge. You just got to seize your opportunity, spider-like, when it presents itself. Anyway, it wasn't Eddie done anything, and he's the only Allen left now.

And besides, she's known since the night Eddie was born she has an obligation to him. She should have taken him away there and then, crazy or not. Whatever happens to him, she won't deny it's partly her that let it happen. She's been watching his whole life to see which way those Allens have twisted his growth.

Sometimes it's a shock, to see the current size of the babies she can remember pulling out of the darkness. With Eddie, there's an extra thing. There's wondering which way his shadow will fall, and how much it's down to her where it does.

The little cabbages have made themselves already, and the kale is high as the dog. After the frost they'll have all that to take in. For now, Jerusha picks the last beans and takes down the poles for Eddie to put away somewhere.

It had to be to one of these outbuildings they took Etta Grace. She wasn't specific about it.

You could never know with her how scared she was. She thought the weirdest things were funny, and she told things most of the time with no expression at all. If Jerusha knew for sure which building it was, she would chase everything out of it and burn it down right now, Eddie notwithstanding.

She shovels the mulch onto a sack to drag it over and spread it onto the asparagus. Nice crown it is. She's been working on it for two years now.

Whatever building they were in, Eddie wasn't there. Jerusha knows that because she asked Etta Grace twice, pretending it was no matter whether he was or wasn't. Eddie was just about seventeen at the time. Years older than when Micky started.

Whether they taught Etta Grace to think it was funny or whether they made her grovel, only Hank and Micky know. Them boys were capable of either or both. They were both there at once, she does know that because Etta Grace told it that way. She gave all the detail of the act itself, believing it was a novelty and Jerusha would be interested.

'I'm allowed to tell, *Maman*?' she said. 'You sure?'

'Yes, child. I'm sure and I'm your mother and nobody else is supposed to tell you what you can and can't say. We been over this, remember?'

She noticed when the girl's monthlies stopped, thinking how to bring it up to her and what to do about it. What to do was more pressing than how she got that way. Jerusha made her drink molasses tea and eat whatever meat they could get. Etta Grace never asked why. She never got sick in the mornings and Jerusha took that as a blessing at first. She should have seen it was a sign of trouble. She knew that well enough, but women don't have near enough distance to see their own children clearly. *Ciel*, look at Julia Allen.

Here comes Eddie through the kitchen door, buttoning his shirt and shaking his head like a dog.

'Let me lift that, Jerusha.'

'I ain't that old. Get outta my way, you.'

'Stop and have some coffee.'

'I just got here. Basket's full of pickled beets. Go and put 'em in the pantry.'

'Yes, mam. Then coffee.' He's funning, but you wouldn't guess it unless you'd been around him from a child.

The dirt is cold. Soon it will be frozen. Even through the gloves, it gets into her finger bones. Must be all kind of things soaked into the earth in this dooryard. Just imagine. Blood and whatever else, sinking in and freezing, and her growing vegetables in it. At the end of days, when things reveal themselves, everything on Allen land will twist and shrivel into black dust, and the hot wind will blow it all away.

Etta Grace did get scared, finally. She cried in the end like any woman does.

Inside at the kitchen table, Eddie has cards out. The hot cup feels good in her hands, and Eddie's milk is thick and sweet.

'Hand and foot?' Eddie holds up three decks.

'I don't have all day. You do any work around here, or just play cards and drink expensive coffee all the time?'

'Been out since still dark, doing that.' He points at the new milk. 'Cleaned the stalls, too. Rummy?'

'Okay, but just a hand of gin. Why didn't you and little Jeanne stop in the other day?'

'She ain't so little no more.'

'Yep, I see that. How come you didn't say hello?'

'She was chattering so much, I couldn't hear myself think. We just kept going out to the road. Didn't realise you were in.'

'She's a good girl.'

Eddie looks through the open door and then over at the case clock. It hasn't been wound in months, but he looks at it like it might tell him something.

'Been raised by two men and it shows,' Jerusha says, 'but she's a good girl.'

'I know it. Anyway, she's been half raised by you and all.'

'Well, so was Etta Grace. I won't stand that a second time, Eddie Allen. Not without killing somebody.'

'My God, Jerusha! How can you say that to me?'

'You're the one stayed. Long as you know enough to be careful.'

'Well, I do. I wish everybody would quit going on at me about it.'

'Everybody, who?'

'Never mind, Jerusha. There's something to Jeanne. I can see that. I'm not blind.'

'No, but you're an Allen. Only lately, I'm still hearing stories about the things your grandpa did, let alone the rest of you.'

Eddie rearranges his cards then lays them face down while he gets up and puts the coffee pot back on the stove. He hands Jerusha a napkin for no particular reason.

'Gin!' Jerusha says. 'I'm old, Edward Allen, but I'm watching.'

'Oh, I don't doubt that. Happy for you to see me, too.'

Now, she's watching. Now that it's too late for all the girls that been through that dooryard. If Jeanne made another, that would be the final thing. That would be the end of Jerusha. She'd do something she wouldn't be able to come back from. Get carried clean away, leaving nothing behind her to signify. Just more blood soaked into the dirt.

Jeanne

Can you see it? Everybody was getting nervous, but nobody was telling each other anything straight. That whole fall was like that. T-Roy disappearing and everybody circling around each other and whispering warnings. Nobody and nothing was clear, somehow.

'Sit down, Jeanne Delaney.'

Jerusha used both my names and that never did bode well. Mostly she just called me 'child' or 'girl'.

'Grampy said thank you for the canning.' I put my boots by Jerusha's back door and pulled the window closed.

'Well, he should thank Eddie Allen, too. It's his vegetable patch. Now sit yourself down.'

'He said to bring you these willows that's extra, for baskets. I dried them and soaked 'em up the creek.'

'I thank you and your *pe'père*. Now stop chattering and sit down. I got a story to tell you.'

'Can I make tea?'

'If it'll keep you quiet. Stove's lit. I been making dye.'

'I saw it out back. What you makin'? Can I help?'

'Jeanne Delaney,' she huffed. I told you, people did that when they said my name back then. 'I need you to stay quiet and listen to me.'

'Okay, I will. Where's the chamomile?'

'Right where it's been your whole blessed life! But don't use that, use what's in the tin there. Gonna tell you an old story, from when there were no cars or trains or steamboats or senators.'

'Oh, I like them. You ain't told me one in ages.'

She just sighed again without even bothering about my name. You see I can talk, don't you? Imagine when I was all wound up and sixteen. Not many would've put up with me.

'They didn't have Children's Aid then, neither,' Jerusha said. She was gearing the story up and getting it started while I made tea in the pot. 'Everybody wandered, and in the summer they had their camps all along the lake. There was a girl same age as you are now.'

There was always a girl same age as me in Jerusha's stories. Funny that, eh?

'She liked to swim and she had a long strength in her that never seemed to get tired. She could pull a bow and skin anything, no matter how big it was, but her mother could never get her to set still long enough to learn to tan hides. This girl left that to other people, ran around the woods and swam back and forth on the lake all day. She brought home enough meat so nobody minded.

'One summer morning, she was swimming while everyone else was still asleep. The dawn had only just started coming earlier and people still got up slow. The girl was the only human thing awake in the land; sometimes she stayed up at night just to feel that. She floated on her back listening to the loons settle down for the day when the sun cleared the hills. When she looked over at the sunrise, there was a boat between her and it, with a man standing up in it. He was just drifting towards her, making himself out of the rising light. It looked to the girl like that man come right out of the sun. When he got close enough, she could see his skin was like the inside of a clam shell and his eyes were pigeon feather grey. Right away, she wanted to climb into that boat with him and let it keep drifting on past everybody she ever knew. Fast as lightning, she was took already.

'He had a different idea. He wanted to stop at the camp where her family was and look at everything. He smiled at her though, and put his hand in her hair. When they got to the camp, he kept smiling and turning over everyone's things. He ate with them and went away again, waving first and then smiling a private smile at the girl.'

'What was her name?'

'What?'

'The girl. She have a name?'

'I don't know! She wasn't my girl. Call her Joan of Arc, why don't you?'

'Okay, just asking.'

'He came back with all kinds of presents. Things made of glass and metal, mostly. Rifles, which hardly nobody had then. He took his time getting into that girl, but he was heading for her all the while. It rained too much that summer and there was a hard winter coming. Everyone saw it and they told the girl to shun that man, this wasn't the time to be venturing out of safety. He came and went, and in the end he started telling lies and taking things. Those people didn't like lies, not at all. Lying was worse than killing people, as far as they were concerned. Before the heat fell off, she was pregnant. The balance of her started changing and swimming felt different. On the land she felt sick and unwieldy, but in the water she was like a fish. She just drifted around on the lake, staring at the sky. Once that girl got a belly on her, the people threw her out.'

'A pregnant girl, with winter coming?'

'I'm telling you she broke the rules, carrying a child for a liar. Going off camping with a man nobody trusted. She wasn't thinking. She wound up begging at the edges of camps up and down the lake, with the first snow falling and starting to stick.'

I threw my chin back then and said, 'I can see you're trying to tell me something, Jerusha. I ain't stupid.' I was cocky like that with the grown-ups, back then.

'Of course I'm trying to tell you something! I did used to be a girl, you know. I remember how it was. The first time the right man lays a hand on you, the blood starts running around inside you to every place but your head. That's why it makes you dizzy. Your brain's being deprived of its normal sustenance.'

'I never been dizzy in my life.'

'Just listen to me, will you? She pushed that baby out in the woods by herself in February. She'd made a little shelter, and like I said she could shoot. At the end of her labour, though, she let the fire go out. Close your eyes and try to see it, Jeanne Delaney. There she is in a lean-to, with the ashes getting cold and blood spilled out onto the snow around her.'

Don't look so horrified, city boy. Jerusha was trying to scare me, but it was for a reason. Life up here's not all pretty like it is for you. All those nice things you have? It's us digs them up out the earth and sends 'em down to you on the train. It's dirty work and it don't pay so good. You see what I mean though, huh? Everybody was telling parables that fall. Hinting me practically to death.

Jerusha was never gonna beat me or stop me from doing anything. The story was her way of trying to bend me into shape.

'She took the baby and put it on her breast,' Jerusha said, 'but she wasn't prepared for the afterbirth. There were no women to tell her, see? When her stomach grabbed her and twisted after the baby was already out, she didn't know what was happening. It came with a big gush of blood that put her out of it. She just let it lay there and rolled away with the baby. Snow was falling and a wind was picking up. All the animals were hiding because they'd felt the blizzard coming. By morning, it had drifted in and buried her. They didn't find her till the thaw. She'd been laid there frozen all winter with that little, shell-coloured baby still latched to her breast.'

I think I said something to Jerusha about maybe telling me a nicer story next time. Something ungrateful, I'm sure, though I can't remember what exactly. She sighed again, and poured some of that tea that was steeping between us. She didn't have any herself. It tasted foul. I could barely swallow it, but she looked at me like I'd lose a limb if I tried to stand up without drinking it down.

'Listen, Jeanne Delaney. There's no sense in not doing what makes you happy. Not till you've got to, anyway. I'm just asking you please, try to keep hold of the fact that a woman's body is a machine especially designed for producing consequences.'

Reading the Will

T-Roy has been walking north from Boston for ten days now, and every mile he walks is colder. He's in a church with a stove, but he can't feel its heat. The stove is in an alcove to the side of the pulpit and doesn't seem to be doing much. There's a good foundation to the church, but the cold still comes up through the floorboards. Bright sun though, and the windows focus it into beams of warmth.

The preacher talks on and on for over an hour. The usual thing about how you can't buy your way into heaven, and a story about a doctor and some lepers on an island somewhere, then a talk about how factories are like the places where they make idols in the Bible. T-Roy isn't listening enough to know how he gets from one thing to the other, but he's sure they must all connect. The man is a good talker.

During his first week walking, there was plenty of work and it was warm enough to sleep outside with the pocket of small silver he'd earned. But snow's fallen now and there's still over fifty miles just to get to Harmony. He's resigned himself to being preached over in exchange for food and shelter. Two towns and two days back, a church lady gave him new socks.

Right here, there's a daughter you can't complain about looking at, and the church has been painted over the summer. The cold coming through the cracks and the watery-eyed daughter make him think of Etta Grace and of the church in his own town. Far as T-Roy knows both him and Etta Grace were only in that church one time, and that was along with everyone else from all around.

It was a big funeral, and an odd one.

Everyone knew there was a dead man in the church, but you weren't allowed to see him. He lay there under the coffin lid and they all seemed satisfied with that. A Yankee way of doing things.

They all went outside and the church was half-painted. There were ladders up against the clapboards and not enough room for all the people who wanted to crowd around that freshly dug hole.

'You all right, Mr Prichard?' The church he is in now comes back into focus. It seems the preaching has been over a while.

'He's cold, John,' Somebody's Daughter says. 'Get him in the kitchen and let Laura give him some soup.'

'I'm sorry, miss. I was praying.' That isn't true, but it isn't entirely a lie either. He is contemplating mortality, which they're always telling you to do.

She sits with him in the soup kitchen, staring. The soup is squash and onions with the taste of dirt just hiding in it. There's a long table T-Roy supposes gets full of workers at certain seasons. Right now, it's just him and two men he guesses are the town drunks. They're playing cards and no one seems to mind, which makes T-Roy like everyone involved just a little bit more, in spite of the preaching. On the wall by the kitchen hatch there's a sign that says, 'Following the path of least resistance is what makes men and rivers crooked.'

The girl is still watching his spoon go up and down. Her eyes have a carrying movement, like she keeps sliding away inside them. Etta Grace had eyes like the stones on Jasper Beach. Black at first, but hiding every colour of a night sky inside them.

'What are you doing wandering in the cold, Mr Prichard?' It's a ridiculous question, considering how many wanderers there are on the roads, but she means it to be friendly, and at least when she speaks she's staring less. T-Roy swallows and wipes his mouth on his own handkerchief.

'I was in Boston. It was windy and I guess something blew into my head. The trains made me mad; they were so picky about time. I just thought I'd rather be walking.'

She laughs at that. 'Just thought you'd head north into the cold? If it was an imp took you over, why didn't it send you south?'

'Because it was an imp, I guess. I'm going home.'

106

'Where's home?'

'Different places. It's a boat. Right now it'll be dry-docked and they'll be up the lake at the border I guess. Or they might've needed me for that. I don't really know, but I'll find it.'

'Who's they?' She wants to know if T-Roy has a wife. Well.

'What's your name, anyhow?'

'Ila.' She looks away out the window, and that's a relief. T-Roy shovels in more soup while she's distracted.

'I'm not being truthful, Ila. In fact, I was in jail. For three days, I think. When they let me out, I just wanted to walk. I just wanted to be without walls for a while.'

Now she won't look at all. She gets up to clear the bowls from in front of the two drunks. They're smoking now. Seems like anything goes in this place.

After a while she comes near again, wiping down the long table.

'The police took my money. I was mad and I guess I yelled in front of the law, but I hadn't done nothing wrong. I'm not religious, but I wouldn't eat your bread and then lie to you either.'

'So, you weren't really praying then. Earlier.'

'Not exactly. I was remembering something, a funeral.'

'And it's not my bread.' She sits down again, but without putting her legs under the table. She sits with a twist in her, looking at him with her body turned away. 'Who lives in the boat with you?'

'The law took my knife too, and the visiting card I had with me. For an important Boston man.'

'Do you want coffee?'

'If it's no trouble.' There is something between them that goes before formality. Or after it, even though they've never met before this. He's holding his hands tight together because he oughtn't to let it carry him away. He probably will.

'It's my *pe'père* who lives on the boat with me,' he says when she comes back with two stoneware cups and a milk jug. 'My Grampy.'

'There's already sugar. I hope you like it like that. We make it that way, in the cold.'

107

'My sister lives with us, too, until the winter comes. It was wrong of me, not going straight back by the train.'

This woman is like the Virgin. Not because she's never been with a man, because of how you just seem to keep telling her things you've done. She sits listening in her blue apron with the star weed under the surface of her eyes. T-Roy is a man who craves softness. Just the hope of it undoes him.

'You don't seem to me like a careless person. Whose funeral was it you were remembering?'

'It was a long time ago. I was a boy and my mother was still alive. I was that age when you're always swiping away people's coattails and trying to see things from around the side of them. I don't know why we went, except that everyone was there. Everett Allen was an important man, for us anyway. We depended on the farmers then, for day wages. The Crooks and the Allens kept everybody going, in a way.

'Everett Allen's boy was little. Eddie, his name is. He was griping in his mother's arms while she stood with that chiselled face on her. She's a brittle woman, Mrs Allen. The grown-ups all threw dirt on Everett Allen's box after the preacher was done talking. I remember thinking at the time how mean that was, throwing dirt at a dead man.'

She laughs, but only just loud enough and a little sad, like. Just precisely the right laugh, which maybe she practises, being a church woman. She straightens her body out then, and takes her legs up over the bench so her feet sit alongside T-Roy's. He's not sure it's polite to keep talking, but he does anyway. One of the drunks is sleeping with his head on the table and the other is playing solitaire.

'Here's the thing. That Boston man, that Edge-Crockett, he was there in the churchyard. I didn't even think about it when I was in his office. It was twenty years ago and I was only an angel still. I didn't have my big teeth yet. *Maman* said that meant I was still an angel and I'd go straight back to heaven if anything happened to me.'

'You just want to talk or do you want me to understand what you're telling me? I don't mind, but I'm just saying if it's understanding or advice you're after, you might want to fill in the details and give me some background.'

Well, then he tells her about all of it. His mother and the boat and the way the Allens sat like crows in that house up the road, coming out every once in a while to rip things open with their saw-edged voices and make dark shadows against the sky. After a while, he follows Somebody's Daughter – Ila – into the kitchen where she says its warmer. He can feel that he's stuck himself to her a little, that it must seem like he's lost or simple, but it doesn't matter. They'll move on by each other tomorrow and then they won't need to think about each other's strength or purpose.

In the kitchen he eats butter cookies and tells her about Etta Grace and the way he used to watch her. The way you could lean into the air around her and it felt like clouds and sweetgrass. Then he leaves that hanging and explains about Jeanne and Eddie alone up at the Allens, about that one-foot brother in town with his flint-hearted mother, and the other brother gone who knows where down the roads.

'Mr Prichard,' she says, 'you seem to me like a man with your shirt caught on someone else's fence. Don't you want your own life?'

'I lost that in the trees, while ago.' He sounds more forceful than he means to, so he tries a joke. 'This is my afterlife. Know what that makes you, don't you?'

'Enough of that, sir. Keep on. What about the man from Boston?'

'He's my sister's father. He was there. At Everett Allen's funeral. I only remembered it while I come up the road here. He stood by the fence while Sloat's driver held the train station cart for him. From where I was standing, he looked practically as tall as the steeple, stretching all black right up into the sky. His skin was the colour of new milk, a little bit blue, and he did that same thing like a cage with his fingers, only they were in black gloves then. His blue face way up there looked like it wasn't attached, just floating on the dark tower of his coat. I thought maybe he was some creature that turns up when a bad person dies. I asked my mother, "what kind of thing is that?" "Lawyer," she said, "come to read the will." I thought lawyer must be a kind of visitation that came with death, not a regular person. I thought "reading the will" was as in what's inside a person, another word for soul. Until I was at least twelve I saw that man in my mind's eye every time someone said the word lawyer. Then it faded and I didn't think about it again until now, only remembered yesterday how he steepled his fingers like that.'

She turns to the stove. He could reach out and put a hand on her shoulder blade. It's there, right in front of him. The small part of her stomach lies under the pocket of her apron and he can picture the tops of her stockings. At the same time, he's thinking about Arthur Quentin Donald Edge-Crockett and how all the dead people scattered over the land up in that valley seem to tie in together. And how he left Jeanne alone with all that.

'When we all filed out of the churchyard, that lawyer moved aside so he could be along of our way up the road. He looked my mother up and down in some kind of way I didn't understand, then bowed his head and gave her a card. They murmured things to each other. He pointed at the cart and she pointed at me, but their voices were too high up for me to hear the words. I'm only now realising, I was right there the day that man drew a bead on my mother. I was standing next to her when the whole thing started. She started to die right there on the road while I was with her.'

'You need some sleep, Mr Prichard.'

'Show me where to go?'

'You'll find it all right by yourself, sir. End of the hall there.' She opens a door to reach for a towel in the linen cupboard by the kitchen door. They're on the bottom shelf and he waits behind her, looking while she leans down in. When she turns around again and sees him there, she laughs and her eyes wash right over and into him. River water, tasting metallic and just colder than skin.

'There's a couple trees down outside,' she says. 'Split them and stack them and I'll feed you for a week.'

Jeanne

We went ferning, me and Eddie and Jerusha, working in the woods behind the cabin, filling Eddie's pony cart with fronds. He drove them to the train station in town, and a man from the city paid us. Maybe that was the best time, the one that lasts. The three of us together under the trees, drawing the sweetness out of the woods and looking after each other.

Grampy went up the north end with the Nadeaus, which had never happened before. T-Roy had disappeared, like I said. I kept trying to get Jerusha worried about him, but she wasn't having it. Said he was a man, and needed to go off by himself once in a while, which is what Eddie said and all, like they'd agreed a story.

The apple pickers came to the Allens and me and Jerusha cooked them deer porridge and johnny cake. There was only ten of them, so one night we cooked trout and potatoes on a fire down in the orchard. They sang in French and Spanish and I tried to save up the words.

Right at the start, winter seemed like a blessing that year, falling down on me and Eddie one day as we came out of the trees onto the road.

The morning had been bright, but cold. Jerusha had me making winter socks, but I'd left them sitting in the basket by the stove. I couldn't sit still long enough to wait for anything to grow on needles.

When I showed up at the back door Eddie put an old wool shirt on me. He measured my feet, too, said I wouldn't last the winter in those boots, which wasn't true, of course.

We went up into the trees early, high up into the larches behind Jerusha's, carrying the two guns and some apples. Eddie had one

111

pocket full of bullets and another with three shotgun cartridges for himself.

He was teaching me to shoot. He had a shotgun and a .22 rifle his daddy took to the war in Mexico. They had a .30 at the Allen house too, but Eddie never took it out. I wanted him to show me the shotgun, but he said just the .22, take it or leave it. I didn't honestly know why I wanted to learn, not then. I guess shooting seemed like something people did when they were in charge, when things couldn't touch them. I don't know. All I'm saying is, it wasn't because I knew what was coming, not exactly anyway.

You should believe that, government man, so you can understand how blank and innocent it all was in the before time.

There were streaks of dusty sunlight coming through the branches and our breath was showing in the cold. We stood still a while and listened to it all, then Eddie started explaining. I got impish and took his hand, just to see what he'd do. He let me. Our palms got slick against each other while all the rest of our skins flushed up and burned into the cool air.

Eddie talked and talked. Keep my opposite elbow under the stock, breathe out, don't rush it. He got cross at me for fidgeting. My toes were numb by the time he fired the first bullet.

The deer were hidden already and the wolverines were travelling. There were hawks up high, hunting over the open scree where there used to be a quarry, circling around over the larches every once in a while. You'd see 'em most days, predictable.

Finally, Eddie made me fire the rifle, standing with the right side of me along a tree. It hardly kicked back at me, and I think I got better after a couple goes at it. Eddie said the .22 was the weapon for me. He explained about the bore and the rifling so I could picture all what happened inside the gun. The hammer would make a spark and the spark would make an explosion. That barrel would gather the energy of that explosion in and focus it. A dark tunnel of metal, directing the fire. I won't lie, I loved the feeling of being in charge of that.

I said, why couldn't I fire the shotgun, the rifle was no trouble? He took me down by the creek and had me stand behind him with my hands up on his shoulders while he fired, so I could feel the kick of it. When the shotgun went off, wings erupted all above us. The crows screamed and the pigeons ruffled away. Then Eddie leaned my right side up against a maple, me being left-handed. Devil's child, according to the nuns in Harmony. Yep, that's me.

Eddie said the shotgun wasn't elegant, see; it wasn't precise. But I said I'd get someone else to show me if he wouldn't. So he stood behind me, took off his wool shirt and folded it over my shoulder.

The kick of it knocked me back into Eddie, but I could take it. It was no worse than standing up while you get belted, and plenty of women do that every day. I was aiming up into the branches, and little pieces of twig and brown leaf fell down in front of us. We sat and ate apples then.

'Eddie, why you live in that farmhouse all by yourself?'

'I believe you asked me that already.'

'Okay, but what do you do in the evenings?'

'What does anybody do? Sometimes I look at the paper. Sometimes I play chess and anyway there's work to do all hours on a farm. You know that.'

'Chess? By yourself?'

'Ay-uh. Or with the man in the paper.'

'Were you sad when they went to town?'

Eddie snorted. A choked sort of sound, but you might have to call it a laugh I guess. 'Guess you don't know them,' he said.

'I do, a little. Jerusha brought all you out of your mother, I know that.'

'Don't know that she would have if she'd known us beforehand.'

'Eddie, did you know my mother?'

'I was only a boy, Jeanne. T-Roy's four years older than me, you know.'

'But you seen her, right?'

'I seen her. She looked like you, some, but the eyes and the nose look prettier on you.' He picked up the rifle and took the bolt out then. 'See the grooves in there?'

'Yep.'

'That's so it goes true.'

'I guess that makes sense. Do you think she would like me?'

'Doesn't have to make sense. It just works. Laws of physics.'

'That's what sense is, Eddie Allen. Things like that are what do always make sense. They just happen the same way every time, because there's a rule that makes 'em. Nice and simple. So? Do you think my mother would like me?'

'How would I know that? She'd be your mother, wouldn't she? Mind you, I don't think my mother likes me much.'

'Why not?'

'My brothers are more her idea of men. Come on along. We'll find a hollow for you to lay and fire the rifle from.'

He made me get downside of a ridge so just my head was sticking up. Then I could lay with my elbows twisted the same side of me and rest the stock against my shoulder.

'Bullet'll go a lot farther and truer than the shot. Time to really aim it here. Nice and slow. Imagine you want that knot in the beech right there. Just think on it while you aim. Don't forget to breathe.'

We were down in the hardwoods then, and Eddie was pointing to a tree about thirty feet away. I actually hit the tree the second time, but about two feet above where I was aiming. The rifle was nicer, he was right. It felt clean and sensible. The shotgun reminded me of an angry drunk. The rifle was like a surgeon, cutting through things. I shoved right up along of Eddie and asked if I done good.

'You'll do. Shove over and give me some room here. I need to open that gun.'

'No.' I pushed harder instead, like a blind puppy looking for warmth. I had no idea what I was doing, but I didn't want to stop it. Don't look so shocked. That's how it is and I'm sure you know it.

Next thing, Eddie was lying over my back with his mouth on the back of my neck. He stayed still like that for so long I started to think something was wrong with him. He was just breathing on my skin and I could feel the whole weight of him holding me down. I couldn't turn over to look at him if I wanted to. I wasn't sure I did want to, anyway. It was kind of nice feeling him but not seeing him right then.

He put a hand up to move my hair away and said my name.

'What?' I said. Just like that. I don't know; it just came out wrong.

'Can I?'

'Well, I guess so.' I laughed a little and he said, 'don't,' and put a hand on my mouth, just soft like.

Then he ran his hands along the sides of me and sounds started to come out of my mouth without me asking them to. I felt my stomach disappear and the blood started rushing between my legs. I wanted to look in Eddie's eyes then, because I felt like otherwise I'd fly off. I wanted to jump right inside him and hide there. I tried to turn over then, but he was still holding me down, me lying on my stomach in the mulch. I closed my eyes so I wouldn't see anything that wasn't him.

All of a sudden he was gone. There was no weight on me and I could feel the absence of him all along my skin. Things were still churned up inside me and I felt a little embarrassed of myself, to tell the truth. I rolled over onto my back and watched some geese, slicing through the sky and making a racket. I was hoping Eddie would wait a while before he came back and looked at me. He was nowhere in sight anyway, but I knew he wouldn't leave me there.

There was nothing about Eddie Allen that ever worried me. I know it sounds crazy now. I knew the family he came from and Jerusha was all the time lecturing me with her stories, but everything about him just always seemed like it was in the right place. Right where I knew it would be all along.

'Come and see how to clean it now.'

I must have closed my eyes. He was standing right over me, and I looked up at him and got dizzy again. Eddie's rasping voice didn't match the words he was saying.

'Never fire a gun without cleaning it after. People lose eyes and limbs that way.' He spread his shirt out on the grass, lay the bolt and the rifle down. I reached for his arm and he slapped me away.

'Pay attention, Jeanne. Someday you might have to shoot something when I'm not by. Knowing half is worse than knowing nothing.'

The snow started falling just as we came out of the trees behind Jerusha's place, like the sky come down to bless us on our way to the road. Eddie looked in Jerusha's back door but she wasn't home.

I was carrying the shotgun breached over my arm, trying to look like Eddie did when he carried it.

'Maybe I'm a soldier,' I said. 'Maybe I'm headed down to Mexico and I get lost and hole up in the painted desert and have to fight off a mountain lion. I carry the gun loaded, ready all the time, and at night I make a fire and the stars are different. Lizards are skitterin' around under the rocks.'

'You're a soldier, why you have a shotgun?'

'So trade me.'

'No. You're okay.' He grabbed the back of my neck then and shook me a little. Thank God, I thought. I'd been worried he'd never lay a hand on me again.

Big flakes of snow came down out of the gunmetal sky and fell around us, promising to cover and change everything, giving us a reason to hold onto each other. They disappeared when they hit the road. On Eddie's sleeves they stayed a while.

'Look, Eddie! When they're big like this you can see how each one is different. They're like every kind jewel.' I tilted back my head and stuck out my tongue, trying to catch one. Eddie's face froze up and he stared at me, then he turned around and walked right out of my line of vision. When I closed my mouth and looked back at the road, he was moving away from me like all of a sudden there was somewhere he needed to be.

'Hey, Eddie Allen! Where's the fire?' I stumbled trying to catch up, and he didn't even turn.

116

'All right, Jeanne Delaney. That's today's lesson finished,' he said to the air out over the valley. 'Give me the shotgun and take the rest of the apples home with you.'

'No! I'm going with you. Ain't nobody up at your house, and this is the first snow of the year. You can't be alone. You need someone to set the fire and heat water.'

'I do all that myself every day. You're still a girl. You can't walk home after dark.'

I snorted at him. 'What the hell are you talking about, Eddie? I been walking from your house to Jerusha's to the lake and back again in the pitch dark all my life. You mad at me?'

'A little.'

'For what? What the hell did I do?'

'Stop cursing. It ain't pretty.'

'What? Eddie Allen, where have you gone?' I made a show of turning every which way, looking. 'Come back here, please! Someone stole your body and I don't like him.'

He just looked at me. I was about to spend the next month trying to make that boy laugh. This was only the beginning and there wasn't so much as a crack in his expression.

'Come on, then,' he said. He huffed and shook his head and sighed and said, 'Jeanne Delaney.'

Well, that was more like it.

A Month of Sundays

The snow won't stick. It's only the weather playing, only a hint and a breath of what's coming. Eddie feels sick and jumpy, trying to think what there is for supper and whether there's any clean sheets. Jeanne goes around leaning against things in the kitchen, waiting for him to touch her. She wants him to save her from the embarrassment of the empty space around her.

'Make yourself useful and go get some eggs.'

She takes the basket and goes down the steps, laughing at him all the way across the yard. It's different than Etta Grace's laugh, coming from the cow barn. That baby laugh Etta Grace always kept, even after her body changed. His mother heard it too, knowing Etta Grace was in there with Micky and Hank. She just smiled at her boys through the clapboard wall, pretending they were all playing in there.

Jeanne's laugh isn't like Hank's laugh either, ringing around the barn and slapping into the backs of the cows. Micky holding the hands of that other girl while Hank laughed that laugh and pulled the dress off her. That terrified girl without a name or a family who went bleeding out into the dark and disappeared.

Jeanne Delaney's laugh is so sure of itself. It looks on at the world and just feels amused. Full of pleasure. It's falling in Eddie's mind like shards of glass. He can almost see it breaking.

The potatoes are boiling and the onions are making Eddie's eyes water. She is behind him now, pushing all of herself up against his back and hooking her thumbs into his belt.

'Shit!' He pushes her off and turns around so he can put his bleeding finger into his mouth.

'Oh, look what I made you do. Let me see.'

'I don't want to touch you in this house, Jeanne.'

118

'Well, what are we doing here then? Let's go somewhere else.'

He stalks out into the yard and starts to work the pump. There's water in the kitchen, but he's ignored it.

'Eddie it's just me, you know. I'm the same wherever I go. It's a special quality I have.'

The words, and then her laugh again, come out of her dark silhouette in the kitchen doorway. When did everything change sides? When did she stop being skittish and get so purposeful? She's barely sixteen. How can a girl like that have so much conviction? She doesn't even know what's going to happen when he lays her down, but she's staring it straight in the eyes. Why on earth did he teach her to shoot? What kind of idiot puts a gun in the hands of a woman like that?

She doesn't move an inch out of his way when he comes back up the steps, so in the end he picks her up and carries her, letting go of her legs for a minute in front of the stove so he can take the potatoes off.

He carries her right past the gun cabinet and the sofa and lays her on his bed, then sits down to untie his boots. It's cold and damp and smells like rancid hide. There are three untanned muskrat skins stretching in the corner. She kneels up behind him and rests her face down along his shoulder.

'Lie down, Jeanne,' and she does for once.

It's a job of work just to look at her. It's enough. He undoes the only button on each boot she ever does up and lifts her ankles out, then lays the boots on the floor next to his. She lifts up her shoulders and stretches her arms so he can get the dress off her. He can see her willing herself not to shiver. The bumps come up on her arms but there's a heat coming off her too. Her eyes are as big as a doe's. He has to look away from them. He ought to cover her, with himself or with a blanket, but he just looks away at the curtain, feeling like the day he first shot something.

She pulls on his sleeves but he doesn't take his shirt off, just lies down along her with a hand on her stomach, looking down at the length of her, because it's good and because it isn't her face. Her breaths are short. She's waiting for him to do something she doesn't have the know-how to imagine. He puts an arm around her waist and pulls her over onto him.

'Ouch. This hurts.' She puts a hand between her stomach and his belt buckle while he pulls the blanket out from under them and covers her.

'Eddie Allen, you gonna look me in the eye or not?'

Instead, he pulls her head down so he can breathe into her ear. 'You can stay next to me,' he says. 'You can stay right here, if you like.' Then he lays her back alongside him and goes to sleep.

Time passes with gaps in it, while he dozes and wakes. He is dreaming of bruised and moaning girls and Hank showing him how to break Micky's fingers when he feels her pressed up against his back. Jeanne Delaney is there in the bed and he has turned away from her, sweating into his wool shirt. For a while they both pretend he's still sleeping. When he turns over, her black eyes are glinting and her breath smells like wet wool.

'You dreaming, Eddie Allen?'

First, he puts just one finger inside her. She is wet and swollen and digs her fingers into his arms. He doesn't take his clothes off, just pulls down his jeans and lifts up onto his arms, holding himself over her and hoping.

'I'm gonna hurt you.'

'Okay.'

She almost does it herself in the end. It doesn't matter. They both call out into the wet darkness. He can feel it when she breaks, and he falls down to kiss her so he won't have to see the tears in her eyes. He moves as slowly as he can, until she clutches him with the kind of desperation only Mrs Crook ever showed him before. She wraps her legs around his back and pushes until he can feel her blood and the wet rest of it against his stomach. Well, that's how long it takes Jeanne Delaney to get the measure of something new. He almost laughs then. But, well, there's no reason to give her everything at once.

By the time dawn makes them out of the shadows they've thrown off the blankets to let their sweat disappear into the morning cold. She becomes strange all over again in the light and he turns away from her. He has to steady his breath so she won't see him shaking. There's blood on the sheets underneath her, blood on her thighs.

'Weren't you about to fry me some potatoes, Eddie Allen?'

'About ten hours ago. I need to be at Sloat's for nine o'clock. City people coming to hunt.'

'Hurry up then. There's eggs already if you didn't break 'em when you manhandled me.'

Eddie lifts his hips to pull up his jeans, then sits up facing the doorway to do his belt and pull his boots on.

'Okay, so I'm no expert. I guess you seen I probably don't do that for a living.'

'That ain't funny, Jeanne.'

'But I think ... you're supposed to kiss me or something.'

'Go and get us some water. I'll make you coffee instead.' Outside the bedroom door he takes a great breath of air that isn't full of their naked bodies. It steadies him so he can turn around just once to look. She's sitting up in the bed with her dress in her hands, looking like some kind of second-hand salvation. Like snow that's fallen on him but won't stick.

It's only a lawyer and two small-time bank officers, waiting at Sloat's Inn when Eddie pulls up in the pony cart. Young men, somehow smelling like soap and Brilliantine even though they've been on the train overnight. They've had their boots shined and their coats brushed by their lacy young women at home in the city. They want a deer, and they've already made bets on who will bring it down. Eddie wasn't in the running.

There's a grey sky, threatening more snow flurries, but they never come. Neither does the sun. It just shows all day like a spill of milk through the cloud cover. He takes them around the other side of Mary's Peak and leaves the pony cart by an old cow shed in Crook's far field. There's a group of deer that live up that side in a stand of yellow birch and ash, three does, with five babies this past year. There'll be a buck around somewhere about now, but Eddie can make sure they don't take him.

They take the deer path up and Eddie tries to keep the men quiet. They've got two flasks between them, which won't help. Once they're in the hide they talk in low voices about senate primaries and floating stocks. Eddie gets in a watching and waiting posture and lets himself drift while they boast at each other. His body repeats to itself everything it can remember and he wonders how long he slept. Long enough to dream, anyway.

After breakfast he'd stuck his head under the pump and rinsed Jeanne Delaney off his fingers. She sat at the table, concentrating on not looking hurt. Laughing at him and telling him about himself.

'Don't stay when I'm gone,' he told her.

'All right, Eddie Allen. I don't want to live in your farmhouse. It don't go anywhere. The view never changes. Don't suit me.'

'Just clear off after breakfast. It's not safe, you here on your own.'

He looked at her dress and now he knew the body underneath he could see it there. No doubt everyone else could too. She's a walking time bomb, with the shape of her showing beneath her little sharp eyes. He can almost feel her ticking now, far away through the trees.

'Well, Allen? You got a line on any?'

'Excuse me? I thought I saw something. Didn't hear you.'

'Girls, Eddie. Where do you get to know some women around here?'

'There.' A doe and two yearlings are moving through the yellow birches up the slope, nibbling and heedless. The spots are gone; they'll survive just fine. 'You'll have to ask Sloat about t'other. Rifles now, sirs.'

It goes on for a month, just like that. Eddie takes state representatives and bankers out trapping bobcats and wolverines and shooting ducks with the shotgun. Brings them back to the train feeling they're more of men somehow, if Eddie can make them believe they've killed things. That's what they're paying for really, to roll in the dirt like dogs trying to get the clean smell off themselves.

Eddie feels dirty himself, dealing with them. But every night, all night, he and Jeanne move back and forth inside each other. They've gone way past whatever was holding him back. And anyway, the push and pull between them in the house seems to force out the ghosts.

At the end of the month, the first real snow comes and sticks. The maples have dried up and the geese disappeared from the sky. The snowshoe hairs have gone white and now Eddie can get one to line the new boots Mr Natale is making for Jeanne in town.

Every night, Eddie tells himself he's doing his best to take all the extra electricity out of Jeanne, for fear it'll burn something down.

Jeanne

Believe me, whatever my body was doing it wasn't asking me first. Every time I touched Eddie Allen I wanted to touch him more next time. Looking back, people must have seen. We must have been like a neon sign, flashing out of that farmhouse into the hills every night. Every time Jerusha could pin me down, she put that nasty tea into me and told me one of her stories. Eddie brought down the buck that circled behind Jerusha's, tanned it in the dooryard and convinced her to make me some trousers.

'Eddie Allen, I ain't seen a woman wear those for fifty years,' Jerusha said. 'People will point and stare.'

'And how long have you known Jeanne Delaney, mam? You ever known her to care about people staring at her?'

'That's what she has us for, you stupid boy.'

'Will you two quit talking about me like I'm not here? Eddie taught me to shoot. I can't do that in the winter in a dress. I seen one of them sophisticated women that donates to the hospital ride by wearing harem pants. Why can't I?'

She agreed in the end. I could see her fingers were getting stiff with the winter cold, though. I got her to let me rub mustard paste into them, sitting on the footstool next to her chair. She looked at me with a sideways smile.

'What?'

'I was just thinking, it's funny how a woman gets made. That boy's turned you into someone who cares about an old woman's aches and pains just by kissing you. How's that work? It's a mystery.'

'I don't know what you're talking about Jerusha Prichard.' I pinched her and she shrieked and slapped me.

Eddie drew all the moisture out of me till my throat went dry and I coughed and had to keep a glass of water by his bed. He drew out all the sound and fury until my arms and legs shook and I couldn't stop them. Then he just held on to me and let me tremble in the dark.

I taught him to look at me while he did all that, but it took that whole month to do it. I laughed up into his face then and he didn't even mind. It was just happiness. Happiness seeping out of us into the timbers of that house where it hadn't been in years. Maybe ever.

We should have known we were shifting things to make room. Rattling something loose.

On that last day we didn't get out of bed, except for the milking. We did that, mucked out the stalls and let the cows out, then took our boots off, made a pot of coffee and got back under the quilt. You get like that, don't you? Like leaving the bed is worse than cutting off a limb, like you can't not be skin to skin for more than a minute or two at a time. It fades, but I didn't know that then. I knew nothing a'tall. I was in the Garden. We were before the Fall.

Finally, Eddie got dressed and started messing around with the parlour stove. I was so loose-limbed, I just lay where I was in the bed and shouted out at him, what was he doing?

'Never mind, Jeanne Delaney.'

'Eddie, I ever tell you about Joan of Arc?'

'Once or twice.' That was him being funny, but you wouldn't know it.

'*She* wore trousers.'

'Yep, I think you might have said. Didn't she also raise up an army and get herself burned?'

'Well, yes, but I don't think that was the end of her. You know, I imagine her to be like Jesus.'

'Pretty sure there's only supposed to be one of those.'

'Well, Eddie Allen, you can't always follow the rules. Joan of Arc wore trousers, and it was about 1550 or something. Nobody told her not to.'

'Not till it was too late, anyway. Come on out here.'

He had the tub full of water and the door to the stove open. Eddie put me in that tin tub and washed my hair with eggs and

125

vinegar till it glistened. I chattered to him about Joan of Arc while the room filled up with steam and the smell of pine tar. All I could put on after was my same old dress and my same old boots.

Once I was dressed, he called me to the window to see the snow. It was blue in the twilight, falling on top of all the sound in the world till it got so quiet not even a wing fluttered out there. The nights were closing in and we weren't going to see the ground again till spring. We stood there while my hair dried, watching the ground fill up with whiteness.

'I'll take you back down in the cart.'

'Look, Eddie. You got company.'

There was a figure coming along the road. No place else it could be going but the Allens. It was a man with a coat he was holding wrapped around himself instead of having it buttoned. He was wearing the kind of hat a city man would wear, but he had work boots on his feet. He came through the gate without stopping to look around first, didn't even have to look down to see where the latch was. That was when I knew he must be an Allen.

'Leave, Jeanne. Right now.'

'I thought you were taking me?'

'Now, girl! Go out the front door.'

'Eddie, you're kinda scaring me.' I laughed a little, but it came out nervous like.

Certain times, you just know, don't you? You just know that things are coming apart. You must have felt that yourself, that feeling when all of a sudden your beautiful things are slipping through your fingers into ugliness and you just can't catch them or make them be still? At the schoolhouse, Miss McLaughlin used to test our reflexes with the ruler. You'd hold your thumb and your forefinger a bit apart around the end of the ruler. When she let go, you had to close them and catch it. That measured how fast you could react. It made you feel helpless, knowing how much time there was between seeing something fall and being able to close your hand and stop it.

126

Or maybe, and this is the thought that won't let me go, maybe we didn't even wake up and try. Maybe me and Eddie just stood still ourselves, mesmerised, until winter fell down and everything turned into ice around us. Until we froze, too.

No one ever used the Allens' front door. It was stiff and I panicked for a minute when it wouldn't give. When I finally got it open it made a scraping sound on the floor. I heard their two voices, saying each other's names in the kitchen, just before I slipped out. They sounded like passing acquaintances on Main Street, not like family who hadn't seen each other in months or years.

'Eddie.'

'Hank.'

Muscle and Bone

Eddie looks at the cold space in the bed next to him, and can almost hear the laughter coming from it. He lies staring at nothing from dark till light, then stays under the quilt for a long time after Hank gets up. He isn't going to sleep much with his brother here. That's something just to get used to. Hank makes slapping sounds with his feet, and then flapping clunks once he's put his boots on without tying the laces.

Next, he hears Hank starting up the kitchen stove, picking things up off the shelves and putting them back again, turning everything over and looking underneath it. He'll see there's been a woman here, but it seems like that's been telegraphed up and down the road already anyway. Eddie looks out the bedroom window into the blue dawn and waits for whatever it takes to gather up inside himself. He can feel the balled-up muscles in his legs and the sick, acid taste filling his mouth and drying out his eyes.

The thing will be not to freeze. You breathe the sickness out and keep your legs steady, focus on the middle distance and make the world stand still.

'I'm only twenty-two,' he whispers into the half-darkness. As if someone will hear him. As if it matters.

Keys jangle below. Hank opens the gun cabinet and shuts it again. He stomps upstairs and into the other bedrooms, where Eddie never goes, turning everything over and making himself master of it.

Maybe Eddie can wait it out, play dead until Hank finishes sniffing and goes away back down the road.

All different kinds of silences, men make. He saw that even as a boy. Speech is for women; they made it up because the silence is all one thing to them. Jeanne chatters all day long, until it doesn't hardly mean anything, there's so much of it.

128

Well, now Hank's come up the road like a blow from behind and swept Jeanne away, back to the rocking water and the places without walls. She'll be moving somewhere between the trees, waving her hands in all directions and breathing the cold air into puffs of diamond mist that give her away, even when she tries to hide. He looks at the orange flush across the sky and pictures her on the little dock, stretching herself up to catch the first of the light in her hands.

Eddie and Hank will sit the hours out in a silence like twisting wire. Something will snap at some point and they both know it already, but whatever it is will make its own time. They know that too.

Eddie misses a step before the sun is all the way up. He is at the kitchen table when he first fails to contain himself.

'I got enough eyes on me, Hank, I assure you,' he says.

'What are you talking about, Eddie? You don't want to know where I been and what I been doing? I'm your family; ain't you glad to see me?' Hank is crouched down putting kindling in the basket. He's been outside with the hatchet and there are splinters stuck to his shirt.

'Well, here I am at the breakfast table with you, all hospitable.' Eddie leans his chair back on two legs, trying to be a boy who doesn't care whether he falls over.

'You don't want to know what's happening in the wide world? Things are stirring up, you know.'

'This is the wide world. I like it here, Hank. It's plenty interesting enough for me.'

'I guess you're keeping pretty busy.'

'Ay-uh, I'm keeping busy making the money those two are pissing away in town there.'

Hank throws the kindling down and shoots up.

'You won't be talking about my mother like that while I'm here, kid. Got it?'

Eddie doesn't even twitch. He is back in control of himself. Here is the thing he has learned, the lesson of the woods and the bleeding

129

girls and the wagon wheel. Keep yourself under cover. Learn how to wait. He balances his chair and stares an even stare out the kitchen door until Hank sits back down.

'Coffee?' Eddie drops his chair and pushes it back to stand up.

'Real coffee?'

'Yep.'

'Who's pissing money away?'

Eddie walks barefoot across the quarry tiles to the stove. Not a speck of grit on the soles of his feet. Jeanne got on hands and knees and did the floor just the day before yesterday. At her age, a woman looks good doing that.

But the day before yesterday might as well have happened when he was eight years old. Some sticky film of time has fallen between then and now. Eddie hopes the picture of Jeanne will stay here in the kitchen, will outlast Hank and time and silence. But already it isn't the same kitchen they were in two days ago, just a copy of it, a spook of a place. Thing about this house is, everything that ever happened in it is still happening somewhere, separate and all at once. Every time you turn your head, there's an echo knocking on the present. If all those ghosts and shadows can hang around here so long, can't she do it too?

'Well if you're staying, there's work to do,' Eddie says. 'Come out with me today. We need to move the sheep to the near field and then we can do some shooting.'

He helps with the milking anyway. He'll do his bit. That isn't the worry, not at all. Eddie doesn't even mind being left with the mucking. That's just the way it is.

'Don't know how you stand it,' Hank says while they're putting the guns in the box and calling Don up into the back of the wagon. 'This place just stifles.'

'It's quiet these days. Anyway, I'm in the woods a lot.'

Don is already whining by the time they have Betty in the harness and the gate open. He knows where they're going. His reason for being is about to show itself and his sinews are singing to it. They're in the same state, Eddie and the dog. About to become who they really are. Only the dog knows what that'll be and Eddie doesn't.

'So, work in the quarry finished, then?'

'This is my home, boy. Just because you're the only one stuck here, that don't mean it doesn't belong to all four of us. I don't have to explain my coming and going.'

'I guess that means Ma sent you a letter.'

'What difference does it make? It's winter, my work is done, so I come home to stay a bit. You're sitting on a pile of cash here and you got no right to hog it from the rest of us.'

There's only an inch or two of snow on the road. Dark patches of rotting leaves are showing in the ruts.

'I got a right, Hank. That's the whole point. Dad left it the way he did for a reason. Know what makes me laugh?'

'I never seen you laugh in my life, kid.'

'He thought it would be you. You and Micky, the real men. He thought you'd be the ones to keep his land and make it work. I was so puny, he thought I'd go to college. He didn't want all you selling land to send me.'

'How do you know what he thought? You were two years old when he died. The world's changing, Eddie. Everyone's moving to the city. These little farms don't work no more.'

'Heard Ma tell it. Anyway, this farm bought them two a house in town and plenty of liquor. Seems to be working all right.'

'I told you to watch your mouth.' Hank says it in a conversational tone.

'So you noticed the drinking too, then?'

'Boy's lost a foot, Eddie. He's a got a right to some kind of consolation.'

'What about Ma?'

'Keep her name out of your mouth if you can't show any respect.'

'You want to do it, Hank? Let's just get out and do it now.' Eddie pulls Betty to a stop, but they both keep staring ahead at the road.

The wide open space weighs in around them. After a minute Don starts whining and Eddie clicks the horse to a walk again.

He's hardly shaking at all.

'Anyway,' Hank says, 'that money come from selling some land, not from working it.'

'Here's me, runt of the litter, the only one who gives a crap.'

'You got a sharp tongue since I been gone, Eddie Allen. When'd you turn so spiky?'

'Not spiky, just practical. You get a long sight on things, sitting by yourself in a house full of ghosts.'

'You got traps out, kid?'

'Some. Got a bobcat and three muskrats in my room stretching.'

'Well, we'll set a couple more trap lines. That's good money. Plenty traps in the barns, right?'

'Ay-uh. I keep everything oiled and working, Hank.'

'So I heard.'

Eddie looks down the top field, thinking Hank is bigger than a man should be at that distance. Out of proportion, like he's kept on growing all this while. Walking down the slope to the wagon, Eddie wonders when he'll be able to get to Jeanne. Rather, his body wonders for him, which is worse.

'I can smell Crook's ram from here,' Hank says. 'You'll have plenty lambs.'

'Ay-uh. And the wool. Got a good buyer the past two years. T-Roy and his friends done the shearing with me.'

'That many sheep don't need half a mountain.'

Eddie ignores that. 'We can take those apples to Crook's later today. He'll press 'em.'

'You already got two extra fields for the cows.'

'Turn around and see, Hank. This valley is the best place on earth.' Eddie turns his body halfway around and lets all that space into his eyes. 'Don't you think that sometimes?'

'You don't need all the fields this side and you know it. Crook'll have that one. And the other, after the pines are cleared.' Hank points up the slope toward the trees below Mary's Peak. Two snowshoe hares are showing against the darker patches in the ground.

'I won't do it. Quit beating a dead horse.'

'You *think* you won't do it. We'll see.'

'I'm changed Hank. You can try me, but you'll find me changed.'

'I been looking at you since before you were old enough to remember me, Eddie Allen. You seem just the same to me.' Hank makes a show of looking Eddie up and down. 'Man built like you got to turn sly. No choice, I know that.'

The cold has made the air clear and simple. Sounds carry. Eddie can hear the growl of a motor around the side of the mountain. Crook's got new machinery with a grant from the state government. Closer to, a quail is calling in the growth under the trees.

'Well, should we go up and get some hares?'

Hank reaches into the cart and takes the shotgun, breaks it and reaches for the shell case. He slings that over his shoulder and picks up the rifle too. He drops the bolt in and trains it on one of the hares.

'Don't think so, Hank. Not even you could make that.'

'Not a breath of wind today. You notice that? Beautiful day for the rifle. I'll go on my own, thanks kid. You take Don and Betty and the cart back. I'll be back later to hang some birds, maybe.'

'Well, I was planning to go myself, 'fore you turned up.'

'Things change, kid. You gotta adjust yourself.'

Now they both go still, waiting. After a minute Eddie gives. It'll make time for steadying himself, anyway. He needs that. He swings himself up on the seat of the wagon and Don looks back and forth between them.

'Take the dog, Hank. You might want him for birding.'

Hank clucks at the dog once and Don heels. People say dogs are loyal. In fact, they're constantly gauging who's master. Loyalty is a human thing, an idea that's sometimes useful to people. Don doesn't

133

need it and it wouldn't be practical anyhow. He sits there now looking up at Hank and waiting for orders. Eddie straightens the traces and then calls to Betty, who seems to be waiting too.

'You watch yourself, Eddie. You're like a scarecrow, sitting up on that seat driving. People are firing guns all over the woods, this time of year. Somebody might hit ya.'

He slaps Betty to get her going and the four of them, Hank, Eddie, Betty and Don, move off into the threatening quiet all around.

Eddie is in the sitting room with the Almanac when he hears Don barking on the road. There's Hank coming up the road, but he isn't the same man he was the day before. This time he's carrying a brace of quail and a rabbit. Don dances around him like nobody ever did anything so exciting before. It's so cold it can't even snow, but Hank isn't wearing a hat or clutching his coat around himself. He has expanded into the world around him. He belongs to the cold air now. Twenty-four hours it took Hank to take hold of the dog and both guns. He's done it just like breathing, slipping in between Eddie and his world without drawing blood. Like a skinning knife between muscle and bone.

Jeanne

Two days after Hank came, I woke up one morning and the whole world had lost its colour under a cover of snow, nothing but the shapes of things showing. I looked at it through the feathers of frost on Jerusha's window glass.

Do you get the frost on your windows in the city? You think you have more of everything there, but maybe it's because you don't know what we have.

I went out into the changed world with a basket of Jerusha's canning, heading up the lake to Mrs Nadeau. There was one set of cart tracks on the road already. I walked inside them to keep my feet dry, looking down at the snow-covered ice on the shallow edges of the lake, the dark deep eye in the middle.

By the time I'd done all the conveying and the visiting, eaten some of Mrs Nadeau's corn beef hash and come back down the road, it was nearly dark. I called three times coming through Jerusha's yard. She didn't answer.

'Hey, Jerusha! You okay?'

'Well, of course. Open that door and stop shouting, child.'

Her door at the back came from an old train car. I kept it painted red with paint from the boat. I took my boots off and tried not to carry too much snow inside. My new socks were two different lengths, and one was knit tighter than the other.

'I called you three times. I got worried.' I tried to shut the door quietly behind me, but it still seemed to shake the whole house.

I was just awkward in the world. No matter how hard I tried to contain myself, something always slipped or stuck out. Jerusha was sighing and huffing my name out before I even had the door closed.

'Jeanne Delaney, when are you gonna learn to think before you

135

use your limbs?' she said. 'This house is going to come down around your ears, one of these days. Sit down and take a few breaths.'

'Jerusha, it's like Christ's tomb in here! Whyn't you open a light?'

It made me sad, the way she sat in the dark like that. You should understand, I did worry about her. I knew what she'd lost. I was an ignorant little thing, but I wasn't totally heartless.

'I'd prefer to be Lazarus, thank you. I do get up and come out again every morning. So far, anyway, but it sure isn't because I'm the child of God.'

'Don't make jokes like that, Jerusha. I need you; you gotta get up every morning. I got something to tell you, anyway. Someone turned up at the Allens' the other night.'

That got her attention.

'Take some breaths and quiet down a minute, girl. What d'you mean, someone?'

'Well, me and Eddie were looking out at the snow, and a tall man come up the road, hulking up out of the dusk like bad news on New Year's Eve.'

That might have been the first time I ever saw Jerusha lose her composure. She sucked in a breath and laid her sewing on the table so she could lean towards me.

'Don't be so dramatic, child! Two feet or one?'

'Two what? ... Oh, it wasn't Micky. It was Hank. Can we have a light Jerusha? I'll make you some tea. I need to ask you about something.'

'You do the light. I'm still sitting and thinking.' She leaned back in her chair and put her feet up under the table, trying to act unruffled. 'You interrupted my thoughts, shouting and banging the door like that. I was years away. Hank Allen say what he come for?'

'I don't know, Jerusha. That's the thing.' I got the lantern, filled it and lit it, then put Jerusha's kettle on top of the stove and shut the door on the fire. 'Eddie acted like it was a mother bear coming up the road and right through the gate. He chased me outta there before I could ask him anything. Show myself to *you*, he said, just like that. Well, of course I showed myself to you. I sleep here, don't I? Why'd he say that?'

'Don't guess he was thinking straight, was he? If he was rattled, I guess it was just instinct.'

'You can't fool me like that anymore, Jerusha Prichard. I ain't so little.'

'I know what you ain't, *mam'selle*. No need to spell it out.'

'Eddie wanted me to tell you so you could explain, but I didn't want to talk about it just then. I want to know now. Tell me what terrified him like that.'

She actually laughed then. 'That boy's been terrified since he could crawl. Haven't you noticed?'

'No. I seen him stare down a pair of spitting wolverines just last week. And you should have seen him go for that poor old photographer at the fair. He don't strike me as the shrinking type.'

'Well, you haven't had another Allen to compare him to. Not since you were grown anyway. How close up did you measure Hank?'

'Yeah, he was big. I could see that from the window, but Eddie wouldn't let him see me. All I heard was them saying each other's names as I was leaving out the front door. Not even hello, they just spit those two names at each other like cowboys in a magazine story, about to start shooting.'

'Eddie's the runt of that bunch.'

'That's mean, Jerusha.'

'You knew the Allens better, you'd see it as a compliment.'

'So, why was Eddie so scared? Why wouldn't he let me stay even to say hello?'

'He isn't ashamed of you, if that's what you're thinking. It isn't you at all. Anyhow, you're just in time to try these on.' Jerusha held up my deerskin slacks. 'Get into 'em. Let's see how they fit and I can fix the ties on.'

'Jerusha, you put embroidery! It looks beautiful.' I had to hold it up to the lamp to see her work. She'd been dying thread and working designs up the side seams. 'You didn't have to do all that.'

'It helps me think. When you're old, thinking is the main thing. You spend a lot of time living things over again. Sewing lets your mind go.'

'Jerusha, you are trying to sidestep me. One time, with Etta Grace, you said I was like a puppy with something in her teeth. There's something going on with the Allens and I ain't letting it go till you tell me.'

'It was Etta Grace I was thinking about just now.'

Well, what was I gonna say to that? Like I told you, I wasn't completely heartless, even then. She stumped me with those two words. It was the same for all of us. Etta Grace was the thing there was no answer to. Turned out though, Jerusha really was answering me. I was just too simple to see the twisting path she was taking to get to the question.

'She liked the lamps lit, remember?' Jerusha asked me.

'Yep, I do. She liked it sparkly at night, she said.'

'I sent you home that day they took her away to the hospital 'cause you were too little to see all that. I was remembering your mother and you, and I didn't want you to think of it like that. I maybe didn't want to connect those two nights up myself. Your mother and Etta Grace, I mean. But that was childish.'

'It wasn't childish, Jerusha. You were saving her. It was me and T-Roy were childish. We panicked.'

'I was the first person ever to touch you, unless you count the inside of your mother. You ever think on that?'

'I don't have to think on it. I know it.'

'Well, maybe I should have let you stay with Etta Grace. I saw you and Eddie the other day, tripping out of the woods in back. There you were, the two biggest mistakes I ever made, hovering around each other and your voices all tangled up together. What I'm thinking now is, why didn't I see it coming?'

'Well, *thank you*. Didn't know I was anyone's mistake.'

'I don't mean it like that and you know it. I mean I failed you both, him when he was born and you later. I maybe should have let you stay and help, that night with Etta Grace. Probably you needed to be with her then. She liked you, and you were about to be a woman. It was time for you to see.'

'Well, here you still are. Tell me now.'

'Telling don't make it sink in. You gotta get the blood on you. You've got to hear the sound death and creation make on their way out of a body.'

'Jerusha, you sound like a Baptist preacher.'

'I don't mean to be all hellfire and brimstone. It ain't like that. That's the whole thing. It isn't the end of days; it's just something that happens every so often if you're a woman. You need to know that so you can keep on going, after.'

'You think I can't look after myself. What is it about me makes you think that?'

She huffed and sighed again. 'Jeanne Delaney, I know you and I knew your mother. I don't doubt you have what it takes to get by. She didn't, if you want the hard truth, but she was a good woman and she loved you right away. She had time to love you. I know, I was there.'

'Yep. You told me before.'

'You don't feel it, though. You got no idea what it is to love a child. You're going to, just like the rest of us. All the things people die for, Jeanne, they're just everyday things. Little commonplaces, buried under all the quilts in all the houses, blood and death and the love of children. They're all tied up together; people just pretend they're not.'

'I don't get you.'

'All right, give it a minute. So, one day, Etta Grace comes home from the Allens' talking about this new thing she did with Hank and Micky. She giggled because she knew it was naughty and, too, she knew some people would go a long way for what those boys were doing. Then she sat down and gave me all the details. You know what she was like, she just told it like anything else she'd seen or done. She said it wasn't as nice as everybody made it out to be. She said it hurt.'

139

I poured Jerusha some tea and pulled those deerskins on. She'd made them with the hair on the inside, warm and ticklish. I kept my eyes on her so she'd know I wasn't taking her words lightly.

'A few weeks later I realised her monthly wasn't coming. I don't think she even noticed. I never was sure if she could count from week to week. Etta Grace's life was made up of morning, noon and night. That was enough for her to be getting on with. Turn around and lift your dress up. Let me thread these laces through and see how they fit.'

'They're kinda long, Jerusha.'

'I can fix that. Once Etta Grace started showing she'd know, and then I didn't know what I'd do. I lay awake every night, turning it over. She never threw up, so I half hoped she'd lose the child and not even realise it. Some of those doctors say a feeble-minded woman can't have good, healthy babies. Anybody my age'll tell you that's not true. We've all seen it happen often enough. I had raspberry leaves and things saved up, anyway. I thought I could get her through the labour.'

Jerusha was bent around to the side of me, pinching seams and talking around the rawhide laces in her mouth. The light fell on the back of her hair, twisted up two kinds of grey. All of a sudden I loved Jerusha so much I thought I was gonna cry. I wanted her to live forever and I wanted to crawl under one of her quilts and let her make me oatmeal and raspberry tart so I could sit up in bed and eat it. I wished I could have a sickness that wasn't too bad, the way you do when you're little and you just want coddling.

'Those lights in the evening,' Jerusha said. 'Every flame was special, far as Etta Grace was concerned. A little hurricane candle was as good as a magic lantern show to that girl. She'd laugh while the warm light bloomed out over her skin and the water in her eyes sparkled.'

By that time Jerusha was talking to herself. I might not have been there a'tall.

'She didn't like the twilight. Every day of her life it frightened

140

her, a little or a lot depending on how much you could distract her. While Etta Grace was with me, I just gave in and spent more on light than I needed to. Sometimes we sat in the cold, but never in the dark. The night the pains started, the poor girl was so scared I lit both lamps and three candles.'

'I remember.' I said it so quiet I don't even know if she heard me.

'When the bleeding got worse, I sent you away. I kept the lights burning all night but Etta Grace felt cold and dark inside, all by herself inside her own body. The child didn't have all the mind a woman needs to take that.'

You look troubled, government man. Have you never thought about how babies get born before? Really thought about it, I mean? Somewhere on the other side of your parlour doors, these things are what happens. Maybe think twice about your women when you get home from here.

Jerusha carried on, words flooding out of her now. 'Etta Grace's skin turned ashy and she started babbling, saying '*Maman, Maman*' and sweating. Every five minutes or so, she'd grab my hand and hang on till it passed. Even then I could feel her trying not to squeeze too tight. That child was always careful not to take up too much space. She kept a lot inside herself, in a way you wouldn't expect from someone made the way she was.

'I'm sorry Jerusha. I thought I was helping. I saw the blood and I thought you needed the doctor. I didn't mean for what happened.'

'Of course you didn't. That's what I'm saying. You were about to have monthlies yourself. I should have let you stay and see what was what. Sending you away from a bloody mess like that frightened you, of course it did. I wasn't thinking.'

'Yes, you were. You were thinking about Etta Grace.'

'I was. And your mother. I didn't want you to see what happened to your mother.'

'I thought Etta Grace was gonna die and I wanted to save her,' I said. 'I woke T-Roy up and then we had to go to the Nadeaus' and borrow a horse. It was dark and we had to go slow on the road. The whole time I kept thinking she'd be dead by the time we got back. T-Roy never said one single word from the minute I woke him up till we got back to your house when the sun was already up. When we got the doctor out of bed, he cursed at us. Doctors never do that in stories.'

'Stories'll make you blind to the way the world is, soon as explain it,' Jerusha said. 'When you have babies, watch out what stories they hear.'

'When I have babies, I'm gonna tell them your stories.'

'After Etta Grace got back from the hospital, I waited for her monthlies to come back. I was ready for it to take more than a month, but after three I knew what they'd done.'

'That won't happen to me, Jerusha. I promise.'

'First, you don't know that. Second that isn't what I'm talking about. It's on those Allen boys, Jeanne Delaney. That's what I'm telling you. I don't know about anybody else around here, but I haven't forgotten it. Sometimes I think it's what keeps me alive, the image of those Allen boys burning under my ribs, right at the centre of me.'

'Aren't you mad at the doctor?'

'Well sure, him too. It's two different kinds of evil, though. Somebody told those men up at the hospital they're gods and they believed it. Gods with needles and oxygen tanks. That doctor believes himself to be incapable of doing wrong, that's his kind of destruction. Micky and Hank Allen done wrong on purpose. They're pure malice and never been anything else. You can believe me on that without me going into the details.'

Of course, I believed her. We all grew up in the shadow of those boys.

'Which is worse?' Jerusha asked herself. 'I don't know. I don't have one of those minds that's made for weighing two kinds of evil and telling the difference. Them boys know they're devils and they find pleasure in it. Their mother's the only one for miles around doesn't think those two should have been drowned at birth. And

'I'm the one pulled them out into the light, Jeanne. Me. I let Hank Allen touch my child, lifting her down out of the wagon the night Eddie was born. I asked him to, then I stood right by and let him. Maybe other times, too. I can't remember.'

I put a hand on her arm, trying to still her. Trying to draw away some of what she was feeling, maybe.

'It's not finished, is what I'm telling you. Everybody's trying to keep you out of the way because we can all see things aren't through happening.'

'You can't know that, Jerusha.'

'Get up on the chair and let me pin a leg up. Might as well finish them now. Looks like we'll be up late.'

'You don't have to, Jerusha,' but I climbed up on the chair while I was saying it. My head was up in the dark between the roof beams then. Jerusha was leaning into the pool of light around my legs, pins in her mouth now.

'Might as well,' she mumbled at my ankles. Then she took out the pins and stuck them in her sleeve. 'You wound me up; you'll have to let me run down now. Stand up straight and be still.'

'All right, but don't poke me.' Neither of us laughed.

'Etta Grace heard me talking to T-Roy about her and then she wouldn't let it go. I had to explain it to her. The way I put it was she was one of the special people who never grow all the way up. That included not being a *maman*. You can guess I didn't fool her.'

'Was that when she got sick? She was so tired that last year.'

'She got slower and then she started to get lighter. Ghostly. I was lucky if I could get a good meal in her once every few days.'

I remembered that too, but only in a selfish kind of way. I was mad at Etta Grace for being so distracted. I remember being confused and a little cross at why everybody was fussing over her.

'Me and T-Roy found her once,' I said to Jerusha. 'In the red pool behind Mary's Peak. It was a cold day, and he grabbed her before she could go in the water. He told me to go home. I guess he took her back here.'

'Yep, he brought her back here and stayed a while,' Jerusha said. 'He started coming around after that, trying to coax a laugh out of her.'

'I didn't really understand the way he put his coat around her that day, the way he took her hand and led her up onto the road. I guess I do now. You ever think T-Roy would have married Etta Grace?'

'Well, if he wanted that, he waited too long, didn't he?'

'That was how I imagined it. Until ... You know, I used to picture them in a suit and a white dress and all that, getting a photograph taken. I thought she could come live on the boat and help us with Grampy. It was one of the stories I told myself when I was littler.'

'He tried to get Etta Grace to fish with him and race him down the road. Trying to lift her heart. But the flesh just kept falling away from her. Towards the end T-Roy looked so helpless I had to quit everything else I was worrying about sometimes, just to spend a minute feeling sorry for him, too.'

Until Jerusha told her story that night, I'd never thought about my brother that way, with an inside life and feelings that got away from him. All I ever noticed about T-Roy was the work he did. Work was pretty much all he did, anyway. I suppose he went to a kitchen junket now and then in the winter, and maybe even danced. I couldn't picture him doing it, though. I suppose he went to school when I was a baby, at least for a year or so. I'd never asked him. I didn't see T-Roy or Grampy much in the winter. They were my summer life. Winter was Jerusha, and in the beginning, Etta Grace.

That year I turned sixteen was when I noticed the separateness of people, when all the things that had happened settled into my mind with a different kind of understanding. I could see the way we're each of us blind to the rest, just occasionally finding each other by accident while we're groping. Then we bump on by into the endless night. People would say I just got to be a woman, is all. The thing about that winter was that everything that had happened was still happening, if you see what I mean. The world was like a grinding wheel nobody could put the brakes on, coming on around.

I thought me and Eddie were different. Of course I did.

'Just for you to think on it, is all Eddie wants.'

'Okay,' I said to Jerusha, 'but I don't get it. You're saying *this* is what Eddie wanted you to tell me? I don't want to be the reason you to have to dig all that up again.'

'It ain't buried, Jeanne. What I'm trying to tell you right now is, you've got no idea what it is that's about to sideswipe you. Eddie wants you to know this is serious. He wants you to know what happens to girls up there. He don't want to look you in the eye and tell you himself, but he wants you to know. You do not want to be anywhere near Hank Allen. You don't want to meet that man on the road or pass by him in the kitchen. Stay away from Eddie until Hank leaves, Jeanne.'

'What if he never leaves?'

'Oh, he'll go. This place is a bed of nails to those Allen boys now. I won't say there's justice, but nothing around here dies either. He won't take it for long. Don't you worry about that.'

We stayed up, burning wood and lamp oil. I wrapped a blanket around myself, threw a log in and pictured the chimney outside. From the road, you'd see sparks dancing up into the snowflakes. You'd see the glow in Jerusha's front window and know there was a circle of light inside. You'd know there were people with fire, pushing back against the winter that was stalking them.

Our voices got smaller the later it got, just naturally. I put an extra shawl around Jerusha and she tutted at me and waved a hand.

'All right then, Mrs Prichard,' I said. 'I'll tell *you* a story now. How 'bout that?'

'OK, *mam'selle*. Amaze me with one of your jaw-dropping adventures.'

'Ghosts, cowboys, trappers or holy soldiers?'

'None of those. Give me something new.'

I took a minute and set up the long fork with some pieces of bread for us meanwhile. There was plenty jam, showing like blood in the jars when I held them up to the light. I made toast while I got my story going in my head.'

By the time I finished telling it, my deerskins were done and Jerusha's head was bobbing up and down where she sat. She woke up while I banked the fire and I put the heavy curtain up, took the lamp over and put it on an apple crate between the beds. The mattress I used to share with Etta Grace felt small now I was grown. I could feel the burden of all my bones, stretching past my earlier self.

I looked over at Jerusha, pulling back the corner of her quilts. There on top of the sheet was her skinning knife, shining yellow in the lamplight. I wondered whether she was that scared, nights I wasn't in the house, that she kept the knife by her. Then right away I knew that wasn't it.

That's when it hit me, what it meant seeing that tall shadow coming up the road. We were past playing. The jokes we told were just to fill up the silence. When we laughed, we were only making cover. Underneath it, Jerusha was getting ready to put herself outside of everything. There was some kind of death, preparing itself there, under the covers with her. The next day and all the days after, that knife stayed with me, lying at the back of my mind, glittering.

I think part of me knew then, it was gonna be me or Jerusha. One of us would have to do whatever needed to be done. And I wasn't going to sit back and leave her between me and Judgement. Later, when I stood in the dark watching what they did to Eddie, I closed my eyes and there was that knife, winking at me.

Time Being

Hank turns over in bed, coming up into half sleep. Right away, the memories start turning inside him like worms. His stomach pitches when the full weight of where he is falls into him. He gets up and starts moving just to stop the things in the corners from making themselves out of the dark and smothering him. Eddie's right. The place is full of ghosts. Things have been sleeping inside him that he didn't even know about until he walked through the gate and the house woke them.

He lights the stove before he's all the way awake. Matches in the tin, same as always, kindling in the basket. It doesn't need thinking about.

Stepping out into the dooryard, he sucks in a great draw of sharp air. It feels like ice prickling the inside of his lungs, gutting him like a knife and pulling the memories out like entrails. Out here there's only cold breath and mists sitting on the bottom of the valley. Snow so bright it pinches your eyes. That feels good. In the patches of shade, the snow is brittle and cracks under his boots. He stands on the frozen mud by the gate, rubbing his palms together.

He's got two rough hands and that's as it should be. Calluses a quarter inch thick between him and anything he touches. He's been making those hands most his life, after his father started them for him.

It was before Micky and Eddie were born, the first time Dad told the story about the wolves. If Hank needed teaching, Dad would make him stand rolling teasels between the palms of his hands while he listened to whatever the lesson was. That day Hank's hands were starting to bleed, but he knew better than to stop. Once his father made up his mind to teach you a lesson, you learned it. The spikes were poking into the cuts they'd made already and he had to lose himself in the story to be able to keep going. It got easier with practice.

Dad told how when his grandfather first cleared these top fields, the wolves would still come out of the woods in packs of ten or twelve. You had to lock up even the big animals good at night.

The point of the story was this: when you shot one of them wolves, the others clamped onto it and dragged it back off into the woods. That, Dad told him, is what survival means.

'You got your schoolteacher and your very own board to carry to your lessons,' he said. 'Your mother makes you rabbit slippers and wool shirts. You get new boots whenever the old ones wear out. In my day, you had one pair of boots a year. When them gone, you went barefooted. You still listening, kid?'

Hank flinched at the change of tack.

'Yes, sir. Listening.'

'Good for you. I'm telling you, the reason you got all those things is because we understood them wolves. Those creatures were telling us something. You survive by being ruthless. One goes down, you eat him and make yourself stronger. So to speak. Get it?'

'Ay-uh. I do.'

He did. It made sense.

Hank's dad gave him these hands and they're his best piece of property. He likes to feel them, and his legs and his lungs, all the power that's in him.

Eddie likes musing kind of work, watching and waiting kinds of things. It makes him a good hunter, even if he is soft. And then there's Micky, sitting in town like a woman, like a wolf that got shot but not eaten. Hank'd rather be moving and sweating, all day long without stopping if he's got a choice. Hard work lets your mind go, your thoughts can wander without getting in your way.

Maybe it's the same for all men. Everyone in the fields or the quarry, spinning separate thoughts in their heads, the work keeping them from going stir crazy or talking too much to each other. You sit still too long, everything on your mind starts to settle down into you like a weight. Before you know it, maybe you can't move a'tall.

No wonder Micky drinks.

In the spring Hank hires himself out to break fallow ground, and after that he goes south to the slate quarries. There's enough to eat and men to drink with, pay and a good fight every so often to make some extra money.

Only bedtime to dawn that he can't empty out.

Even at the quarry, Hank dreams about Etta Grace. In his dreams he watches her from behind a tree with different kinds of light falling on her, changing her body and her face.

Etta Grace could swim, and run like a doe. Sometimes, there'd be just a flash of colour in the woods behind the old logging camp where they lived. You'd see it out the corner of your eye and know it was her. In the summer, she spent all day by the pool at the bend in the river underneath Mary's Peak.

He looks down to the creek now, winding black through the bottom of the valley with a pillow of cloud on it. When the pickers used to come to work the fields around, that pool there was full of kids every evening and all day Sunday.

She could have only been eleven or twelve, wearing that yellow dress she swam in that didn't do any good once she'd been in the water. There was nothing to her body then, anyway. She was more like an eel than a woman. He watched her dive under. She didn't come up for more than two minutes. Kids were shouting and splashing, their voices clanging off the surface of the water. Bud Crook was with some other boy, standing in the shallows trying to catch crayfish in one of his mother's coffee cans. The ripples from Etta Grace's dive spread out and disappeared and none of them others paid any mind. The shouting and splashing faded into the background while Hank looked at the still water in the bend, wondering what his father would want him to do. Let her drown or pull her out? He tried to lay the story about the wolves onto the problem, but it didn't fit.

In the end, he jumped down and went into the brown water after

149

her. When he pulled her out she kicked him, then stood up and pulled the long braid over her shoulder to squeeze the water out. She shivered and wrung the water out of her skirt, too. Goose bumps came up all over her arms and legs. She came and dripped on his boots while he was tying them back on. When he looked up, she pointed a finger at him, laughing.

'Fooled you, Hank Allen. Fooled you.'

In his dream she doesn't say those words, but sometimes she is that girl, soaked to the skin, dripping on his shoes, looking like the day he fished her out of the red pool. She points at him and laughs, calling him weak, soft. Her lips aren't moving, but her voice echoes all around the two of them without bothering to come from her closed mouth.

Hank turns his back on the valley and walks back into the dooryard. Eddie's boot prints show here and there between the dog's and the mess made by the cows.

Hank's strides take just a bit more ground than Eddie's. Not much, though. Eddie is a lanky son of a bitch. It's in thickness more than height that Hank beats him. Eddie's built like an extra tall kid instead of a man, looks like you could snap him in two without straining. Then, he was born like that. Micky bellowed like a cow from day one, but Eddie just whimpered. There was no flesh on him. He looked like a bird just hatched.

Their mother looked once at Eddie, then mostly left him alone. Two years later, Dad got sick and left them. Eddie never got the benefit of a father, and it shows.

Hank and Micky took things up after Dad died. They tried to make Eddie into a man, but maybe it was a lost cause from the first. Hank's seen other men like Eddie. No strength in 'em, so they turn sneaky, womanish.

He takes longer than he needs to closing the gate. He doesn't want to go up past the outbuildings and into that kitchen. Nothing's the same without Micky stomping around, without Ma talking sharp in the kitchen and Etta Grace singing in the woods down the hill.

He only had Etta Grace the once, and that with Micky looking on laughing. She could have been any no-name girl, any day of the week, but she wasn't. She was the only girl they ever took to the barn who had two names to her, and folks they knew.

He was gentle, as far as that goes. You didn't have to be rough with Etta Grace. You could convince her pretty much anything was a game. That was the first time he'd ever been inside a female with a past, a girl he could recall from before and would see again after.

She was crying and trying to get away, but it was easy to hold her still. He tried not to break anything on her and he's still not sure why.

At the end of it, a retching groan came up out of him and he was ashamed in front of Micky. When he let go of her, she slid down the pole and he turned away, walked out and left her to him. He stopped to button his jeans in the doorway, blinking at the light. Behind him, he heard the soft sound of Micky dropping down out of the loft.

That day with Etta Grace, that's when it all started emptying out and falling away. He can see that now, looking back. Micky lost his foot soon after, and everything started changing.

Finally Hank left, saying he'd find work and send money just so Ma'd let him out the door without a fuss. Micky was still in bed recovering, been there for weeks, cursing at anyone who looked in the door and swigging the Donnatal straight from the green bottle on his bedside table.

Hank packed a cloth bag and leaned on the doorframe upstairs, nodding to Micky. Micky nodded back and that was all they needed. Ma said her pointed goodbye at the stove and Hank walked out of the gate alone. Eddie was up in the deer hide and nobody thought to go get him. There were muddy ruts in the road. Hank's boots were dirty before he got down the hill. He hasn't really been home to speak of since.

And right on time, the first night back, he had the dream again. In the dream he leans against a tree somewhere and that retching sound comes up out of him. He feels ashamed, but he can't stop it.

Etta Grace hears and turns towards his hiding place, pointing and laughing.

Jerusha should have kept that girl in her place. It was delinquent, letting her run wild like that. It upset people's lives.

One thing Hank learned from Etta Grace though, don't fuck a woman if you know too much about her beforehand. Tangles up your mind, that does.

Jeanne

I see your coffee's got cold. Is it you're wrapped up in my story, or you just dislike my coffee?

And have you guessed yet? Yep, I went back to the Allens. I was turned sixteen years old, with the smell of Eddie Allen soaked right into my skin. Foresight wasn't my ruling quality at the time, and there wasn't enough room in the past behind me for hindsight. I did wait a week, and then I hid up off the road in my deerskins and watched for Hank to leave with the guns. Days were shorter, but Hank Allen didn't care about that. He owned the dark road and he believed the animals would always answer to him. All the animals, including us.

Eddie was in the dooryard stretching and scraping two snowshoe-rabbit pelts. He wore just an undershirt and his bootlaces done loose. His arms weren't big, but they were ropey. The kind of strength Eddie had was like a snake, or maybe a hawk. He'd survived by slipping sideways away from great big, lumbering things, and that grew him a certain shape. I thought about his twisting ways and smiled at him.

'Don't yell at me, Eddie Allen. I'm here now, so just say hello and be nice.'

'You're here after I said you weren't welcome. So why's that?'

'You were lying and we both know it. Anyway, I watched from the road. No one here but you. What ya doing?'

'Making a lining for your new shoes, funny enough.'

There was snow working through the flaps of his boots and his forearms were red with the cold. Everything that happened showed on Eddie's skin. He was like a glass lampshade, with the light shining right through him. I thought about him breaking and it made me choke, so I turned away and slapped my thigh for Don. He was tied,

153

though. That was new. He yapped and strained up onto his hind legs until I went to where he could reach me.

'You're freezing, Eddie. Come inside. I'll make you coffee.'

'When I go inside, you are not coming with me.'

'I am, too. And I'm staying until you kiss me and say hello.'

I clomped up into the kitchen in my old boots, took them off, put them by the kitchen stove and forgot about them, going around in my lopsided new socks. So there those boots were when Hank came back later and we were behind the bedroom door. Might as well have hung my underwear out like a flag so he'd know I was naked in there. Young people are that stupid. Or reckless is maybe the word.

It was hours later when we heard Hank come back in. We were in Eddie's room without even a candle going, breathing into the darker darkness under his quilts and whispering to each other. I kept talking because I didn't want to tell him about the things Jerusha said to me. They were pushing at the back of my throat, so I covered them up with a bunch of babble about nothing a'tall. Eddie kept his hands on me all the time. He'd put a latch on his door and we were to stay behind it; I knew without him telling me.

'It's like we're bandits and your big brother is the law,' I laughed at him.

'Not funny, Jeanne.'

'Oh, Eddie. Don't worry so much about your proper family. They're gone. Jerusha says Hank will leave soon, says your brothers can't stay put here anymore.'

'What else Jerusha say?'

'Nothing. Never mind. I made up a good story for you. Practised it on her the other night.'

I pushed his arm out with the top of my head and lay inside it, talking into his chest. He put his hand on my waist all soft, but the muscles in his upper arms got tighter and tighter on me until I could hardly breathe.

'Let up, Eddie. You're crushing me.'

'Just stay still, little woman. You're like a jumping bean.'

It's nice though, isn't it, to feel that kind of power around you? Well anyway, some women feel like that. Women who don't understand about guns, that is. Once you been up close to the things a bullet does to muscle, you never feel safe again.

I had to go out that door eventually, for water from the pump and to the outhouse. We both did. Once I'd come up that road like a blind child onto a train track, the rest of it was just follow through. It isn't like nobody warned me; I just didn't think I needed to listen. Simple as that. I swear, young people'd throw themselves off cliffs if you let them, convinced they'll never hit the ground.

The house filled up with silence and we thought Hank must have gone to bed. We didn't say that to each other, but it was what we were both waiting for. We went in the kitchen and shut the door. Eddie stoked up the fire and I made some biscuits and coffee, me giggling and whispering like a kid. Eddie sat still and put on a face like there was nothing bothering him, nothing wrong in the whole world. I don't know how it would have seemed to a stranger, but I sure didn't find it convincing.

When the door from the sitting room flung open we were across the kitchen from each other, me at the stove. Eddie stiffened up at the table and Hank took his bulk right through between us and outside onto the porch. He left the back door open and stepped down onto the dirt.

'Say hello to Jeanne, Hank.'

'Hello,' he said and unbuttoned his fly.

He looked right at me and smiled, holding himself and pissing up against the back of the house. Eddie couldn't see him from where he sat, but he could hear.

'Coffee, Hank Allen?' I needed to say something before that brittle silence exploded. And, too, I wanted him to know he didn't scare me.

Eddie looked straight ahead at the doorway. He wasn't going to flinch, but the moment for reacting had passed. I could feel the cold size and shape of the space between us.

'I just made it fresh,' I said. 'Mine's better than Eddie's.'

Hank buttoned himself up and came back through without even turning his eyes in my direction. He stood still between us for a whole minute while he looked at Eddie and Eddie looked out the door. Then whatever kind of silence they were trading ended and Hank moved on.

'Whether she's here or not,' he said with his back to us. 'It don't matter. We'll take care of things,' and he shut the door behind him. I guess he went back to sleep. Somebody like Hank Allen just does things like that and then sleeps on them. I'm sure you know the type if you've been around the world enough. There must be a city version.

Eddie took me back to Jerusha's then. He took the biscuits out of the stove and wrapped them in a kitchen towel, sat me down and put my socks and boots right on me.

'I'll have your new boots soon, Jeanne Delaney. Just stay put until I bring 'em, would ya?'

The night was black as cow eyes. We could only stay on the road because we knew where it was. When we strayed onto the edges, blades of grass crunched under our feet, stiff with frost. There was a tang in the air, and no hint of snow. Just glass fingers of cold clamping down on the world, changing it. In that kind of weather, the water draws up out of things and cracks them. Trees popped in the night.

'Where the hell is T-Roy?' Eddie said into the black air. 'Whyn't he back yet?'

'I don't know. I think Jerusha knows but she won't tell me. Maybe he went straight up north to Grampy.'

'He wouldn't do that. He knows what's happening around here.'

'T-Roy and Grampy are always gone by this time. You know that.'

'Course, I do. What I didn't know was Hank. T-Roy shouldn't have left. I should maybe ride you up to your Grampy.'

'Don't get rattled, Eddie. Hank'll leave eventually. Spring, if not sooner. He don't bother me.'

'You don't understand, Jeanne. They want things from me, and I won't give. Anything could happen next. Anything a'tall.'

I found him in the dark then. We were almost at the cabin and I wanted to get him around me before I left, so he could weigh the outside of me down and stop me from flying apart. I was only pretending not to be frightened. Between them, Eddie and Jerusha were trying their best to scare the living daylights out of me, and it was working. Even if I wasn't the kind of girl that showed it.

Eddie put his wiry arms around me and rested his chin on top of my head. He put his lips on my ear and said both my names. I took his hands and put them on my waist. That made me feel steady, contained. When I looked up into his face a star fell out of the sky behind him and the fiery streak of it made me look away from him.

Go ahead and laugh, city boy. It happened. I swear to God.

A Breath

After breakfast Ila asks T-Roy what he'll do now. The wood is stacked against the back of the church hall and already covered with snow that fell in the night.

'Moving on. No excuse to do anything else.'

'Wait until I clean up breakfast. I'll drive you up the road some,' she says.

'You were right, you know,' T-Roy says to her while she talks to the horse and tightens up the harness. She's made coffee and thrown in a pile of blankets. There's fine snow in the air but it's hard to tell whether it's still falling or just blowing up off the ground.

'It happens,' Ila says. 'What was I right about this time?'

'I wanted to be away from them. I wanted to help, but I mostly wanted to be away for a while. Get in the middle of my own life.'

'Well, you've come through here. There's a purpose.'

She has on blue wool stockings and boots. A wool skirt, too, and a coat made for a man even bigger than T-Roy. No one seems to mind where she's going with a swarthy stranger who came in off the road just last week. She hoists herself onto the box and he reaches out to help, too late. There's a bell on one of the traces and she shakes it and laughs.

'Tell you what,' she says.

'What?'

'Let's call this your very own life. No funerals and no family. Me and you are strangers. I don't know anybody who knows you. I could be imaginary. So could you.'

'I told you this was my afterlife.'

'Well, maybe it's mine, too.'

They drive through the next town, drinking the milky coffee from her insulated bottle and not talking about much. She teaches him a union song about a world where no one ever has to be sick or cold and everyone gets enough food. She says she's on the road a good bit of the time; all of them are used to it. She sings a ballad about a whole town that got flooded for a dam, and he sings *C'est l'aviron*.

This is who T-Roy was supposed to be.

After the second town, she pulls over and lifts the pile of blankets out of the box. She goes through a gate and throws them down near a tree, then wanders off. T-Roy stands by the cart until he and the horse are both breathing out the same cloud. The air is that still and cold. The horse leans into him and then Ila reappears under the tree.

'Scared?' she says.

'Little bit. Mostly just wondering.'

'You'll still be wondering later. No point dwelling on it.'

He is about to feel her coffee mouth and kneel down to reach under and touch the tops of her stockings. And then he'll be alone on the road with himself. He can see that from where he's standing.

She isn't new, of course, but she is warm and she never looks away once. He can smell the musty iron smell of her in the sharp air. The size of the world opens up all around them and they fill it right up. She cries once like a hawk and after, when he tries to put his head down on her stomach, she pushes him away.

'None of that, now. I'm not your mother. Look me in the eye when you touch me.'

So he lies for a while looking at her with his hands inside her coat until she says, 'All right then,' and stands up. 'Time to get on now, T-Roy.'

'I'm gonna look at you a minute first, so just stand still and take it,' he says.

Yes, these are the people they are supposed to be.

'Get back now, Mr Prichard.' She tosses her head up the road away from the pony cart. 'Your sister's carrying everything by herself. Winter's here and your Grampy is getting cold. Time for you to go on back now.'

159

T-Roy walks until the world turns black and then just keeps walking. There are two more towns, but his feet are warm enough and he doesn't want to talk to anyone. The first words anybody says at him will wash away the smell of Ila Somebody's Daughter. Women are like that. Or T-Roy is, maybe. He never can manage to lie down next to a woman long enough to fall asleep and dream.

In the end he dreams while he's walking in the stony dark. The whole rest of his life, T-Roy remembers that night as if it were full of people. As if he forgot the exact size and shape of himself and the edges of him blurred into the trees. Some breath he breathed past Ila's shoulder has filled up the world.

Real and ghosts and angels, women have shaped the whole of his life. The feel of Ila's body fades into the memory of Etta Grace, which even T-Roy knows is one of those things you don't never tell the women concerned. By the time the sun starts its low arc above the hills, T-Roy is more than halfway to Harmony. He laughs.

'Getting further the closer I get,' he says to the road.

Every Inch of Empty Air

There are footsteps above Eddie, falling down onto his dreams like clods of earth. It takes him a moment to remember it's Hank, wandering back and forth across the floorboards, in and out of the upstairs bedrooms. Eddie dresses, and then pushes through the tension in the house to the kitchen door. He and Hank move around the house like magnets with opposing sides, keeping a fixed distance and feeling each other's force.

There's ice on the slopes, but not enough snow cover for a sled. He'll have to travel into town with the wheels on the cart, but there is a storm coming. All the creatures can smell it. Even the winter birds have gone quiet, hidden somewhere with their feathers puffed up against the cold.

When Micky turns up, Eddie is loading the guns and Don into the cart. It's almost a relief to see him coming through the gate, something to break the stalemate and move things on. Straw, camel, back. Today the balance will tip and something will happen.

'It ain't even all the way light yet, Micky. How'd you get up here so early?'

'Bud Crook stayed the night and drove me out. I walked up from the bottom of the hill. You ain't glad to see me?' He cocks his head and sniggers.

Just like Micky to get out and drag himself up around the ice patches in the halfway dark, instead of asking for a ride to the door. He'll take a bit of fuel for his bad temper anywhere he can get it.

'Well I'm going in. I could have brung you back with me.'

'I don't need you to get me anywhere Edward Allen.' Micky looks away over the valley.

Eddie stops a minute to listen, like there's maybe a sound from the woods that means something. Then he shakes his head and rolls a milk can into the cart. When he throws the box of cartridges under the seat, Don's ears perk up and he gives one sharp yap.

'I done the milking and the mucking,' Eddie says. 'You two want to check the fences?'

'Maybe.' Micky pushes open the door with the bottom of his crutch.

'There'll be biscuits if you're hungry. Coffee's on the shelf.'

Eddie drives out onto the road and stops to get down and close the gate. The valley stretches out below in black and white, dirt and snow. There's a long, thin cloud sleeping on the river, but everything else is clear. So clear it feels brittle, like the air right around him might soon shatter and drop to the ground in pieces. It'll have to warm up before it can snow any more.

It seems like there's nothing moving in the whole valley, human or animal. Where is Jeanne now? Sleeping still? Or wandering like a crazy thing, pretending she's the Pathfinder and freezing her feet? Be like her to get up and follow some fool idea back through the trees, leaving her boots half buttoned and Jerusha sleeping alone. Eddie stretches his hands open and closed, to try to get the ghost of Jeanne Delaney off them, but it moves to the skin inside his shirt. The feel of her up against him knocks him right out of the present moment. Alive or dead, the girls around here just seem to be able to rise up out the ground and grab onto a person. It's an effort now to remember that Jeanne is more than just a haunting. She's got a body, all tangled up with his now. He startles and feels a sick hollow in his stomach.

When he swings up and onto the seat of the cart he can feel every inch of empty air in the valley, focused on him. Don thumps his tail against the boards, thinking they're going straight out with the gun.

'Town first, Don. Lie down.'

Micky'll be with Hank at the kitchen table now, saying whatever it is. Things are in motion, and they'll know he knows it, too. Before this time tomorrow, everybody will have shifted position. All of them will be in whatever new places they're going to occupy. Today

162

is what Eddie has been waiting for, the brittle cold and the sudden twist. He turns away from the farm and leans back to help Betty down the hill, doing his best to fill his eyes with the blankness of the valley, the road wide open under the milky sky. Eddie prays to the hills and the river that Jeanne Delaney will for once stay still, indoors.

Mr Natale, the cobbler, has his stove burning hot and smoky. Eddie can smell fruit tree wood in the air outside his door, still a little green. Inside he can smell the stiff sheets of boot leather stacked up and the pot of glue warming on the stove.

'Mornin'. You muffled the bell.'

'New baby. A girl, big one.' Natale looks happy with that, like he can keep his babies out of harm's way and everything is right with the world. Like girl babies are just as good as anything else. He's got two boys already. The older one works in Sloat's yard and brings back the skins for his father.

'Congratulations. Mrs Natale doing okay?'

'Fine. Easy this time. Not like before.' He talks in little bursts with the happiness coming out of him.

'My boots ready?'

'Not your boots, Eddie Allen. Girl's boots.' Natale laughs and turns to reach up onto the shelf. 'Heard you Allens are selling off.'

'Don't listen to the gossip at the store, Mr Natale. Not selling.'

'Your brother told me.'

'He was just storytelling. He gets bored, you know. Let's see.' Eddie reaches out for the boots.

'Special, eh?'

They do look good. He's made double seams and overlaid the stitching. Somehow, they're big enough for fur lining but they still look like ladies' boots. The toes come to a rounded point, which isn't practical or necessary, but it's right. Eddie pays in quarters from a roll he has in the box with the shells. Then he goes out to the cart to fill a pail with fresh milk for Mrs Natale. The town is rolling over and getting up now, people moving from the store to the schoolhouse, the slaughter yard and the dairy.

Everything is ticking on, fitting together. The day is moving forward. All Eddie has to do is ride the current to midnight.

Setting

Julia Allen is shovelling coal into the stove when Eddie drives up along the side window. One boy gone and another arrived. She nods to herself. Making men, that's the job and she's done it. They go out in all directions, but you're the middle of the wheel, the centre of the strength. Pull them in and turn them.

Eddie isn't perfect, but he's there for insurance. The other two have done their best to toughen him. He wasn't old enough to remember his father, that's the trouble. Everett was good for Hank and Micky, made them into little men. Eddie come out of nowhere, like he wasn't even from her body, not even an Allen. He doesn't understand about being a man.

He calls out from the mud room and stops to take his boots off. Every time she hears that voice she wants to slap him. It settled a few years ago now, but it's still higher than Hank's or even Micky's. Not enough size on him to put the gravel in it. A man's voice ought to be too big for indoors.

She sees his hands on the doorframe first, then he sticks half his body around into the sitting room.

'I guess you sent Micky now, too.'

'You don't even say hello first?' She drops the shovel back into the coal scuttle. 'You come here to pick a fight?'

'Sorry, Ma. I forgot myself. You okay?' He bows his head respectfully, even if she did have to remind him.

'I'll do. Come sit down. Not that chair. Over here.'

'I brought some milk, and cider from Crook. Potatoes, too.'

'Do you want tea, Eddie?'

'No thanks. Had coffee early. Now, you going to tell me why you sent Micky stumping up that hill at dawn?'

165

She reaches over and slaps his leg. Hard as she can. 'Don't joke like that Edward Allen.'

Whyever God set what he did on Micky, it was right and Julia's grateful. Imagine being in this town place all alone? No man to lock the windows or send away the tramps from the back door. Now she's got Micky. It hurts to look at him that way, but it was necessary. Keep quiet and pray hard, that's all. Things come around to you, if you keep still and wait.

Her own mother did that and learning it got Julia through all those babies, living and dead. Through Everett's black days, too. Kitchen chair days, she called them in her own head. Days when she thought it safest to sit still by the stove. When Everett was mad, it was better not to move around and try to talk him down. You just sat with maybe some darning or knitting. Sometimes it broke over you, sometimes it didn't, but it was gone quicker if you set still and kept the babies quiet as you could.

Well, that was her work. No harder than cutting and swamping and tending sheep and cows like Everett did. No harder than God intended, which was no harder than she could stand. A whining woman is a curse on everybody, 'specially her own self.

Micky has those black days, of course he will with what's happened to him. Mostly he disappears, but sometimes he just stares at the pictures on the walls and rubs on both thighs with his hands. Even then, Julia can't help looking at him in the way that makes him mad.

'I ain't some kind of diamond prince that landed in the middle of your life, Ma,' is what he says. 'I'm only here 'cause I can't be anywhere else.'

He was always the brightest, and the handsomest too. Better looking than Everett ever was. Micky is the spitten image of Julia's own father. He came on the heels of all those bloody creatures born too soon without enough limbs and their stomachs outside them. She sat still through all that, and Micky was the prize. Now here he is, made to stay by her in her age. Who says you don't get your reward in this life? That hay wagon saved her, but she's quiet as she can be about it.

166

'Micky called me Edward, too. Everybody's using my whole name today. Looks like I'm a stranger now.'

'You're family, Eddie Allen. We ain't the ones forgot that.'

'Oh, I see. The thing is, our dad left that land so we'd stay a family right there. I ain't left it. You all did.'

'You didn't even know him. He wouldn't have wanted things like this. His big boys all broken and scattered and you living with some vagrant in his house.'

'She doesn't live there, Ma. She lives with Jerusha. She will live there one day if I can get her to. I'm done lying about that. You all do your worst.'

Eddie might just as well be named Afterthought. Inside him he's like one of those dead babies, whole in the body but there's something missing from the man of him. He acts like a poet or the handsome young preacher from a newspaper serial. No sensible woman wants to marry that when there's wolves at the door. What you need up here is a man like a bottled storm. You get raged at, sure, but no one comes along your family with bad intentions neither.

Julia picked Everett right after she seen him knock a man cold from behind. They were all in someone's dooryard during a kitchen junket, one year just after Christmas. The snow packed down around the house and all the young ones getting ready to pile on the sled. The man was twice Everett's size and thought the fight was over after he'd flattened Everett one time. He turned and spat and started walking off. Everett picked up a short rail that was laying in that dooryard and sideswiped him. That was when Julia felt it, the string that connected her and Everett.

She could see herself, walking behind the Crook girls out of church, sitting behind the doctor's daughter at school in Harmony, all those stuck-up girls who wouldn't invite her on their picnics. She used to dream about cutting all the hair off them. But in her dreams, pigtails bled. Lined up behind all the pretty girls with parlours, she'd just breathe deep and picture them scalped and patchy with blood running down their dresses. Julia Allen got through school by

167

feeding herself pictures of revenge and retribution. Then that same kind of satisfaction was all of a sudden made real, in the good arm of Everett Allen. When Everett swung that rail, a world of memories and hurt was swiped clean away.

The big man Everett hit went down and lay in the snow with blood coming out his ear. Julia looked at Everett flinging the short rail away, and her body said, *Him. I want him.* She made sure to sit with her thigh pressed along Everett in the sled. The one time she was ever forward with any man, but it was do or die and she knew it. A man like that would make you good sons to take care of you in your old age. Anybody came along that man's family with the wrong ideas, they'd wind up bleeding.

Julia looks over at Micky's empty chair. It had taken her days to wind him up to it, but he'd gone up to the farm in the end. It's time to move things along and Everett isn't here to do it. Julia has the kind of men you have to manage without seeming to. Except Eddie, who never seemed to have anything to manage until now.

Everett was rough, and she knew right away she was safe next to him. If you played your cards right, you could turn that man around, wind him up and point him at anything that was in your way.

Growing into men, Hank and Micky ran around in all directions making up to people they shouldn't be and toying with girls long before they had whiskers even. Until one day the hay wagon turned over and left Micky sitting in her good chair for comfort.

'You really going to do this to me, Eddie? Don't you know how people are going to talk about us? The only grandchildren I'm gonna get will be mongrels.'

'I'm sure you got a few grandchildren, Ma.'

'Shut your mouth.' There's a kind of satisfaction in being able to talk to a man like that, but it goes off quick.

She looks at Eddie and he looks at her. He knows his time's run out; she can see it in the way he holds himself. However much of him there is inside, he'll finally show it now. Then they'll all know.

White Drifts

The valley is another kind of empty when Eddie takes the road home. Not even a whisper of mist or a ghost in the corner of his eye. He turns up Widow Road instead of passing straight through.

Once Betty and the cart are settled in Crook's old potato house, Don takes off up towards the blind on Mary's Peak without even stopping to check with Eddie. Eddie has a bottle of coffee and Jeanne's new boots in a sack with the box of bullets. The .22 in his other hand. There's just about half a moon rising on the other side of the mountain, and a couple of hours till dark anyway.

There's a burden of long dark hours left in this day, might as well spend them in the woods with the rifle. He clucks once for Don, who struggles up the wooden steps and settles himself on the floor of the blind.

Across the valley and up the hill, time is stretching tighter, pulling all the Allens into their places. Eddie can see Hank and Micky in the barn as if he were there with them, the two of them laughing with their sleeves rolled up. Whatever will happen later is making itself between them now.

A moose and her young one step out of the trees. Their fur is thick and full of tufts and the young one scratches herself against the trunks of the larches as they move down the slope. Eddie loads and cocks the rifle, rests it in the shooting window but doesn't sight. He isn't really here for that, and anyway he'd need the .30 and perfect aim to bring down a moose.

Once they've gone Eddie lets the focus out of his eyes. Snow is falling. The dark trees and the white ground blur into a pattern that might be anything. Restful for a little while, until thoughts creep into the quiet. The sight of Jeanne covered in ash, of Jeanne's mother with a belly like a full moon stretching above him, the look in Etta Grace's open eyes.

169

The one girl he and T-Roy managed to save was the one he didn't even know. He never heard of her again, or maybe he did but didn't realise. He had no name to recognise if it was spoken. He might even have seen her on the road and not known it. He was only up close to that nameless girl once, and it was night.

It was T-Roy she looked to that night, while Eddie tried to make out the side of her face. The moon was full but there was no colour. Her hair might have been black, but it might have been anything, really. She had strong calves, like maybe she lived in the hills or did field work. The blood made curves where it ran down the bulge of her muscles.

Anyway, she would be broken and stilted now, twelve years later. She maybe sells herself behind the paper mill in Harmony now. Or maybe she covered it all up and someone married her.

Etta Grace he never even tried to save, but he'd know her anywhere, especially if she spoke. Sometimes, when he's under the trees, he just knows that Etta Grace is still speaking somewhere, still throwing her sing-song words into the wind. Hank hears it, too. You can see it when his eyes get fuzzy and his arms tense up. He'll go away, or he'll go mad. Already, he wanders around the house half asleep in the dark, muttering to himself.

One of them could just light a match and make it all go away. That is one way this day could end. In his mind, Eddie can see the house burning, the bedrooms and the smokehouse and the barn where Hank and Micky used to play. Flames could unravel the whole history of the Allens, turn all their years and generations into a blanket of ash. It might be the one act they ever agree on.

There's a coyote, stalking something through the slow-falling snow. Quail, most likely, or maybe a fisher cat. The coyote looks mangy. When it stops and raises its head, the glint in its yellow eyes makes Eddie realise it's almost dark. The coyote starts and takes off on a turn, leaving long, sliding tracks in a patch of snow. Leaving nothing but silence. Don is sleeping patiently. It seems for a few minutes like he and Eddie are the only animals for miles around.

There is the first star. A planet, Jeanne says. She learned that from her birthday book, which planets you can see when and how you tell them. It's Mars maybe, glinting pink and low in the sky between the branches. Eddie lifts the rifle into the shooting window and sights. He lowers his eye along of the barrel and lines it up with that point of light. When he pulls the trigger he'll make a burst of fire inside the chamber, a flame in the dark so fierce and fast it can drive a bullet. He holds the trigger halfway and feels the world waiting for him, then squeezes his finger and causes a spark in the chamber to match that star. The sound of the shot startles Don and unsettles a hawk, who takes off and dissolves into the sky.

Eddie can hear Hank and Micky laughing from the road. There is a lantern on the kitchen porch and the door is open. Don jumps out of the cart and slides under the gate, heading for the pump, where he sniffs at the layer of ice under the spout. Eddie opens the gate and says, 'Hey'.

'Hey, yourself.' There is Micky, leaning against the wall with a crutch in one hand and a hot poker in the other.

They're making hot apple jack. Hank put the small cider barrel out a week or more ago, as soon as things started to freeze. For just a minute, Eddie thinks maybe this is all Micky came for. Maybe Hank sent a message in with Crook, saying, come and help me poke the hot apple jack, let's drink and play some cards. If that's it, they'll be up all night and something ugly will happen before morning anyway. Even if it isn't planned.

He leads Betty in and rubs her down, taking his time. The warm smell of horses is dirty and comforting. He cleans the stalls and climbs up to throw down some new hay. From up in the hayloft he can hear them, laughing while they poke through the ice and draw off the liquor. There is no light up there, but Eddie doesn't need it. He can see the yellow hole of the trapdoor and he's known the feel of everything else since before he could remember. Known that laughter, too, of course. It could have been a good sound, and he used to pretend it was. The shotgun and the rifle are still below, laying in the wagon, but he has the rifle bolt in his pocket.

It's important to move slow and keep your eyes level, no matter what comes in front of them. Eddie makes his steps deliberate, moving across the yard and past them, through the kitchen door with the rifle in his right hand and a lantern in his left.

He takes the keys from the kitchen shelf, puts the rifle in the gun cabinet, the bolt in the box on top, goes back for the shotgun, then locks the cabinet and puts the keys back in their place in the kitchen, next to the crystal. None of it is secret. Anyone named Allen knows where all these things go. Almost nobody else does, but even a stranger would work it out. It's accidents they're trying to guard against, not meanness. When he puts the keys back, three of their Grammy's sherry glasses are out of their places, circles of dustless shelf showing where they were.

'Come on then, Eddie,' Hank says. 'Let's make a toast.'

Eddie puts the lantern on the table next to the one that's already there, goes out onto the porch and takes a glass. He raises it up, looking them both in the eyes before he nods and drinks. In the silence, the alcohol fire goes down between his lungs.

Micky bends then and lifts the jug with one hand, moving his crutch into his armpit with the other.

'It's freezing cold out here. Let's go inside and do some real drinking.' He rests his forearm on Eddie's shoulder to hoist himself over the kitchen doorstep.

'Forgot exactly how good that was,' Hank says. 'Where you been today?'

'Town and then the woods. Seen two moose and a coyote, all wearing their winter coats.' Eddie looks out into the yard. The half moon is up now, throwing patches of light onto the snow between the barns. The dead black stalks of brussels sprouts sticking up out of the snow are all that's left of Jerusha's vegetable patch.

'Didn't shoot nothing?' Hank looks relaxed. When Eddie thinks about this moment later, that's what he remembers. Not a muscle on Hank shows Eddie there is anything behind him. That's the real difference maybe, between people and animals. People can hide their instincts, teach themselves not to flinch.

A flash of white and then darkness.

Eddie wakes up with snow in his mouth. He is lying on the ground below the porch. There is Micky standing up on the kitchen doorstep, with the jug still whole in his hand. Hank is there too, leaning like liquid on the railing, and that is how Eddie knows how little time has passed. Hank is in the same position, with the same look on his face.

'Reckoning time, Eddie,' Micky says. 'You've had enough time to fuck around up here. Tonight we fix this, and tomorrow we get things done.'

Eddie pushes up on one elbow, but his arm shakes so hard he has to fall back down on his back. He looks at Hank, not Micky.

'I won't do it. You know I won't.'

'I'm the one talking to you. Look at me when you answer.'

Next to Eddie's head there is slushy place that smells like apples and alcohol. Up close, Micky would smell like that, too.

'I know it. I know it all, everything the two of you did. I guess you're proud of it. The place is mine now, unless you want to sit and wallow in your own mess.'

It's Hank that hits him then, flying off the porch and landing on one of Eddie's arms with a sickening sound. The next time Eddie wakes up, he's bleeding and tied to the pump. His boots are full of snow and his toes are burning with cold. He flexes both arms and it seems like neither is all the way broken. They are tied, though, and losing circulation. When the poker hits his thigh he feels the impact first. The burning comes after. It feels good to scream. The wire in his gut finally snaps and his voice comes steaming out of his mouth into the cold.

'You ain't going to die, Eddie,' Micky says. 'Just so you know. You're just gonna sign a couple papers is all.'

Eddie can see now that the two of them are glad for this

173

opportunity. They're glad he resisted, glad to be back together in the dooryard, drawing the blood from some helpless creature. They're pretending to be whole again, even though they must know it's temporary.

'Ask Hank, Micky,' Eddie lisps around the blood in his mouth. 'Ask Hank about the ghosts.'

Hank hits him so hard he cracks his head against the pump handle. The sound is like a rifle shot. The metal so close to his head, maybe, or Hank's fists so quick, that the impact sounds like gunfire. Warmth floods down into Eddie's arms and legs and takes him under again. It's summer there, in the place where his mind goes. Everything is bright and the air smells like warm earth. There is Etta Grace, talking, and Jerusha stirring something. Jeanne Delaney is a kid again. He watches her running down to the creek and feels nothing at all. No one else is there, just Eddie and the three women, in the time before they all changed.

When he comes to again, Micky is lying across his legs leaking warm blood. There is something like blood in Eddie's eyes and all, and he can't turn his head around far enough to find Hank. There is a bubbling noise, and it takes Eddie a long time to realise it's Micky breathing. Then that stops too. He can hear Hank talking by the gate.

Micky's back stops rising and falling, and Eddie is alone in the dooryard under the sky. The cold doesn't matter anymore, and anyway the heat of Micky Allen is draining into him. When he looks up, the moon has gone down and there are so many winter stars they look like dust. Whatever Hank has gone off chasing might swallow him in the dark. He might never come back. Could be no one will come to untie Eddie and he will freeze here. The big snow will come before Jerusha or Jeanne thinks to check on him. The kitchen door will swing on its hinges and let the weather into the house. He will sit quietly under the snow with Micky, waiting for spring while the house fills up with white drifts.

Jeanne

I'd only come outside that night because I couldn't sleep. I'm sure I don't have to tell you. Teach a sixteen-year-old body about sex and then tell it to stay away? Leave that to the ladies at the Children's Aid, who incidentally have never yet managed to keep girls in shacks from having babies soon as their bodies are ready. I didn't tell myself that Eddie was why I'd taken those soft steps past Jerusha and out the door, why I'd carried my old boots in one hand and sat on the back stoop to put them on. But it was, of course.

I was wearing a hand-me-down sweater of T-Roy's and my new deerskins. I wanted to be out in the cold so I could feel that deer's coat turned in against my own skin. Some creatures are born with their flesh and blood wrapped up against the snow like that. Humans have to steal somebody else's skin to make it through winter, which is maybe what twists us. I don't know.

Oh, anyway, there was something like a sideways gravity operating on me is what I'm saying, something pulling me out into the blue night. I went down to the creek so I could look at the light on the water. It was frozen black, since there'd been a sharp drop after the snow. I thought about stepping onto it and then about falling through into the slicing cold. All the trees were bare and the summer birds were long gone. It wasn't weather for playing at staying still in the woods. I'd have lost some toes. I hadn't got my new boots from Eddie yet, see.

Them days, I was always standing at some place in some season and trying to picture my mother doing the same. Something about becoming a woman, I guess. Maybe this strange thing taking over my body made me need her, and feel like I was her at the same time.

Maybe the trees were different when my mother was under them. Maybe the oxbow wasn't made yet, the creek a different shape then.

But there might once have been the fish under the ice and every moving creature and snapping branch echoing across the blue blanket of snow in the night, and her standing just where I was standing. I tried to fill in the blank in her thinking, tried to get inside who she was. It was easier for me to imagine being Joan of Arc than it was to imagine being my own mother, but I tried.

There was no book about my mother, no information, nobody to write down an imaginary life and a heroic death. Jeanne Delaney bled out onto old quilts one night at the end of a summer, maybe holding Jerusha Prichard's hand, maybe looking down at me, squalling there.

And here was Jeanne Delaney still looking out into a winter night, breathing and talking to herself. It was never going to make sense. I was the thing that killed her, the noisy, bloody knife. Then I was me, something extra and unnecessary, sticking out from the edge of the world. Jeanne Delaney had already been and gone but here I still was, running through the same woods and the same houses, never shutting up.

I don't know why I was thinking all that just then, but there wasn't much else to think. I'm glad all that wondering is over, these days. I've ripped my own hole in the world now.

I wandered up to the road without thinking why, leaving a trail in the snow a mile wide, I guess. Eddie would've scolded me. I came along the side of Jerusha's maples and through the trees down the slope.

'Twasn't till I got down onto the road that I saw her.

She was coming straight towards me. I must have stood out like a shadow against the half moon over the hill behind me, but that snowy owl didn't swerve an inch out of her path. She came low down the middle of the road, throwing the moonlight right back at me out of her yellow eyes. Owls have eyes like wolves, yellow and sharp and right outside of anything like pity or sweetness, or evil either. They're not bad creatures, just deadly.

Something else came swooping down the valley along of her, too.

Something I didn't see at all at the time, because it was the exact same colour as the night. I could say that something jumped into me and made me do what I did, but that'd be a lie. It was just the cold, midnight colour of our new lives, rolling in ahead of all the things we were about to bring on ourselves. It was just the shadow falling in front of what I was about to do.

The owl kept coming straight on at me, with her white wings spread out and her head forward. She must have stretched five feet, wingtip to wingtip. I couldn't see the specks of winter black on her, there in the dark. She looked like she'd made herself right out of the snow and the cold grace of the curving hills around us. She only flapped those wings one time. Not a yard from where I was, she brought them down together in front of me, then opened them up and rose over my head and on past. I turned around and she'd gone dark between me and the moon, fading into the shadows over Jerusha's trees.

When I couldn't make her out anymore, I turned down the road again and ran into the dip and on up the hill. By then, I knew full well I was running towards Eddie Allen.

I thought I just wanted to tell him what I'd seen. I thought what he would have done if he'd been there, standing saying nothing and just soaking the sight of that ghostly bird into himself. I'd have tugged on him and chattered, but it wouldn't have touched him. He'd have been somewhere I couldn't get to, blending himself into the land. That was Eddie's version of joy. Once you knew him, you recognised it for that.

But he hadn't been there, so he'd have to take it second hand with me telling it my way. If I told it right, I might get him to smile or hold me. I was proud of myself for understanding what Eddie was teaching me, thinking he would be proud. I was full of what was in the woods, in that way that makes you bigger than your own body, that melts you into everything all around. My plan was to throw a pebble at his bedroom window and get him to come out to me.

I wasn't even thinking about Hank until I heard his voice in the yard. Certainly not about Micky.

I'd slowed down at the top of the hill, breathing hard through my mouth, and thank God for that. I heard the words barking out of those Allen men and the sound of Eddie's bones cracking, I swear. I went still and waited a minute for the situation to sink in. I was a fool, okay, but I wasn't simple. I went to the side of the road then, and came slow along the cow barn. Once I got to the space between that and the chicken coop I climbed down into the ditch and put my head under the bottom fence rail.

There was a lantern sitting on the kitchen porch, throwing the shadows of Hank and Micky Allen all the way along the slushy yard to the smokehouse. The two of them stood looking down at their little brother and barking words at him. Eddie sat against the pump with his head hung down to the side. His hands were behind his back pulling his shoulders up. The light was on his hair. It hung forward in clumps, throwing his face into the dark. The ground was all churned up between the three of them and Micky Allen stood with his foot in the slush, leaning on his crutch. Hank stood the other side of him, watching Eddie's blood drip black out of his mouth onto the snow.

His legs'll freeze, was the first thing I thought. I thought about how cold to the touch Eddie's skin would be. Well, listen, it's not like you get born all mentally prepared for a sight like that. I don't know, maybe you do and then your soft mother breeds it out of you with blankets and warm milk.

Then I thought of the day I saw Eddie under the pines, and of the last time I saw Etta Grace. If I said that was why I done it, I wouldn't be lying. I wouldn't be telling the whole truth either, though. I guess in your city newspapers and your marble courtrooms you get to pretend the truth is simple. We don't.

I told you I didn't have a mother. Did I tell you already I was a girl who did what was necessary? You've heard a fair bit of my life, now. You tell me. What else was I going to do with myself but the

178

things that needed to be done? It took a minute or two, but I got there. I arrived at the only decision that made sense, quick enough.

The snow in the ditch crunched when I scrambled back up onto the road, and then I tripped over a stone and slipped. Every sound is loud when can get you killed. If them two Allens had found me then, I'd have been scooped up into that scene in the yard. I'd have been just another one of their bleeding girls, without a name I could call my own.

The wheel ruts were full of icy mud. I went slow as I could around to the front of the Allens' and forced that sticky front door. The worst thing was going into the kitchen for the key to the gun cabinet. I took a deep breath and moved without wasting one step or stopping to lift the jar slowly. If either one of them had turned their head, they'd have seen me through the window. I picked up the jar and took it with me back into the sitting room. If I stopped to cover my tracks it'd be too late anyway, once whoever was left noticed it missing. If I didn't do things right, I guessed Eddie would be dead and none of it would matter.

The bolt for the .22 was in a box on top of the gun cabinet. That was the gun I knew best. There were bullets in Eddie's room.

I dropped the bolt in and loaded on the front porch and then went back to that same spot in the ditch between the cows and the chickens. When I heard Don whine, I nearly pissed my new deerskins. Well, sorry, that's the truth. He must have been tied or he would have come straight to me there. That's one more way I could've been dead by now.

Hank went into the barn and kicked Don so he yelped. I guess they thought he was just upset about what they were doing to Eddie. I leaned the rifle up onto the bottom fence rail, then shifted my weight from one foot to the other until the ground under me was solid. Then all of a sudden, I wasn't scared anymore. The fear just drained away. I started to breathe, to close the world down to that one thing that was in front of me.

I wasn't quick at it. It took me much too long to get calm, but I did learn from Eddie Allen. I had to travel to get to that place in between breaths where Eddie seemed to live. He'd been showing me the way, though. I knew how to breathe the whole world right into my lungs and breathe myself back out into a different world, one with a bullet flying through it.

Eddie dragged his head up and mumbled something at them. Hank moved while he was still speaking, so fast I didn't even see the short rail in his hand. Before the words were out of Eddie's mouth Hank was done swinging and I swear I thought he'd snapped Eddie's neck with the force of it.

I took a long breath in through my nose and mouth, and let it out nice and slow through the trigger. Before the shot was done sounding Micky crumpled. It looked like someone had just snapped their fingers and made his bones disappear. The sack that was left of him dropped down right where it was. His crutch fell one way and he fell the other, down across Eddie's legs. His head twisted to the side, facing me with his cheek against the wet ground.

There was some kind of blank space in time then. I saw Hank looking every which way and realised he didn't know where that bullet had come from. Next thing I was on the road behind the chickens, reloading. I knew he'd come through the gate eventually, but he'd go to the gun cabinet first, and I couldn't let that happen. People tell you their fingers fumble, times like that. Not me. I got to the gate while Hank Allen was still five feet from the kitchen porch.

'Stop there,' I said and pulled the bolt across.

'Jeanne Delaney?' Well, that was a new way of saying it.

'Jeanne Delaney was my mother's name. Keep it out of your mouth, Hank Allen.' I don't know why I said that. Things were coming out of some cold place inside me, bullets and words and some other woman's strength, I think.

'Jesus,' Hank said, and sort of fell sideways to lean against the porch.

We were both quiet then and I could see the panic and the anger sliding out of him into the night. I didn't put the gun down, though. I just stood there, pointing it at him and trying to think how I was going to open the gate without putting the rifle down and giving him a chance to kill me. I wasn't shaking, though. I still had the power up in me from the shooting, I guess. The main thing I remember was how steady I felt. I shook later.

After a while, Hank said, 'I guess I'll be leaving in the morning. You should come with me, Jeanne Delaney. Can't you see you're too many for Eddie?'

'What?'

'I'm saying a woman like you needs a man like me. I could take you with me.'

'You want to sleep next to me, Hank Allen?'

'Don't be coy, girl. I know my little brother's been right into you.' He gave a slow look down along the rifle. 'I'm gonna go ahead and guess you liked it.'

That's right, Hank Allen asked me to go with him two minutes after I shot his brother. Unless he done it while I was behind the chicken house, he hadn't even checked to see if Micky was breathing. If you find that strange, you haven't understood a thing I've been telling you. That man had two brothers bleeding out into the yard, and already he'd moved past that and started thinking on what he could walk away with. And the thing he wanted was me, me with my violence still fresh on my skin. That there was the definition of an Allen.

'You want to sleep next to me?' I said, 'Yes, please. I'll get up in the night and cut your stomach open, then lay back down to sleep in your blood, Hank Allen. Etta Grace was my friend.'

He jerked his head like I'd slapped him. I'd like to say he looked ashamed or cried, but he didn't. I didn't have that much power. No one does. There was no kind of satisfaction to be got from Hank Allen. Whatever was happening, it wasn't justice or redemption. Whoever died next, it wasn't going to mean anything. There wouldn't be a reason.

Any one or all of us could have lay there dead for days before Bud Crook or the dairy man come along us and reported it in town. Our reasons would have blown away down the valley long before then.

'Get out of here before I shoot you.'

And you know what? He did. Hank Allen didn't even stop for his coat. We threw it out later, together with his grandfather's knife and his extra shirt.

Snow started falling again, though I wouldn't have known it except for the lantern. The moon was down, the stars were gone behind clouds, and we were just shadows in a circle of lamplight that could have been in the middle of anywhere.

I backed out of that light and away from the gate to let him through, aiming at him the whole while. Hank Allen went down the hospital road in his shirt sleeves and I never saw him again. Far as I know, word of him never come back to his mother or the brother he left living behind him. One time, I dreamed it was that snowy owl that swooped down over the road and took him up and away.

But first, almost every night for a year, I dreamed him coming back.

Immemorial

Jerusha has the heavy curtain open so she can stare out into the light of the setting half moon, blinding the stars. The thing that has been stalking through the snow is here tonight. Jeanne has lit off somewhere and the fire's gone out. The whole world is holding itself between breaths, expanded, about to let go. Whatever Jeanne is off doing or seeing in the cold dark, it will change everything.

If Jerusha can feel this coming, how come she never knew about Etta Grace? Spend your whole life learning sharp lessons, but in the end you lie in the dark and turn to brittle bones without the one thing you needed to know.

That morning, more than three years ago, Jerusha woke up and looked into the grey light for a full minute before she felt the empty bed across from her. Etta Grace was off again, walking and walking and wading through the creek, breaking the branches off things and talking to herself. Shrinking into the woods and dropping the flesh off her own bones with the whole unfocused power of her sadness. Talking to the ghosts of her children, maybe.

Anyway, that was what Jerusha thought when she opened her eyes and looked over at the empty bed. She thought Etta Grace was off in the trees somewhere, talking to her ghosts.

So she moved slow, getting a shawl and some boots on. She even lit the fire and shut the door on the stove before she walked up over the hill through the sugar maples. It was spring, one of those mornings when the air is cold but the sun is warm as long as it's on you. She stopped and stood in a piece of light by the spring house, thinking the danger of frost was maybe past, she could put beans in. She stopped for a minute to feel the world on her skin, knowing nothing. Then she went the long way around, on the edge of the creek, because it was such a good morning and because Etta Grace liked the tadpoles that were growing in the stagnant pools in the little oxbow below the beeches.

When she saw Etta Grace's legs, she actually shouted at her.

'Etta Grace! Don't come down from a tree that way, you'll break your legs, girl.'

Then she understood, though she couldn't say how. Seeing how things move and gauging different kinds of stillness is an animal thing that's left in us. Etta Grace was speaking her absence in the way she hung there.

Jerusha didn't hurry. She took even strides, cutting her way through each piece of space and time between herself and her child. She did that because if she stopped, she might turn around and run away.

Away from the sight of her daughter, hanging from the oldest beech. The trunk was so big around, Etta Grace and Jeanne would have to join their hands to get their arms all the way around it. They liked to do that, a few years before.

Once, she caught Jeanne Delaney sleeping up there and was afraid to shout in case she startled and rolled off. That time, she had one of those perfect pictures you get in your mind of an accident that never happens, of a limb snapping and a white bone sticking out like a moose's tooth. Not today. Today she saw only what was in front of her and not until it was.

Etta Grace, hanging long and drawn out with some of her chestnut hair in front of her face, with her brown eyes open to meet her ghosts.

Eddie was on his way to the creek with a rod and some coffee when Jerusha came up the muddy road with her boots untied and her hair loose. It was early and the sun was still striking sideways across the road. Jerusha wasn't shouting or crying, not even moving fast.

'Need help, Eddie.' She sounded like she was still half asleep.

'Sure, Jerusha. What?'

She just turned back and starting walking, so he followed,

straight past the cabin and up the slope through the sugar maples. There's people would have thinned out the beeches from between those maples, sold the wood and maybe got more syrup and more money. Jerusha wasn't one of them, of course. So the beech tree was there for Etta Grace to find, on the other side of the hill where the trees grew down towards the creek. Eddie would have seen her anyway, on his way through to his fishing.

It was not entirely a graceful tree. One fat limb grew out lower than the others with a great bulge of a knot in it. No beautiful symmetry, but its bark was smooth and silver in any kind of light and those girls liked to put their feet on the knots in the trunk, climb up and lay on top of that fat branch. That was all he thought of, at first.

He ran towards the tree as soon as he saw her, then stopped when he realised. Something about the way she hung there was already outside of time.

'We need to get her down before T-Roy comes and sees her.' Jerusha's voice was so cold Eddie reached out to put a hand on her. She slapped it away.

Seemed like it took hours to climb up and get his hands onto the rope. You get like a machine or a puppet, times like that. You just move through it. Eddie'd had practice long before then.

Etta Grace had made a bowline knot. It was the same knot she'd been making for months, over and over, ever since T-Roy taught her to tie it. She could learn to do most things with her hands if she took it slow.

Jerusha stood still while Eddie climbed, hugging Etta Grace's legs and waiting. The girl had fouled herself, but it didn't matter. Looking at Jerusha's face pressed up against those skirts, you'd have thought the daughter was alive, needing comfort.

Eddie stretched along the silver branch and tried to get one hand under Etta Grace's arms while he cut with the other. She must have shimmied along there with the rope in her hand. She maybe lay down and put the rope around her neck and then just rolled off.

Maybe she stood up and jumped, or sat and pushed off with her smooth, pretty arms.

The little beech flowers were out under the new leaves, with the green so bright it reminded him of summer thunderstorms. No storms that day though, just the sun, lighting everything and no sympathy.

You'd know the place if you were from around here, city boy, but you can't see it now. It was just along the creek by the oxbow. Some willows have been growing in there ten years or more. Back then, it was a patch of swale. It looked solid enough covered with leaves, but you could sink up to your knees in it if you didn't know the woods there. I went up around it, playing my Joan of Arc game. It was early still, and the light was gold and slanting, the kind of light that made you feel beloved of God. I could stand in the dusty shafts of it and become a saint. I was using a stick for a sword, stalking stray English cowards and chasing them away from the river and into the woods around Beaugency. When I found one, I'd call out the Virgin's name and make them turn to look at the burning light all around me before I put the blade right into their hearts.

Well, I wasn't but thirteen years old at the time.

I'd left Grampy and even T-Roy sleeping on the boat, I was out that early. It was good when winter was over and they were back, nice to lay there rocking on the water at night, knowing they were near me. But you don't stay in bed on a morning like that. Well, I didn't anyway. I guess girls who stay in the beds they're supposed to be in don't have to carry the memories I do behind their eyes. But listen, government man, I'm not sure I'd trade, even now.

I saw Etta Grace through the trees. She was on the other side of the creek and up the slope a little, in our favourite beech. Hanging, I mean, from our favourite beech. I didn't know what I was looking at for a long time, but something in me could smell it. I stayed where I was, behind the branches across the creek, level with Etta Grace up the opposite slope. She was swaying there, in and out of one of

186

those yellow shafts of light, moving in between the saints and the shadows.

After a while, I saw Jerusha coming along the opposite bank but I didn't shout. For an hour or more I wasn't sure I'd ever speak again. Things happened in my body that morning, things were growing and changing and trading places. My voice was one thing; it left me for a while. I just crouched in behind the leaves and watched. Jerusha stopped at the bottom of the slope, looking up at Etta Grace and the rope, then she moved like a soldier across the space between them. She stood and stared, then she looked away and down at the creek. A sound like a coyote makes come up out of her, a kind of screeching yelp, just once. She turned around and walked away, and still I didn't move. You need to believe me; I don't think I could have.

By the time Jerusha came back with Eddie Allen, the sun was higher. Pieces of it were stabbing back off the creek into my eyes, making me see purple spots after. At first, when I looked up at the three of them, they disappeared behind the sunspots between us. Jerusha hugged Etta Grace while Eddie climbed the tree and cut her down. She fell back over Jerusha's shoulder and sprawled out on the leaves. I thought maybe they'd cracked her head.

I stayed hid there, watching the three of them. Jerusha turned her back while Eddie Allen knelt down and laid Etta Grace out straight. He folded her arms, then put one hand behind her head and lifted it so he could gather all of her hair in the other hand and pull it forward in front of her shoulder. Sometimes, those few years later when Eddie touched me, I would think of that.

Don't look at me that way. You ever know how someone you sleep with would touch the dead? It matters. I had my eyes on Eddie Allen when he thought there wasn't anybody looking. I saw right into him, and that's why I never felt scared of him after.

187

CONFIDENTIAL

Etta Grace Claire: 24 yrs old, feeble-minded
Father(?): Tubercular
Mother: Vagrant

The patient came to us in the miscarriage of a pregnancy, in the capacity of a medical dependent. She and her mother, Jerusha, are known locally by the name of Prichard. William Prichard (died tuberculosis) is said to have been the father of the patient, though there is no legal record of a union, and the patient should properly be catalogued as illegitimate, under the mother's maiden name of Clare, or Claire.

She seemed to present with serious loss of blood, and was barely conscious, but these symptoms were no doubt exacerbated by poor nutrition and degenerate living conditions. She came to us with a collection of dirty rags packed between her legs, having been given some of the noxious herbal concoctions usual with such women as the mother. Thankfully, her bleeding was not serious in spite of this treatment. Though the mother claimed the patient had been haemorrhaging, the local physician reports her hysterical at the time he collected the patient. Miss Claire had perhaps aborted naturally and might have survived without care. The pregnancy had advanced five months.

The patient is clearly feeble-minded, with the sexual promiscuity that often accompanies that condition painfully evident. No physical deformity, beyond whatever has caused her infertility, is immediately recognisable. In fact, the patient is known locally as a beauty. She might be classed as a moron, functional and capable of independence, but sub-intelligent.

William Prichard, if we are to believe he was the father, was of ameliorated Amerindian stock. The mother, Jerusha Claire (known

188

as Prichard) is called a 'Gypsy' by the locals, which suggests an indeterminate lineage. When interviewed, the patient claimed her mother came from Canada as a child. Given her mental incapacity and distress, however, this information should be considered unreliable. Jerusha Claire did revert to a base dialect of French when hysterical. Certainly, both mother and daughter are evidence of that social deterioration which results from the ingress of immigrants of inferior stock.

Jerusha Claire is a granny midwife who has served many of the rural women, including some from respectable families, with the usual ignorance and lack of hygiene. She lives with the patient in one of the disused logging camps along the lake.

The patient is apparently sound in body, with anaemic blood but strong lungs. I have performed a preventative sterilisation. As can be inferred from the information herein contained, she is sexually incontinent, and likely to commit further breaches of chastity. She is, in any case, a great temptation to local youth of all backgrounds, and would no doubt become pregnant again. Whether or not she is genetically degenerated to the degree that she cannot carry a child to full term, she surely does not have the wherewithal – mental, moral or financial – to care for any living issue without becoming dependent on town or county.

I present this case as data for your Eugenic Survey of the area. Its use may be limited, her grandmother having come from outside the locality alone and her claim to paternity unsubstantiated. There is some connection, however, with one of the 'pirate' families on the lake. I have not been able to ascertain the nature of the relationship. Further inquiry may perhaps reveal more illegitimate unions which could explain it and add information to your genealogies. Certainly, this 'pirate' family also has a history of sexual incontinence and general shiftlessness, though they have never been dependent on town or county and so may have escaped your notice. There is another illegitimate child shared between the two abodes, nearly grown and sadly of the expected character.

I was visited by two respectable local farm wives, who petitioned for the patient's release back into her mother's care. As there is no history of dependence, I have complied. Spaces in county facilities are woefully limited.

This branch of the Claire tree will end with the patient. I hope this case history may be of some help to your project.

Jeanne

I was gonna need a quarry pick. First, I was gonna need to get Micky into the pony cart and Eddie into bed.

The stars had come out again, shining off the snow, and the lantern was still burning on the back porch. The moon was down and there was a good piece of the long December dark in front of us still. I had time to keep on doing what needed to be done, and plenty of blue silence to do it in.

I got Betty in the traces and had to make Eddie help me lift Micky. I took the quilt off Julia Allen's bed and rolled him off Eddie's legs and onto it. Eddie opened his mouth and shut it again, but he didn't seem to know how to make a fuss about his mother's good blanket. He hardly spoke at all, nor looked at me.

'I didn't mean it, Eddie.'

'What?'

'They were killing you.'

'They said they weren't. I told you to stay away, didn't I?' He said like it was an actual question, not like he was mad at me. He sounded like he was talking in his sleep.

'You did Eddie, but I saw something I wanted to tell you and then I heard them in the yard. Jerusha told me, too. About them.'

He stood up and then stumbled, caught his hand on the pump and flinched. Something was wrong with his arm and it wouldn't hold his weight. He pulled on Micky with one hand and I used two. I made a ramp out of barn boards and climbed up into the back to pull from there. Betty could smell Micky. She danced around and put her ears back. I should have waited till we had him in the cart to get her out of the barn.

Well, you good at getting rid of bodies are you, government man? I didn't know.

191

Eddie just stood there staring at the wheel of the cart. I snapped then, and started shouting.

'I had to, Eddie! They killed people before now. What was I supposed to do?'

'You don't know that, Jeanne.'

'I do. And you do, too. It's me, Eddie. It's just me.'

'Jeanne Delaney.' He looked away at the gate while he said it. He looked at his own feet and then at the place where his brother's should be. He looked up at the prickly sky and then over at the lantern on the porch.

'Come on, Eddie Allen. Bed,' I said. Like normal. Like I was his and had a right to speak to him in that way. Like we were married people and this thing in the cart was maybe a deer for butchering or a sack of potatoes.

I tied Betty to the fence. Inside the house, I cleaned and bandaged Eddie's legs best I could. When I saw the burns on them, I couldn't believe he'd stood at all. I used ointment and then covered him with a clean sheet under blankets. They had a good medicine cabinet, being a farm. I didn't know what else to give him besides peppermint and chamomile and headache powders. Later, Jerusha took me through it and said the headache powders were wrong.

First, she stood looking on while I buried Micky Allen.

I left Eddie on the couch with a fire going. Once I got the cart out onto the road, I went over to shut the gate. What if Betty spooked and ran? I had a crazy vision of her taking off through the valley like some ghostly horse from Washington Irving's *Sketch Book*, with the corpse of Micky Allen in the back of the cart. In my head it was like a moving picture on the bioscope at the fair. That horse'd streak into town while everyone slept and bring Micky to his mother. I could almost hear her screams drifting over Sloat's fields and up the road. I shook my head a little to clear it, then got up onto the seat. While we started down the road, I talked to Betty like it was a nice, calm thing, driving a body around the roads in the small hours of a December night.

Betty knew Jerusha's yard even in the dark. She took me up between the trees off the road and I let her loose before I went inside. I didn't take my boots off, just walked through and stood for a minute over Jerusha in the bed. The outline of her body took shape for me in the shadows. I could smell the rosemary oil she put in her hair, hear her rustling movement and her shallow sleeping breaths.

I could feel and smell and hear everything that night, like somebody else's senses got added to my own. I could have done anything. I could have fought a bear in the dark and won. I could have outsmarted a family of wolves by myself. I didn't much want to do any of it, but that didn't matter.

From the outside, the heroes in stories look like people lucky enough to have a shining thing to aim themselves at. They're like arrows full of the force that shot them, flying towards the light. Now I'll tell you what those heroes feel like on the inside. Trapped. Helpless inside moving time, like down dead pieces of wood in a river in spring.

I reached out and put a hand on Jerusha's shoulder, waking her as gentle as I could.

We didn't use any words at first. I had that same lantern off the Allens' porch and we filled it with Jerusha's oil. She followed me out in a shawl with her boots untied. I put out a hand to stop her and climbed up into the cart. When I rolled Micky Allen's body out onto the snow, she didn't even gasp. She just stood looking down at him.

'Where's the other one?' she said.

'Gone, Jerusha. I promise. Gone.'

We were quiet for so long a rabbit came to the edge of the yard to look at us. Then Jerusha put her hands either side of my face and looked right into me. After a minute, I guess she saw whatever she was looking for.

'Okay, let's get the rest of this done,' she said.

'Jerusha, I shot somebody. He's dead.'

'It needed doing and you know it, Jeanne Delaney. I'm sorry it was you, if that helps.'

'Something's backwards, Jerusha. I'm not sorry a'tall. Something's dropped out of me. It's like a dream came out of my head and turned real.' I could feel myself choking and drowning, even though I knew it wasn't happening.

'Listen to me, girl,' Jerusha said. 'You know you weren't never like everyone else. Neither you nor Etta Grace, in different ways. I can't say if your mother would be proud, but she would have been safer with you around than she was without you. Your mother was my friend, so I'll go ahead and be proud of you.'

'I killed someone, Jerusha.' I don't know why I kept saying it. Words weren't helping.

'You're gonna have to put that out of your mind, Jeanne. It can't be undone, so you'll just have to keep going. It might take some time, but after a while you'll go days and months without it even occurring to you. You'll see.'

Maybe you know that wasn't true, but I don't know whether she meant it to be. Jerusha died before she was proved wrong and so I never asked her whether that was just a sweet lie about the forgetting. And anyway, how would she know?

I needed the quarry pick to break the ground. It was only a few weeks till Christmas and the hard frost was inches thick already. It would get harder, but already there was no way into it with a shovel, not for someone my size anyway. Jerusha watched through all the hours it took, and she brought me a big mug of something bitter and steaming. The night was so long we had to stop once and fill the lantern again.

I guess we could have put Micky in the ground under Etta Grace's beech tree. That would have been a kind of justice, but it would have felt more like blaspheming. Anyway, I'd dragged the man far enough by that time and I had a lot of digging to do. I'm not a shiftless woman, in spite of what the social workers might say. I never have shied from any kind of work, but that night was the hardest I ever worked in my life.

By the end of it I was standing down in the hole. Did you know, three feet underneath the winter ground all the life is still there, just sleeping? Once you break through the freeze, you can smell the rot and the growing. On a night like that, it's enough to hypnotise you. I wanted to lay right down in there myself and ask Jerusha to cover me over so I could go to sleep inside the smell of warm earth.

From that day to this, I've never been scared of being buried. I was ready that night, and I've been ready ever since. I'm not saying there's been no pleasure, all these years, just I've been content with where I'm going to wind up, is all. Faced up to it that night, years ago.

There they still are under the maples, I guess. The incomplete bones of Micky Allen. Wherever that doctor threw his foot away at after the accident, I don't know. Once, in a Hooverville, I heard a preacher say that at the end of things we'll all be raised up whole in the body. I wonder whether God'll be able to find where I hid the rest of Micky Allen.

As time went by, I started to think maybe Hank laid down somewhere and died in the cold that same night. He wasn't hardly wearing anything and I can tell you first hand, the ground was frozen hard as diamonds. After a couple days it was clear he hadn't gone to his mother in town. Maybe he lay down somewhere in the woods. Maybe when spring came whatever was left of Hank Allen thawed out and faded into the mulch. Vultures carried away his long bones.

After it was all done, I sat inside with Jerusha till broad day. When it got light I went out the door and that guilty piece of bare earth stared over at me, like a black eye in the snow. I got back to find Eddie still on the couch, snoring through bubbles of blood and his skin burning in the cold room. Don lay along beside his legs, staring at me. I rubbed Betty down and fed both horses, then I did the milking. I got Eddie into his bed and made him drink cold chamomile, and then there was nothing left for me to do. I'd finally run out of purpose.

The snow started coming down outside and I pulled the curtains on the new day. Eddie was like a furnace under the blanket. I took off all my clothes and lay down in the circle of his heat. The room filled up with milky winter light from behind the curtain and all the sounds in the world got softer. But nothing slowed down inside me. I could taste acid in my mouth and my thoughts were so clear it was painful.

After a while I started to shake, waves moving through the muscles in my arms and legs and on into the centre of me. When the shakes hit my stomach I retched and then carried on trembling. I might as well have been lying naked on the river ice for all I could get warm. There was Eddie next to me like a sleeping pillar of fire, and me just glazed over, frozen.

I started shaking again every time Eddie touched me after that. But we did try.

We tried hunting in the snow and bathing in the tub by the Allens' wood stove. Until Julia Allen came back from town. Then we started spending afternoons holed up at Campbell's old farm. The house'd been empty since Campbell went out and shot himself in his own barn, two or three years before. His kids were in the city and didn't care.

I remember lying there one afternoon, trying not to fall asleep and dream about Hank Allen coming back to get me. Eddie woke up and slid his good arm under me. He took a sharp breath in when he tried to follow with the other one. I kept as still as I could, trying to steady myself and seem comfortable.

'Jeanne.' Eddie sounded surprised to find me there.

'Yep, that's me.' He tensed up and I could feel the waiting memories pouring back into him from the edge of sleep. His arm went loose.

'What happened, Jeanne?'

'Your brothers are gone. It's just me and you here, Eddie.'

'What happened?'

'Your arm's getting better. Jerusha says we just have to look out the fever don't come back. We could go out and lay a trap line soon. You need to get back out under the trees, Eddie Allen.'

He gave up and quit asking then. To this day, I don't know what he remembered.

Of course, I should have told him, should have got it all out into the air. Wept or bled or vomited, done whatever it took to get it out of me. We could have shouted it out at each other and wound up closer again. Instead, me and Eddie Allen became separate territory. A river came between us, separating my language from his. After that day, the silence around us got crowded with half-formed things.

We did go out and lay traps, though. A few days later I was at the farm, waiting on the packed snow at the edge of the road like we agreed. You ain't been up here in February. You fall off a path then, you're up to your neck. Sometimes folks get buried and they don't find 'em until spring.

Anyway, I waited at the corner of the house, in front, away from the windows so Julia Allen couldn't look out and see me. Don heard me and barked hello, telling Eddie I was there.

In February, there's nothing but the outline of things. The river wound through the valley as white as everything else, you only knew it by its flatness. I looked down at the dark branches of the trees, the fence wires and the black gates. There was so much light throwing itself back at me, my eyes couldn't make out details. The long sweep of it made you feel on top of something though, masterful. I could imagine those first Allens or whoever picking the spot. They maybe had to climb a tree to see the ghost of what I saw now, cleared and cut twice since then.

Eddie came through the gate with the traps in a sack and I stepped out into the road to meet him. Julia Allen came out onto the front porch. She was a dedicated user of that front door. Someone had oiled the hinges, so she could swing it out and no warning. I was caught there and had to say hello.

Nothing.

'Ma, say hello.'

'Jeanne Delaney.' She nodded.

'Mam. I think you knew my mother.'

But Julia spoke to Eddie. 'I'm making apple brown betty today, Eddie. Maybe some cookies, too.'

'All right, Ma. I'll be in just after dark.'

'You'll do what you need to, Edward Allen.' She smiled a tight, satisfied smile. 'Men,' she said, like they were something delicious you could eat.

You get what I'm telling you? Julia Allen knew. She didn't make a fuss about her other boys because she assumed they both were dead. She thought it was Eddie done it, and that made her happy. Complete.

'I'll do your socks,' she said.

Eddie laid a trap line in the trees along the river, for muskrats and things. I went along him, chattering, then we put on our snowshoes and went up through the spruce to the deer blind.

'Come on up here and sit still, Jeanne,' Eddie said.

We climbed up and Eddie opened his insulated bottle to let the steam and the smell of coffee out.

'You know, Eddie, the world is huge. We could...'

He put his finger to his lips, didn't even say hush. We sat for a long time then, while Don struggled in the drifts, and then turned himself around and around into a hollow in the snow underneath the blind. I was warm, in my new boots and a fur on my head, too.

All I could do with myself was contemplate Eddie Allen and I didn't want to do that. I just wanted to feel him and smell him and pretend there was no such thing as time. If there's too much distance between you and another person, you have to see each other. What you want when something that strong starts to go bad is just to fall into their body, so you don't have to look at them. You just try to hang on to your own blindness.

I don't know what Eddie told his ma. I'm not even sure what he knew, but I could see he was settled in to wait for that woman to die. He was going to stick by her until she did.

Well, it seemed to me he could be waiting forever for that. Julia Allen wasn't going to turn back into earth with the rest of us. She wasn't made of any yielding substance. As time passed over that woman, she'd just harden like the things at the bottom of the ocean. Turn into bone, turn into stone. She was some kind of eternal thing, too many for me. There wasn't a bullet anywhere on this earth made for Julia Allen.

'I'd better go before dark,' I said. 'Jerusha gets nervous these days. She's turned snappy.'

I laughed and Eddie made a little smile without bringing his eyes into focus.

He didn't say anything. I leaned down close until I could feel the heat of him and breathed in. I sat on a rung of the ladder to put on my snowshoes, then went the back way down the mountain and around through the beeches over the frozen creek. There was a fox out on the ice. She didn't run, just stood fifty yards away from me and pointed her yellow eyes.

I cried for a few days when I realised me and Eddie were never gonna be all the way alone again. All those ghosts were hovering every time we touched each other. Not just those Allen men, but Etta Grace and my mother, too. That day in the deer blind was the last time we made any kind of effort.

Together, we were outnumbered by our dead. We couldn't carry 'em.

Even that year, the thaw came. You'll have no idea, city boy, how you get so you think the snow will never melt. T-Roy came back before it did, stopped to show himself and then went up the north end.

It was time for me to work. After they all came back from the border, Jerusha stayed with Grampy on the boat while I went with T-Roy out to the farms.

We were putting in Crook's early beans the day Ila showed up. It was too soon for beans, I thought, and so did Jerusha. Crook swore the frost was past, but the dirt was cold. I got tired of stiff fingers and bending over, so I took a pail and went to the pump for water.

A woman with the weirdest eyes I ever seen was standing there. They weren't blue in themselves, more like clear, thick glass with something blue-green behind it. They made me feel the way I did when the Nadeau boys grabbed hold of me and tossed me into the lake in April, falling through the air and then so cold my lungs contracted.

'I'm looking for a man named T-Roy Prichard,' she said.

'Union woman,' Mrs. Crook shouted from the kitchen doorway. 'Come up here to make trouble.'

'Trouble for her, I suppose. Not for you. We're only here for the men at the paper mill in Harmony.' She smiled and it relaxed me right away. I took a breath, liking her better. That's Ila, steps right into your life and just takes things over. Mostly she does it right.

'T-Roy don't work at the mill, never has. Can't stand the stink or the staying in one place.'

'Oh, no. I didn't mean that. T-Roy's a friend of mine.'

'A what?' That came out before I realised it wasn't any of my business. Then I pointed to the rise in Crook's three-acre field and told her T-Roy was behind it. That was that.

Ila was there when we buried Grampy at the end of that summer. She wasn't there when T-Roy said goodbye to Etta Grace, though. It was me he took along for that.

We came down to the creek from the other side, pretending we were going to fish for trout. That gave us an excuse to sit a long while, looking at the beeches across the water. The sun was still in the south then, leaving the branches of the trees in the morning light and the trunks in shadow. I love T-Roy, so I tied some flies and helped him pretend.

Once he was ready, T-Roy said, 'She might have died young anyhow.'

'There's no might have. She just did. Things happen like they do, T-Roy. Nothing from any of us changes it.'

That wasn't true, of course. In my mind, I could see Micky Allen crumpling into the slush and Etta Grace rolling herself off onto the short jerk of that rope. We'd all done plenty.

'She was happy for most of it,' I said.

'Laughed all the time.' T-Roy smiled in his quiet, far away fashion. 'Mostly I remember the singing. To hear her sing, you'd have thought she had more brains than anybody. Every shade of feeling.'

'Yep.'

We stayed quiet a longer time then, watching the sun roll down the hill and listening to a warbler who'd just made his way back. I put my fingers in the creek and watched three trout slide by. We weren't pretending to fish anymore.

'I loved her, Jeanne.'

'Well, we all know that, T-Roy.'

'I didn't want to take advantage, so I waited and waited. Then she turned into a ghost right in front of us, and nothing we could do to stop it. She was like water slipping through our fingers.'

'No. She was solid and real and people killed her, T-Roy. Same as if they'd done it with their own hands. She wasn't anybody's fairy tale.' Maybe that was hard, but I didn't mean it to be. Anyway, he took it.

We stood up and looked at the beeches. I was glad we hadn't put Micky Allen under there. It was a church, not a graveyard.

By full summer T-Roy was living with Ila in a house on dry land, a house that didn't move a'tall. He wanted her to have a proper wedding with him, but she said church was against her religion.

'I met you in one,' he said.

'I've been converted since.' Ila laughed her educated laugh. 'I had a revelation. Saw the light.'

Everything she said had two meanings, and she talked like a summer visitor. She settled down and stayed the winters, though.

Had her babies up here in the woods and travelled around with them in the summers, trying to convince the loggers to unionise.

There wasn't any place for me in their house, so I stayed with Jerusha. Ila Prichard, that's what we all called her, had come along and washed me out of their lives with those cold-water eyes. I didn't go up to their house much. You might catch them two at it in the bedroom any time of the day or night. T-Roy got to looking like some kind of angel man, a light coming off him and somehow taller than anything he stood next to. It was good to see him like that. It was.

Jerusha lived long enough to pull my baby out. I didn't have to knock on her door bleeding, because I was already right there in the little bed next to her. About an hour before dawn on an August morning, I felt a pop like a balloon and the little ocean inside me spilled out onto the quilts.

You won't know anything about it, city boy. I don't know how to tell it. Imagine there's a hurricane in your body. Imagine a hurricane *is* your body. An earthquake. The Seaway. Imagine you swallowed the birth of a star.

Jerusha did like always, boiling water and rolling me back and forth to change the quilts under me. She made me eat teaspoons of honey and drink something foul. She made me get up and walk around the room. I cursed her, then felt bad.

She'd seen two of the people she loved most in the world die with babies, and she thought it was her should have saved 'em. I couldn't see a flicker of fear in the way she looked or moved, but I knew. In between two of those birth pains, I finished learning about sympathy. I was about a week shy of seventeen. I'd shot and killed a man half a year before I fully understood how to feel someone else's pain.

I held Jerusha's arm to stop her bustling, and looked her right in the eyes. 'I'm gonna live, Jerusha. Hear me? I'll do it; you'll just have to help me.'

I swear to you a ghost flew up out of her then, something like a smoking chimney or a cloud of steam. Or I don't know, maybe I was already dreaming awake by that time. She smiled at me, then we both went back to doing the work of our separate bodies. My son came out squalling. She put him down in a basket while she propped me up so I could push the afterbirth out into a bowl. Later, I lay with the baby wrapped on top of me while she went out and put the rest of it under the mulch.

Jerusha brought me a cup of molasses tea and said, 'My last job is done.'

I didn't name the boy Edward. I named him John, because that was the tuneless way Eddie said my name. Trying to get it right and failing.

Jerusha wasn't lying when she said it was her last job. She only lived six months more. I think she died happy as she could have. She was proud of me, but she didn't like to say.

Grampy died first. By the middle of September, he was buried and our boat was empty, floating high on the water because all our possessions were in the house with T-Roy and the woman who refused to be his wife.

The day I took the boat out onto the lake for the last time, I didn't bother untying it. I cut the ropes with Jerusha's shiny knife. The sun was getting lower then, but the days were still long enough. The lake was full of dark yellow light when I got to the middle and cut the engine. The boat threw a long shadow east towards the *batteur*, and beyond that the few square miles of trees where I'd spent most of my life.

My baby boy was up there in the woods, asleep by Jerusha's chair.

Like I said, the boat was riding high. It bobbed and pitched in the middle of the lake. I stood for however long in the cabin where I got born and my mother died. We'd buried Grampy's Saint Barbara with him, but I could still feel her there, demanding all our heat and our light. I threw open the hatch and searched the wood on the walls and the floor, looking for some forgotten stain of our

203

blood that hadn't got scrubbed away. You know what? I wouldn't have been able to tell that blood from anything else. It might have been there and it might not. That was how much the world noticed us and all our violence.

I can't have stood there too long because the sun was still above the horizon when I came up for the fuel can. I went around the boat in a circle, letting the gasoline soak into all the boards. It crept up, invisible, and took over the air around me. I threw a couple of matches in the bow, as far from the engine house as I could get, then ran back and waited until the flames rose up over the forward cabin. Then I jumped.

That colder seam in the middle of the lake was there waiting for me, where it still is, I guess. I held my breath and swam all the way through it before I came up. By the time I rolled over and looked back, the sun was down but the sky was all kinds of colours. The burning smell on the breeze was stronger than I thought it would be. Soon people along both shores would be coming out to look. I was away in the shadow though, looking back and waiting for Saint Barbara to appear.

And she did. The engine house went up and the flames shot all the colour back into the sky. There she was in the fire, with her dark hair and her sword, while the wave of her heat rolled over me and I choked. I said goodbye and went under again, swimming towards our little dock for the last time.

There was no one there to see me scramble up onto the *batteur*, but I guess all around the valley people knew it was me that done it. They didn't care. I wasn't hurting anybody, not that time. They just put it down to grief, I guess.

A few months later, after we buried Jerusha, I took my son up over the border and found work where I could. I took the lesson from my mother and Jerusha, moved my child back and forth across the borders, county, state and nation, so they wouldn't smell his blood and come take him from me.

Mostly, a border is an ugly thing, made for people in rags to go back and forth across of. We make the most of ours, though, even if it is painted through the woods in a line of dried blood.

Didn't I tell you, government man? I'm a fool, but I ain't stupid. I'm not saying any of all that into your tape recorder. I been moving up and down this country since before you were out of school, and no one's put anything on me yet.

Where was it? In the woods, under the trees with the martens and the bobcats and the moose, that's where. Under the wings of the owls and the sharp-shinned hawks. You can pretend I made the whole thing up if you want. You got nothing to go on, really.

Well, write me down, then. That's what the government pays you for, isn't it? What you gonna do with all them tapes anyway, when your Federal Writers Project is done? When there's a new government and the money dries up, where are all those stories gonna go? To sleep under dust somewhere, just like the people that told them. What difference does it make?

Make me into book. Make me a hero. That's what I should have been all along. I always knew it, from a little child.

Miss McLaughlin gave me the Pathfinder. Give some other girl me.

Historical Note

This book is purposefully set in a non-specific area of New England in 1913, though some will notice its similarity to the shores of Lake Champlain.

Eugenic sterilisation was widespread across Western Europe and North America in the late nineteenth and early twentieth centuries. In the US, it was enacted chiefly as a form of racial violence against women and communities of colour, but was also practised on poor and disabled white women. While writing this novel, I depended on the important historical work of Nancy Gallagher, who documented this state-sanctioned practice in Vermont. See Gallagher's *Breeding Better Vermonters: The Eugenics Project in the Green Mountain State*, as well as the online archive at the University of Vermont. The letter in the chapter titled 'Confidential' is based very closely on actual historical documents. We carefully considered its language and, though we mitigated some of it, felt that it would be wrong to 'whitewash' it completely. This is our history; we didn't want to let that be ignored. Do not assume, however, that this practice was confined to the dim historical past. I have personal knowledge of eugenic sterilisation enacted as racial violence in Brooklyn New York in the early 1980s. This is not just something 'our grandparents did'.

During the environmental research for this novel, I learned about hunting and fishing tourism and the ecology of the mixed boreal woodlands of New England, which are unique on earth. Dona Brown's *Inventing New England: Regional Tourism in the Nineteenth Century* tells a story that will be familiar to people in Wales and elsewhere. If you're wondering why people in New England spoke French, and what happened to them if they did, you might read Gerard J. Brault's *French-Canadian Heritage in New England*.

The wonderful archivists at the American Folklife Collection in the Library of Congress provided me with recordings made in the early 1930s. I was able to choose specific areas on the map and receive local oral histories in digitised files. In these recordings, elderly New Englanders, both colonials and First Nations people, recalled their lives in the late nineteenth and early twentieth centuries. These stories provided a wealth of detail about daily life, as well as a priceless record of local dialect.

Acknowledgements

I depended a great deal on my mother and father when drafting this novel. Both were born in rural upstate New York about fifteen years after the action of this novel takes place. They told me about spring houses, fur trapping, .22 rifles, sleigh blades on pony carts, common farming accidents and much more. I am grateful to them for sharing their history, and for everything else.

Diolch o galon to all the wonderful women at Honno for your trust and hard work. Thanks to librarians and archivists everywhere, to readers and book bloggers for your wonderful responses to *Fall River*. Thanks to my family for everything, always.

ABOUT HONNO

Honno Welsh Women's Press was set up in 1986 by a group of women who felt strongly that women in Wales needed wider opportunities to see their writing in print and to become involved in the publishing process. Our aim is to develop the writing talents of women in Wales, give them new and exciting opportunities to see their work published and often to give them their first 'break' as a writer.

Honno is registered as a community co-operative. Any profit that Honno makes is invested in the publishing programme. Women from Wales and around the world have expressed their support for Honno. Each supporter has a vote at the Annual General Meeting. For more information and to buy our publications, please visit our website www.honno.co.uk or email us on post@honno.co.uk.

Honno
D41, Hugh Owen Building,
Aberystwyth University,
Aberystwyth,
Ceredigion,
SY23 3DY.

We are very grateful for the support of all our Honno Friends.